The critics on Mich...

'Sheer good writing of the kind which sustains the reader from page to page without wanting to skip a single line . . . warm, but also seriously creepy' Frances Fyfield

'Michelle Spring joins the ranks of our best crime novelists . . . her touch is deft, her insight enlightens and the suspense grips' Helena Kennedy, QC

'With each book Spring is maturing as a writer discovering how far she can push her talent and exploring the darker recesses of the human psyche' *The Times,* designating Michelle Spring as a Master of Crime

'The author, with great skill, makes us love the characters we cared for least' *Mail on Sunday*

'Cambridge-based Laura Principal is one of the more believable and astute private investigators' *Sunday Telegraph*

'One of our more assured feminist crime writers' *Good Housekeeping*

'Powerful emotional intensity . . . Spring's subtle, highly charged evocation of menace indicates extraordinary skill' *Washington Post Book World*

'A female private eye comparable to V. I. Warshawski and a twisty psychological plot worthy of Elizabeth George' *Alfred Hitchcock's Mystery Magazine*

'Astute, entertaining, right-minded and carefully constructed' *Times Literary Supplement*

Michelle Spring was raised on Vancouver Island. She worked for many years in England as an academic and turned to fiction as a way of coming to terms with two particular incidents that cast a shadow of fear over an otherwise fulfilling career. The ploy worked. Writing relieved the nightmares, passing them on to her readers instead in the form of suspense. Michelle Spring has left university teaching now in order to write full time. She lives near the centre of Cambridge with her husband and two children.

The other three novels in the acclaimed Laura Principal series, *Running for Shelter*, *Standing in the Shadows* and *Nights in White Satin*, are also available in Orion paperback.

EVERY BREATH YOU TAKE

Michelle Spring

ORION

An Orion Paperback
First published in Great Britain by Orion in 1994
This paperback edition published in 1995 by Orion Books Ltd,
Orion House, 5 Upper St Martin's Lane, London WC2H 9EA

Reissued 2000

A CIP catalogue record for this book is available
from the British Library.

Printed and bound in Great Britain by
Clays Ltd, St Ives plc

For David, Rosa and Joshua

ACKNOWLEDGEMENTS

This is my first venture into the world of fiction and I am indebted to a number of people who have smoothed the way. Very special thanks are due to my partner David Held and to Yvette Goulden, Jane Chelius, Ruthie Petrie and Michael Thomas, all of whose insightful comments helped to make the book a great deal better. Thanks also to Terri Apter, Lizbeth Goodman, Marianne Hirsch, John Thompson and Barbara Trapido for advising me well, to Tracey Hodge for providing peace of mind, to Julie Held for showing me her studio and to Felicity Bryan for finding the book a good home.

Every breath you take
Every move you make . . .
I'll be watching you.

(Sting)

CHAPTER 1

———

I only drive fast when I am not in a hurry. The rhythm of speed, the fluid changes of gear, the split-second, single-minded calculation involved in overtaking a lorry on a steep Norfolk slope can be depended upon only when I am relaxed, when there are no deadlines to meet, when I can abandon myself to the present.

So I arrived early at Wildfell Cottage. My Saab 900*i*, six years old but still sporty, swung into the drive at too fast a pace, spraying bits of gravel onto the patch of meadow that Helen euphemistically refers to as 'the lawn'. I parked under the apple tree – something that can't be done in summer, when the branches are heavy with fruit – and stepped out with a jauntiness tempered by relief that Helen hadn't arrived yet to register my reckless progress up the drive.

Inside the hatchback, the car was tightly packed: a briefcase, two carrier bags bulging with groceries, a pair of wellies and a case of wine. First things first. I hefted the box of wine onto my hip while fumbling in my jacket pocket for keys. Once all the goodies from the boot were secure within the cottage, I undertook a prowl of the ground floor, turning on the lamps on the mantelpiece, and drawing the curtains across the French doors. The wine and groceries I placed on the old oak table in the dining area, the briefcase in the lower cupboard of the dresser. It had been a hard week, and I had no intention of doing any paperwork until Sunday. Then I settled down to my favourite Friday-in-the-country job of laying the fire.

Helen thinks it's perverse that I never wear gloves to handle the logs. But for me the scratch of bark on my skin is an essential offering, the intimacy that entitles me to the comfort that the fire provides. When she walked into the living room an hour later, I was stretched out in an armchair in the fire's glow, the neighbour's cat on my lap, woolly worksocks on my feet, a jazz recording by Elizabeth Welch on the compact disc player, and a smile on my face.

'You look cosy, except for one thing.' Helen gestured with her chin to the cardboard box on the table. 'Even if that case of wine fell off the back of a lorry, it won't do to let it sit there untasted. Shall I fetch you a glass?' She made her way in search of the corkscrew, without waiting for me to reply.

So I didn't – except to suggest that we begin to behave like adults where drink is concerned. When you often meet for weekends away in a remote area of Norfolk, letting the contents of your wineglass depend on *ad hoc* visits to the local off-licence shows a serious lack of foresight. When Helen handed me a glass, I proposed the obvious toast: an end to the days of paying over the odds for drink of inferior quality.

'You certainly couldn't describe *this* as inferior,' Helen pronounced. She pushed the sofa a little nearer to the fire, installed herself in it and enjoyed a long satisfied sip. 'I'm all in favour of thrift when it means the purchase of a splendid case of wine. But tell me, Laura dear,' she said, wriggling into the downy cushions, 'how are you going to square this charming extravagance with our agenda for the weekend?'

That's Helen, direct as ever. We had agreed to concentrate this weekend on solving the recurring problem of our mutual shortages of cash. It is not that we are poor, either of us. Helen was promoted last year to Assistant Chief Librarian, astonishing those acquaintances who had mistaken her modesty for mediocrity or lack of ambition. She is set fair to replace old Evans as Head of Library Services at Eastern University when he finally settles for retirement. And while the recession hits other forms of business hard, a tightening of financial belts has *increased* the demand for the services of private investigators like me. So, it being an ill wind, my current income is nothing to sneeze at.

But we had, as they say, commitments. Helen takes the major financial responsibility for her daughter. Despite his

2

stated intentions, Virginia's father has never found it easy to part with money. After a few years poised between frustration and litigation, Helen decided that Ginny's relationship with her dad was more important than cash. As for my commitments, there are no children to feed and clothe, but there is a house to look after, and expenses to contribute towards Sonny's London flat where I stay during the week. Add to that the rent on a boathouse, a season ticket to Cambridge United, and the odd case of wine, and you can be sure that my Visa statements are never short of entries.

And we have Wildfell.

The cottage had come to us by an extraordinary route. The key landmark on this route was Clare Atkinson, who grew up with me in Bristol. We attended the same grammar school. My father was a lorry driver, hers an architect, but against the odds, we became friends. Clare's father had seen the potential in a decaying barn long before the trend for designer outbuildings was established. Eventually he bought for himself a corner of a farm that nuzzled up against a wood, providing three acres of graceful land bisected by a gentle stretch of stream. He made the barn into a glorious home, with high ceilings and stunning light-filled spaces, before his own private pain caught up with him. He hanged himself from the central beam. After that, Clare could not bring herself to live here – but neither could she consign the house to strangers. Wildfell Cottage represented everything she loved and everything she feared. She insisted we buy it, at an absurdly low price, on one condition (a condition we would have granted in any case) – that she could return from New York to stay with us occasionally. Several years on, she has not yet felt able to do this.

So Helen and I became the unlikely co-owners of a country retreat. In recent years we have visited Wildfell Cottage less than we used to. In the winter months we may meet here only occasionally, just enough to warm the place up and shake the city off our shoes. In the spring and summer we come more frequently, often with other friends in tow. Myself, I far prefer a wellie-clad week on the Norfolk coast to a holiday in the Mediterranean. No anxiety about passports, no queues at

Gatwick Airport, no aggressive taxi-drivers – just fresh air, plentiful food, feet up by the fire and lots of lovely sleep.

It's not that we don't have other homes to go to. Helen and Ginny live in Cambridge, an hour and a half's drive away from Wildfell. My job takes me all over, but my office – such as it is – is located in London. More important, so is Sonny, who's my partner (though I seldom use the word) in both the professional and the personal sense. You can usually find me in London during the week. On weekends, if you are one of the select group of friends who have my ex-directory telephone number, you will probably reach me at my house in Cambridge, the only legacy of value from my marriage to Adam. None of this alters the fact that both Helen and I count Wildfell Cottage as a kind of spiritual home.

The pity of it is, even a spiritual home needs maintenance. And the joint account that Helen and I run for the purpose of funding Wildfell – for paying gas and other utility bills, for the monthly cheque to the neighbours who caretake when we're not around, for occasional repairs to roof or plumbing – has to be topped up regularly from other sources. You could argue that a country home, however cheaply acquired, is an extravagance for people like Helen and me. You could, but it is something we never do. Our agenda this weekend involved solving the problem of upkeep, not questioning our commitment to Wildfell.

Helen was on her second glass of wine. It was clear that she was beginning to feel WEEKEND in her bones. Now seemed as good a time as any to drop my little bombshell. 'I may have the answer,' I proclaimed with more assurance than I actually felt. And I proceeded to tell her about Monica.

I had heard about Monica from a friend who works for the Eastern Arts Foundation. 'A remarkable painter for her age,' Chloe declared. 'Beginning to get some recognition, too. She needs a place in the country to get on quietly with her work, somewhere near the sea.'

My ears perked up precisely as Chloe, who is a dab hand at matchmaking, had known they would. Wildfell is only a five-minute drive from the most beautiful stretch of shoreline on

4

the Norfolk coast. Other bits of information about Monica also interested me. In particular, that her mother had recently died, leaving a substantial house in Newcastle for which a buyer had been found. Monica would soon, in other words, have money to burn.

It took until Sunday morning to persuade Helen that Monica might represent the solution to our financial problems. I suppose she feared she might lose the tranquillity that Wildfell represents. It was eight years ago that Clare signed over the cottage to us. Two months before legal formalities were complete, James, Ginny's father, went walkabout, leaving Helen in a misery of uncertainty. Two-year-old Ginny was bereft. James did show up again eventually, a chastened man, aghast at what he had done, but it took several months and considerable tact and effort on Helen's part (and even some from me) to repair the relationship between father and daughter. The fact that Ginny now chooses to spend alternate weekends and a portion of vacations in Bristol with James is a tribute to Helen's generosity of spirit. Her own emotional confidence, however, has not been so easily restored. She has had one or two relationships in recent years, but these were fragile from the beginning, and Helen has found it more rewarding to put her energies into her job, her friends and her daughter (not in that order) than into a lover.

So perhaps it is not surprising that Helen regards our weekend life at Wildfell as her salvation. Here, during the weeks that James was missing, she and Ginny had escaped from the clamour of relatives, police and casual enquirers. Here, Helen had marshalled the confidence to convert a friendly library job into an impressive career. And here, she and I had cemented the friendship that had begun when we were both undergraduates in Cambridge.

As soon as I arrived at university, I found an ally in Helen; she was more sophisticated than me, but no less distanced from some of the more hierarchical aspects of Cambridge life. We lived on the same hallway in Newnham College, shared a kitchen, sat up late together giggling and letting off steam, checked each other's essays, revised together for exams, and eventually were witnesses at each other's weddings.

In fact, Helen's unswerving friendship throughout my ill-fated marriage to Adam – clever, cold, demanding Adam – was one of the things that enabled me to see just how shallow my relationship with him was. Other friends reasoned with me, rejecting the comparison: 'But Laura, you can't expect that kind of understanding from a man.' 'Why not?' was my curt and persistent reply.

So Helen's resistance to the idea of Monica was not altogether unexpected. In Wildfell, Helen and I had created together what few people maintain from childhood to adulthood, an unambiguous sense of home. And now I proposed to threaten this by introducing another person, a third term, into the shelter of our little circle.

In the end it was the money that won her over. Not that Helen is a mercenary woman. On the contrary, she is very unworldly in some ways, slow to calculate costs where something or someone appeals to her. I took care to offer a Sunday brunch that appealed. We ate on the patio. Helen softened over orange juice that was freshly squeezed; she relaxed as she bit into warm bagels with smoked salmon; she smiled as I swiped at a curl of cream cheese on her chin. And by the time I set a dish of fresh mango in front of her, she was able to view the prospect of Monica with something approaching enthusiasm.

'Splitting the bills three ways instead of two, investing her rent money to provide for large repairs, we could save – well, Laura Principal, how much do you reckon?'

'Let's put it like this,' I replied, the scent of victory fuelling my launch into fantasy. 'With the money we save, we could install a greenhouse on the south wall for your seedlings. Or buy a grand piano for the sitting room. Or we could plan a holiday for you and me and Ginny in Lanzarote.'

Helen turned her deckchair to put her face in the way of the pale morning sunshine. 'The Caribbean,' she corrected. 'Antigua, to be precise. So it's settled. We invite Ms Monica Harcourt to visit – next weekend? – and see whether she is good enough for Wildfell.'

CHAPTER 2

It's just as well my weekend was restful, because the working week began early on the Monday morning, in the plush surroundings of the Regency Park Hotel in Central London. I had an appointment for half-past eight with an executive of one of Italy's largest companies, Ceresa Nazionale. I drove through the dark, reaching the hotel just after eight. In my business, it doesn't pay to be late for a briefing with a new and influential client. The first appointment of the week means they are serious about needing your help. It also means you are being tested.

I was offered a breakfast of fruit, cheese, croissants and coffee, and a job that any private investigator would relish. I'm quite adroit, but it is still easier to concentrate on a new brief with my hands free and my mouth empty. So I refused the breakfast, and accepted the job.

Ceresa Nazionale was expanding its operations in Britain. This process entailed delicate discussions with potential partners throughout the UK, and for these the services of a London-based interpreter were required – one who knew the nuances of business etiquette in Britain. Since the negotiations were highly confidential – and since Ceresa's competitors would love to have early warning of the deals being struck – my brief was to run a security check on the top-ranked applicant for the post, and to produce results by the middle of next week.

I gave the case top billing. There would be more work if this panned out. I made a lot of phone calls, and spent a lot of time sitting in London traffic jams in my smartest business suit. It doesn't do to look dowdy when interviewing Italians.

I followed up in person the list of referees that Mina Harrison had provided with her application. Her former and current clients included haulage firms, importers, exporters, tourist agencies, entertainment promoters . . . Most were medium-sized companies, the kind that can't afford a permanent interpreter on the payroll but need someone on tap for difficult assignments. They all spoke well of Mina Harrison. She was fast, efficient, polite, they said. Their Italian contacts liked dealing with her. Her fees were steep, but you get what you pay for, and she was certainly one of the best. One mentioned, with a look I didn't like, Mina Harrison's short skirt. None mentioned problems with discretion (or rather the lack of it), although I gave them every opportunity to do so.

The paperwork checked out, too. Mina's credit rating was fine, she had no history of bankruptcy, and those aspects of her financial affairs that I could probe seemed to be in good order. Her landlord described her as a model tenant. Her mother appeared to be a respectable widow living in Surrey. No obvious skeletons in the Harrison closet.

The final interview took place in the young interpreter's office-cum-flat in Mayfair. It was one of those modern, mock-Georgian buildings, where the doors to each suite are made up to look like external doors, all matt almond paintwork and brass fittings. Mina's sitting room was in fact refreshingly light and modern, with whitewashed walls, a pale sofa and a striking abstract oil painting in shades of blue on the wall opposite the window. The room looked classy but not necessarily beyond Ms Harrison's means. Mina Harrison looked classy, too. She was well-groomed, graceful and extremely pretty. Her intelligent-looking face was framed by brown bobbed hair that shone and shook as she spoke. Her voice was pleasant, her manner friendly and, yes, her skirt was exceedingly and most becomingly short.

She answered my questions with apparent candour. Her answers corresponded with what I already knew. Then she showed me her office, occupying what otherwise might be a second bedroom of the flat. It contained the usual equipment – filing cabinets, fax machine, two telephones – and a brisk and prosperous atmosphere. On the wall, a charcoal sketch of a nude with wild, tangled hair provided the only personal note, a contrast to the restrained elegance of the sitting room. I wondered whose taste that reflected. Perhaps the audiotypist, a sad-faced woman who worked school hours and looked as if she'd rather not. While Mina fetched some documents, the typist wittered on and on, apparently under the illusion that she had an obligation to entertain me. She explored a variety of points she thought we might have in common: the plots of Sue Grafton thrillers, her trip to Cambridge last year to visit her student brother, the fact that her osteopath had his surgery near my office. I stared at the nude with the wild hair, nodded occasionally and breathed a sigh of relief when Mina Harrison returned.

I explained to Ms Harrison what additional checks I had run and why, and asked her if there was anything else that she thought might be relevant to the interests of Ceresa Nationale. She considered for a moment before replying with a shrug, 'No.'

Seldom has a case been so simply and unambiguously wrapped up – or so I thought. I dictated my report on Friday morning, and delivered it to the Regency Park Hotel myself, well ahead of the deadline. Then, intimations of future work chiming in my ears, I nipped into the washroom, changed my business suit for a sweatshirt and jogging pants, and set out for Norfolk.

An unqualified success – that was how Helen described her telephone call to Monica. Yes, she *was* looking for a place to work at the weekends; yes, she *was* interested in the sort of arrangement we had in mind and finally, yes, she would be delighted to join us for a getting-to-know-you session this very Saturday.

The most unexpected 'yes' was Helen's exuberant endorsement. No longer the reluctant partner, Helen had become in the space of one phone call Monica's advocate. And I was rather surprised to find that the greater Helen's warmth about Monica, the cooler I became.

The account of Monica that Helen provided on Friday evening can only be described as effusive. The fact that the other woman was a colleague, based in the Art Department of Eastern University, seemed particularly to capture her imagination.

'How can it possibly be,' Helen asked rhetorically, 'that she has been at the University for over a year now, and yet this weekend will be the very first time we meet? You can't imagine, Laura – it makes such a difference to know there's another OK woman, a kindred spirit, around.'

I refrained from taking her up on the 'you can't imagine'. She seemed to have forgotten that I had, after all, spent my early years as a history tutor. And most women in academic life know precisely how lonely it is to work without a kindred spirit, without someone who shares your sense of humour, someone who will wink at you across the table and soften an intolerable meeting with a flash of empathy. But I bit my tongue. Clearly, Helen was on the first wave of enthusiasm for a new friendship. Who was I to pour cold water on her fun?

Instead, I dragged the conversation brusquely back to the business at hand. 'So, you gave Monica a PR job on Wildfell, she jumped at the chance of a home in the country at knockdown cost, and you've set up an interview for tomorrow.'

Helen looked put out. 'Don't be so cold-blooded, Laura. I would hardly call it an interview. Monica is simply coming to see the cottage and to talk to us about the possibility of sharing.' Her voice took on a pleading quality which did nothing to improve my mood. 'Laura, if only you'd spoken to her. She's had such a disappointing year, what with moving to a new place and her mother's death and breaking up with her boyfriend. She was thrilled when I told her about Wildfell.' Helen looked anxiously at me. My frown did not encourage her train of thought.

'Look,' I interrupted. Why does appearing inconsistent make me awkward? 'Let's not rush into this. We scarcely know this woman and – '

'But it was *your* idea to involve her in the first place! And Chloe recommended her, after all.'

'That's just it.' Finally, I managed to come clean. How is it that in the toughest conversations with my clients (who often are, as Sonny likes to say, 'real hard men') I stay on top, but here I was making a hash of an important discussion with my closest friend? I put that question away for another occasion.

'Look, Helen, about Chloe. I popped into her office on the way here, to thank her for putting us onto Monica. But when I told her about the arrangements for the interview—'

'Meeting,' Helen insisted firmly.

'All right, meeting,' I conceded, 'Chloe's reaction was not what you would describe as pleased – more like panicky. She began to make excuses. You know the sort of thing – she didn't actually *recommend* Monica, she only mentioned her in passing. She didn't really know Monica all that well, she had no idea what she would be like to live with, and so on.'

'Disclaiming responsibility, by the sound of it. Could it be that Chloe's the sort of person who thinks it will reflect badly on her if she recommends someone that other people don't like?'

'Could be,' I concluded lamely. 'Perhaps that's all it is.' I was calmer now that I had Helen's full attention.

We were in the kitchen, putting away groceries for the weekend. Helen turned aside to grind some coffee beans. For a moment I couldn't hear her over the crunch of the grinder. The noise stopped. Helen looked thoughtful as she poured boiling water into the filter on top of the ground beans. The invigorating aroma of Kenyan coffee filled the air. 'Did you ask her if she knew anything specific about Monica? Anything bad, I mean?'

'I tried to, but nothing concrete emerged. Anyway,' I demurred, feeling for some obscure reason rather guilty, 'it's not Chloe who might be sharing future weekends with Monica, it's you and me. So we'll just have to suss her out as best we can, and make up our own minds.' I filled our cups, and added, almost as an afterthought, 'But maybe we should be careful.'

'Careful? Come on, Laura Principal, spell it out. What exactly do you mean by *careful*?'

'Well,' I said, pausing to think what I *did* mean, 'assuming we all get on well tomorrow – and assuming of course that Monica likes the cottage – maybe we shouldn't talk serious

11

business right away. Don't you think we should save a decision until we've had more time to get acquainted?'

'A probationary period?' Helen asked drily.

'On both sides – a chance to think it over before we commit ourselves. I wouldn't mind setting up another weekend with Ginny here as well. After all, this is her place too and she loves her holidays in Norfolk. What do you say?'

Helen was silent for a moment, then she gave me a quick hug. 'It's a good idea. Let's hold off on a decision for a while, then. I'm sure Monica will go along with that. Actually,' she added, looking faintly embarrassed, 'I was afraid you were going to turn thumbs down on the whole arrangement. You seem so grudging about Monica, as if you've already decided you don't like her without even meeting her first.'

I assumed a face of exaggerated innocence – 'Who, me?' – refilled our coffee cups, and shifted the conversation to food. We decided in the end to wander down to the Unicorn. A stroll down the lane, a couple of pints of Abbott Ale and the Friday evening special of steak and kidney pie were just what we needed to put the awkwardness of the conversation behind us.

It had been agreed that Monica would arrive in time for lunch on Saturday, and stay until Sunday afternoon. First thing Saturday morning, Helen and I prepared the cottage for her arrival. We swept the polished floorboards downstairs, straightened the unruly wellies by the kitchen door, and set flowers in every room. I cast a critical eye over the bedroom that would be allocated to what we this morning called the Monica-person. (The ground had subtly shifted in a short period of time. Now we were certain that a third co-resident was the answer to our problems; the only question – in my mind at least – was whether Monica would be the one.)

Nothing to worry about in the bedroom. The floorboards were sanded and stained a delicate pale grey, through which gleamed the grain of the wood. The roof was sharply peaked, with a skylight that caught the morning sun and a small round window peeping down towards the stream. The room contained a lot of light, but only three pieces of furniture, all secured with more expenditure of time than of money from junk shops in the Norwich area. A small but comfy double bed (the kind my mother Dorothy describes as a 'three-quarters bed') with a patchwork coverlet and enormous fluffy pillows occupied the centre of the north wall of the room. On the opposite wall was a narrow pine cupboard, fitted up as a wardrobe with two deep drawers. A small wooden trunk doubled as a bedside table. With a ceremonial flourish, Helen placed a delicate porcelain bowl of pot-pourri on the trunk. 'If she doesn't like this room, we don't want her,' she declared. A show of bravado. Anyone worth knowing would adore this room.

And Monica did. There was no mistaking the pleasure in her voice as she explored Wildfell. The sunny kitchen, the large airy living room, the patio . . . for all of them she exclaimed her approval, but her greatest delight was reserved for the bedroom. 'I could be happy here,' was what Monica actually said. Neither Helen nor I were ever quite certain whether the declaration in that quiet statement was, as it sometimes seems in memory, overladen with surprise.

From the moment that Monica drew up in front of Wildfell, hair all wild and woolly, T-shirt paint-stained, laughter uninhibited, she was the focus of Helen's considerable powers of concentration. In no time at all, Helen had winkled out highlights of her life story: the cosy childhood in Newcastle, the glamorous years at art school in London, the isolated life of the artist-in-residence, the move to Cambridge. Monica opened up to Helen effortlessly, suggesting someone for whom a good dose of self-revelation was long overdue.

In fact, the two women hit it off like a house on fire. For a start, they expressed very similar views about college affairs. Together, they bemoaned the process whereby women in academic life become overloaded and undermined – their heavier and largely unacknowledged pastoral role, the effect of being patronised by administrators who see teaching or providing library services as a disruption to the central activity of meeting each other in committees. And yet Monica wore these problems lightly. Perhaps it was because she had come over the past six years to see herself more as an artist and less as an academic.

Monica's wry amusement was a pleasant change from the heigh-ho, here-we-go-again style that Helen and I had evolved over the years. Her accounts of students had even me rolling in the aisles. There was the talented textile designer, always on the verge of quitting on Friday, who had invariably forgotten this by Monday morning, and who seemed oblivious to concerned tutors left mopping their brows in her wake; the promising water colourist who followed Monica about, longing to be on equal terms but not quite able to pull it off; the young printmaker, hovering on the edge of sexual encounters, who thought his rather arch images of naked women were deeply expressive of some universal truth.

Monica's conversational portraits of people were generous as well as vivid. It was common knowledge at Eastern University that the Art Department shared some of the less endearing qualities of a den of hungry lions, but Monica seemed undaunted by the fearsome reputations of its members. Even Ella Grimsby, over whose decidedly angry head Monica had been appointed Course Tutor, came in for pastel treatment. 'No, really,' Monica protested, 'one of the most articulate women I've ever met.' Her wry smile suggested that she would prefer not to spell out what precisely Ella had articulated. And, in what I later came to think of as a typically good-hearted gesture, she claimed to be angling for an invitation to share the afternoon tea that Ella dispensed to protégés and friends in her office.

Yet for all Monica's bonhomie, I wouldn't say she was comfortable during that first weekend with us. For one thing, she was given to sudden bouts of nervousness. Like many city-dwellers who scarcely register the raucous squawk of sirens, the aggressive shouts of men at closing time, the thunder of a train, she flinched nevertheless at the softer sounds of the countryside. When the source of her alarm – a sharp metallic bark – was revealed to be a fox, Monica blushed, and she was even more embarrassed when I explained that the scratching in the roof was due to nothing more than mice in the thatch. Helen made an effort to take the sting out of these revelations.

'You'll feel better once you get to know the ghost in the

woodshed,' she said soothingly, with a conspicuous wink in my direction.

Monica looked puzzled. 'You've got a ghost?' she queried. 'I thought they went in for stately homes, not modernised barns.'

'Early on,' Helen explained, 'we resigned ourselves to the fact that there were some noises here we simply couldn't place. We learned to recognise the fox, that barking sound you heard a few minutes ago, and owls and wood pigeons and a small assortment of country sounds. But both of us,' Helen said, nodding in my direction, 'are city girls at heart, and we are forever hearing thunks and snorts that we can't begin to explain. So we invented a ghost to account for them. Her name is Miranda. Romantic, don't you think? Every so often, we have an evening by candlelight and invent spookier and more melodramatic legends to account for Miranda's wanderings.'

'Why the woodshed?'

'Well, you saw that shed, down the flagstone path at the edge of the copse? We always keep it locked. Or at least we try to.'

'A safety precaution,' I interjected. 'We keep garden tools in there, as well as firelogs, and we don't want any of the local children messing around with the axe.'

'But in spite of our best intentions,' Helen continued, 'we sometimes hear the door banging in the middle of the night when the wind's up. And then, instead of having a go at Colin – he does the gardening – for leaving the padlock undone, we blame it on the ghost.'

'Poor Miranda!' exclaimed Monica. 'Doomed for ever to take the blame for other people's misdeeds!' Her tone was playful, but the image stayed with me of someone whose surface good humour masked a watchful, uneasy self.

And there was something else I couldn't shake off. During the evening as I sat in the old armchair, scanning our guest's face, less involved in the conversation than Helen, I was haunted by a certainty that I knew Monica from somewhere. The tilt of the head, the woolly hair, the angle of the cheekbone were familiar to me, stored in some out-of-context file in my brain. (Of course I later asked Helen, 'Does she look familiar to you?' but Helen only replied, 'God, yes, it's as if I've known her for years!' That wasn't at all what I had meant.)

Whether or not it was the tale of the woodshed that influenced Monica's reaction to Colin I'll never know, but his appearance on the Sunday morning signalled the other really odd thing about her behaviour that weekend. Colin and Polly are our nearest neighbours at Wildfell, and useful people to know. Between them, they keep an eye on the place while we're in town. In exchange for a small regular income, Colin obliges with numerous chores we're pleased to be spared ourselves.

He appeared suddenly around the side of the cottage on Sunday morning, just as we were returning from a walk in the woods. I waved a greeting, and turned to Monica to introduce her. I stopped short when I saw her face. She looked – well, not surprised exactly, but frightened. Poised for flight. Her eyes held a shimmer of panic. At my halting introduction, she regained her composure, but no one – least of all Colin – was convinced. Helen, with her usual tact, engaged our neighbour in a spirited discussion of plans by the Parish Council for a new drainage ditch near the main road, but he was not mollified. I saw him cast a wary glance over his shoulder at Monica as he made his way to the meadow.

Monica never offered to explain. On my part, there seemed little point in bringing the incident up again. We arranged for another weekend, and a business discussion, in a week's time. But watching as Helen posed for photos on Sunday afternoon, her arm around Monica's strong shoulders, watching their goodbyes as Helen embraced her and reluctantly allowed her to settle into the car, then watching as Helen skipped down the drive behind the retreating Renault, waving like a child and making absurd faces, I could see for myself that any discussion between the pair of us about Monica's future at Wildfell would be merely a gesture.

Helen's decision had already been made.

CHAPTER 3

Sonny had been gone too long. That was the first thing that struck me on Monday morning when I settled down to work in the office. The heating had come on hours before, so the room was warm, and the caramel-painted walls reflected the light in a welcoming way. My desk was as I had left it; that is to say, the wood, though not expensive, had the depth and beauty of age and the surface, busy with files, spoke of challenges to rise to and money in the bank. But I had a powerful sense that something was missing. And that something, I realised with a jolt, had warm brown eyes and went by the name of Sonny Mendlowitz.

The jolt came because, by tradition and training, I am not the sort who misses absent friends. Sonny spotted this quality in me early on. 'There are two sorts of people in the world,' he mused, sitting on a black vinyl bench at the airport. 'The missers, who border on desperation when their loved ones are away. And the repressers, who pretend nothing's happening. The missers spend fortunes phoning home whenever they travel. The repressers act like they're too busy to take the call.'

I wasn't committing myself. 'And which do you claim to be?'

'A misser for sure,' Sonny said. I was on my way to meet a client in Barcelona, and he had insisted on getting up at five a.m. to drive me to Heathrow. Greater love hath no man . . . 'I shall wait by the phone the whole time you're away,' he declared, hamming it up, 'endlessly scan the news for reports of Spanish planes falling out of the sky, leave reams of fax messages at your hotel desk . . .'

17

'Promise me you won't do anything to embarrass me,' I interrupted. My identity as a serious investigator still hung a little loosely on me, and I didn't want to be exposed as merely a woman.

'And you're a represser,' he finished softly. Sonny loves to tease, but he's one of those people who also know when to stop.

'It's a fair cop,' I acknowledged. Somehow my childhood had put paid to missing. My father was a long-distance lorry driver. With a name like Paul Principal he should have owned his business and dictated his own hours. Instead he worked for a firm that transported goods between the West of England and the Continent, so my childhood was punctuated by his absences. By the time I was in infant school, I had learned to block out the fact that he was away. I had stopped running into my mother and father's bedroom first thing in the morning, unable to bear the disappointment when Paul's side of the bed was empty. Well, it's empty all the time now. Paul died a few years back, after eighteen months of discomfort with everything from ulcers – the lorry driver's curse – to thrombosis. But even after my father's death, I clung to the habit of refusing, consciously at least, to miss someone who is away.

That's why I was surprised to find myself missing Sonny that morning. Actively missing. So, I said to myself, this is what it's like: a sense of incompleteness; something maddeningly glimpsed just at the edge of your vision that you can't bring into focus.

As it happened, I didn't even have the option of a phone call. For the past week, Sonny had been holed up in a rustic cottage, no mod cons, in a remote corner of the Orkney Islands. His sons, Dominic and Daniel, are just old enough to relish the adventure of trekking gentle hillscapes in the company of their father, so Sonny had headed north with them for a rugged boys-together half-term holiday. I could just imagine how thrilled the lads would be at their first sighting of a puffin off the Orkney coast. They wouldn't necessarily be as enthusiastic about the absence of a video recorder, but that was Sonny's problem, not mine.

Sonny's hands-on involvement with Dominic and Daniel was one of the things that had attracted me to him in the early days of our relationship. To see them together – Daniel was just a baby then, and Sonny was unfazed by the chaos and the mess of infancy – made me feel secure somehow. Here was a man who didn't find the stuff of life distasteful. And he made me feel that I could love and still be myself. Sonny, it was clear, needed a woman for many things, but he wouldn't depend on me to provide all the warmth and caring in his life.

Dominic and Daniel are lovely kids, both with a keen sense of fun. I've enjoyed blending them into the pattern of my life, taken pleasure from the way they have learned to trust me, to confide in me, even sometimes to tell me off. Dominic, in particular, has his father's emotional insight and I've learned quite a bit about myself from his reactions. But I've never felt the desire to turn the four of us into a family. We share confidences, pizzas and the occasional football match. But Morag, Sonny's ex-wife, is mum to Dominic and Daniel, and I like it that way.

So I share Sonny with the boys. The working week belongs to me; many weekends and much of the holidays, to Dominic and Daniel. Though occasionally I chafe at the way this eats into our social life, most of the time it suits me to a T. But this morning was different. My commitment to our arrangement didn't prevent me from working my way through the files on my desk with one ear cocked for the sound of Sonny's return.

In the event, an urgent message enticed me away from the office before Sonny reappeared. The rest of the day was taken up with the sleazy affairs – financial, that is – of one Michael Loizou, whose current address is the third door from the end on the south upper wing of Bedford Prison.

Mr Loizou's solicitor Diana Murcott claimed that her client was a quiet, unassuming family man, convicted two years ago on largely circumstantial evidence of a series of raids on building societies. When she had visited him at the weekend, he had been in an agitated state, insisting that he needed a private investigator to check out a rumour that was troubling him. She claimed to have no knowledge of what the rumour might be.

Now, some private investigators, with an eye to preserving their licence, will act for prisoners awaiting trial but draw the line at working for convicted criminals. I take a different view. The courts in Britain have had a bad press in the last few years, what with the Birmingham Six, the Guildford Four and others. Give or take a little hysteria, that bad press has been justified. Only the most ill-informed could take conviction in a British court as an infallible guide to guilt. If you think about it, there may be almost as many innocent people incarcerated in our prisons as there are guilty ones roaming the streets outside. And it is the innocent ones inside who have most need of the kind of services a private investigator can provide. So my working week is often punctuated by visits to Her Majesty's Prisons. But it doesn't mean to say that I don't draw lines.

'I won't be involved in anything illegal,' I warned her. 'And since Mr Loizou had no regular employment, I'll need some guarantee of payment.'

'Payment's no problem. Loizou deposited five thousand with me for future legal fees before he was sent down, and I can pay you out of that. It's five hundred pounds in advance, and the rest of your fee when Michael indicates that you've done the work to his satisfaction. And if you can't do what's asked of you – if it should turn out to be illegal – you keep the advance and no questions asked.'

She wrote me a cheque then and there. I took it straight to the bank, rang the office to say I wouldn't be back until late afternoon, and set off for Bedford Prison.

Leaving London by the A1 is a curious experience. This stretch of road on the outskirts of the city always seems to me a little like something out of science fiction. A graceful perimeter of trees beyond Barnet brings to mind a residential avenue, and yet this impression is sharply belied by the blasted and barren landscape beyond. The sensation of unreality is heightened by a blandly-lettered sign that announces the road's traditional name: *the Great North Road*. I often wonder how visitors from Russia or from Canada, where the North means icy wastelands, react to this grandiose name for a small English highway. The Great North Road does of course go north: it moves, small and determined, in a virtually straight line, through Hertfordshire and Bedfordshire, and on up to Lancashire and Yorkshire, pointing the way at intervals to Cambridge or Peterborough or Lincoln or Doncaster or York. For those in pursuit of romance, there is the sign near the turn-off to Nottingham that signals the way to Sherwood Forest. The fact that the sign is set in the tarmac parking lot of a shabby transport café tends to dampen a sense of adventure.

My adventure on the Great North Road was short-lived. After an hour's drive, I turned off towards Bedford. I had to remind myself not to be lured by the outstretched fields and big skies around me into relaxing, for the road itself is given to sudden twists and hairpin bends that test a car's brakes and a driver's nerves. The only reason I can imagine for wishing to meet a road engineer is that perhaps he or she could explain to me why, in largely flat countryside, that particular road corkscrews in this fashion.

In Bedford, I stopped for a ham and cheese croissant and a cup of coffee at a tiny shop on the High Street. The croissant and coffee were freshly made, and my request for directions to the prison met with a precise and willing reply. Still, I couldn't wait to get away. From the moment of the enquiry, the customers and the neatly-dressed woman who ran the shop abandoned all semblance of English reserve. I became the undisguised object of several pairs of eyes, some merely appraising and some frankly hostile. It made me shudder for the humiliations endured by those who have a friend or a husband in prison. It also put me on the side of Michael Loizou in a way I hadn't been before.

Bedford Prison turned out to resemble a downmarket holiday camp for the unattached. I parked in a large lot on the opposite side from the driveway used by prison vans for transporting inmates to and from the courts.

Diana Murcott had provided me with a certificate sealed with a Home Office stamp. According to her instructions, on arrival at the prison I was to present myself to the duty officer.

Locating him was one of the easier parts of the day. His title, on a wooden sign nailed on the wall next to a green metal desk, was the first thing I noticed when I entered the main door. A set of black letters on small plastic squares, like pieces from a Scrabble game, gave his name as *Evan Lewis*.

Evan Lewis inspected the letter Diana had provided, and peered at my identification. His inspection had a cursory quality. I realised then that Diana Murcott must be more influential than her poky office suggests, since she had managed, at short notice, to wangle me the kind of pass usually reserved for legal representatives. Eventually the duty officer cleared me, waving me on to a junior prison officer who scanned attentively through the papers in my briefcase, as if there might be a bazooka tucked away between the sheets of A4. Finally, I was escorted to a waiting room. There, for want of anything better to do, I waited.

I came within seconds of falling asleep. When finally I was summoned to the visiting room, I had to rough myself up, mentally speaking, before I could give a passable imitation of a private investigator. But Michael Loizou seemed ready to buy my act. He immediately took me into his confidence.

Mr Loizou vociferously denied any involvement in the series of building-society raids for which he had been found guilty, but admitted that his arrest did not find him completely unprepared. He had done time before, and he knew that he was under surveillance by the police. In the weeks before the dawn raid at his house in Wimbledon, he had invested large sums of money in a profitable restaurant-cum-nightclub in Soho run by his older brother, Dmitri, and had arranged that his wife, Sonia, should hold the title deeds to two substantial buildings adjoining the restaurant. Michael had every intention of returning to civvy street as a man of property. So discreet were the Loizous, Michael and Dmitri and Sonia, that the police had not managed to establish that these little investments were in any way linked to the convicted brother.

But now Michael had heard an unsettling rumour from a newly-arrived inmate, of imminent property development on a grand scale, of luxury apartments and chic galleries for tourists, in just the part of Soho where Sonia and Dmitri had their holdings. Nothing wrong with that; it could even signal a spectacular return on his investment. Except that Sonia Loizou, who visited regularly, only shrugged and looked blank when her husband asked with studied casualness whether anything was happening in the Soho area. Michael was rattled. He called for me.

I agreed to check out the property scene in Soho. Michael, who was younger and far better-looking than I had expected, smiled a trusting smile. He displayed a set of perfectly shaped teeth, the kind that any male model would trade his orthodontist for. I took my leave, wondering whether Sonia Loizou had found it in her heart to betray a face so apparently candid.

In the parking lot, I rang the office and received a message that made the return drive a pleasure. Sonny was back from Scotland, and looking forward to a reunion. He proposed, and I accepted, that we should meet for a walk before dinner.

After the atmosphere of the prison I felt stiff and stale. I needed some fresh air, and I needed Sonny. As it happened, the traffic was on my side. I drove back to London at a relaxed pace, singing all the way, and managed to pop into my brother Hugo's house for a wash and a change of clothes, have a quick chat with my sister-in-law Justine over the heads of the children, and still arrive at Hampstead Heath within two minutes of the six o'clock pips on the radio. Sonny's blue Vauxhall Cavalier was pulled up on the shoulder of the road, a hundred yards further up. There was no one inside. I found Sonny himself lounging near the side entrance to the Heath. He looked as he always did after a few days' absence, warmer and stronger and more appealing. Knowing this is one of the things that stops me in moments of weakness from contemplating a more structured relationship. We embraced each other, and leaned against a tree trunk to re-establish contact.

For a moment, I considered coming clean, telling Sonny that for once I had missed him. But I couldn't find a form of words that seemed sufficiently low-key, so I let the impulse die away. Why break with tradition, I shrugged to myself. Then I tucked my hand into the capacious pocket of Sonny's greatcoat, he wrapped his arm around my shoulders, and we set off with long easy strides across the woods and over the hill.

As we walked, Sonny took me through the ups and downs of his week with Dominic and Daniel. It turned out I was right about the video. The boys were quite put out at the lack, and positively alarmed to discover that the television only received one blurry channel. But they rallied, and Sonny reported with some pride that by the third evening they were clamouring for another game of *Cluedo*?. Daniel invented a prize, which he called 'a black belt in *Cluedo*?'. I promised on my honour to take part in a tournament as soon as I had a Saturday free.

Then we exchanged news and views about work – the job Sonny had put on hold when he left for Scotland, Ceresa Nazionale and Mina Harrison, and Michael Loizou. Part of the fun of a case like the one I had taken on that day was talking it over with Sonny.

It was Sonny who first introduced me to the investigative business, at a time when I was having difficulty coming to terms with some emerging truths about the fragility of both my marriage to Adam and my career as an academic. We met at a jazz club near Chesterton Lane, just around the corner from my house in Cambridge. I had taken to playing saxophone there occasionally with a small local group. Sonny was a friend of someone in the group; he came along one night and played the clarinet like a dream. He was a few years younger than me, tall and clean-shaven, with thick blond hair. He had a soft voice, a rough chin and the manners of a gentleman. He didn't at all look the part of a private detective.

After that encounter, though I tried, I couldn't get our first conversation about investigative work out of my head. I'd known lots of people in academic life who were good at their jobs. I'd known a few who were obsessive workaholics, and others who got high on the sweet smell of success. Sonny was one of the few people I'd ever met who took pleasure in the work itself.

It was months before I could persuade him to let me have a go at detective work. Sonny was dubious at first. I don't know which he found more unlikely, a woman or an historian. But a time came – oh, some eight years ago now – when he needed someone to infiltrate the front office of a West London firm.

'You?' he asked. We were wolfing down lasagne in the saloon bar of the Eagle, the old un-reconstructed Eagle before the brewery invested two years and ten of thousands of pounds in tarting it up. Sonny lifted his eyes to the blackened ceiling where hundreds of American ex-servicemen had signed their names in candle-smoke. He was not so much composing a reply, as waiting for me to make my pitch. When it came, I think he was probably surprised to find that it made a lot of sense.

I fixed him with the same look I used on undergraduates who failed to grasp the central point of an argument. 'You can't run from this one, Sonny. Look, the way you've described the problem to me, there's a security leak in the external relations office of that firm. You can't seem to plug it. You've tried introducing decoy documents to see where they end up, without success. You've tried bugging the office, ditto. The only thing left is to put someone in there.'

'You?' he asked again. There was too much scepticism in that tone for my liking. 'Of course I have to put someone in, Laura. By why *you?*'

'Isn't it obvious? The only vacancy coming up is for a clerk-typist to cover vacation absences. And let's face it, this may be the age of the breakdown of gender barriers, but no one in their right mind is going to buy the idea of you as a temp. I, on the other hand, can type after a fashion, I can file, I can join in the office gossip and I'm the right sex for the job. Voilà, Laura Principal, junior clerical worker extraordinaire!'

By the time we had picked up our coffee from the bar, I had agreed to drop the French phrases and Sonny had agreed to arrange to slot Laura Principal into the external relations office. The rest was up to me. I cancelled my teaching, pleading illness, and threw myself into the assignment. Having worked in an insurance office during the holidays when I was an undergraduate, I knew enough of office routine to be able to blend in at Permex. A two-day crash course with a temping agency left me with a better technique and a deeper respect for office machines.

Sonny gave me the once-over before dropping me around the corner from Permex. The thrown-together look preferred by academics wouldn't do for the external relations office, so I had invested in a manicure and a neat two-piece from Marks & Spencer. Sonny could scarcely hide his amusement. 'Not bad,' he said, pretending to admire my naïve attempts at make-up. 'Keep this up and perhaps I'll take you home to Mother.' This comment didn't do a lot for my confidence.

That assignment was the only time in my life that I can recall being really afraid of failing. I wanted desperately to succeed. It was more than just interest in a new career, more even than wanting to impress Sonny, though I guess that played a part. No, it was something to do with taking my future into my own hands. The effort of trying to establish myself as a historian in Cambridge, in a world where women – unless, that is, they had a one-in-a-million kind of brilliance – were undervalued and undermined, had worn me down. I was tired of living on the margins. Tired of taking on too many students to supervise because I dared not offend their Directors of Studies, tired of spreading myself in the process too broadly outside my area of expertise and then hearing myself deprecated as a generalist, tired of never having the space and financial security to go all out on my own research. Add to that the squabbles with Adam, and his frequent implication that what I lacked was constancy, and the result was clear: I was desperate to prove to myself that I could be effective.

Well, it worked. I blended into that office like butter into a sponge cake. No one blinked an eye. The place was friendly enough and I was, after all, just another woman. The accounts clerk invited me to eat my sandwiches with her on the first day, I got the hang of the collator on the second, and on the third, without further ado, the marketing manager included in a pile of material for photocopying a set of documents that were strictly confidential.

On the fourth day, I brought Sonny evidence to prove that the marketing manager was up to mischief. There was nothing grudging about his response. 'You brilliant thing,' he said and, putting the briefcase aside, he wrapped me up in the nicest hug I had known in years.

The investigative business, I've since realised, is chock-a-block with cynics. It's populated with ex-police officers and others who believe that the best you can hope for in this line of work is to take a stab in the dark at nasty things that crawl out from under the rocks. They approach their work with dread, and at the end of the day make straight for the nearest pub to forget what they've seen. Enthusiasm is a rare quality. Sonny appreciated mine. We savoured every detail of that assignment, and then experimented equally successfully with a few more.

The only fly in the ointment was my husband, Adam, who was none too pleased with this career move. Oh, of course he wanted me to work, but at a job suitable for a future professor's wife. He approved heartily of typing and its professional variants – administrative, managerial, and Civil Service. Or why not a real career? Retrain as a solicitor, a personnel consultant. Or, have babies . . . Well, we continued like this for more months than I care to recall. I was lazy. I used my absences, working nights, time in London, as an excuse not to talk to Adam about the emptiness in our relationship. And I noticed that, even after all our years together in Cambridge, I didn't miss my life with him one little bit. None of our joint friends were really intimates of mine. So when Adam told me about Isabel, I was relieved. We're on civil terms now, Adam and I. Whereas I was rather an embarrassment to him as a wife, having an *ex*-wife who is a private investigator gives him a certain glamour at dinner parties. It establishes him as something more than a stodgy academic. With me, he has a 'past'.

So by the time Sonny proposed a working partnership, the door had closed on my marriage and I was free to re-locate. Professionally and emotionally, these were the best moves I ever made.

CHAPTER 4

While I was wrapped in nostalgia, the afternoon light had retreated from the Heath. Sonny and I ran down one of the hills towards a lake, our coats outstretched like bats' wings behind us. When we slowed to a strolling pace, I began to tell him about Monica Harcourt. He didn't make it easy, and he refused to share my view about the riskiness of the proposed arrangement.

'So far,' Sonny said in a teasing voice, 'Monica sounds like the perfect housemate. You tell me she's talented, warm-hearted, amusing. You and Helen landed on your feet when Clare sold you the cottage, and it sounds to me as if luck is on your side again.'

We looked at the stone finery of Kenwood House, visible across the Heath. On the crown of the hill, the trees engaged in a vibrant display of colour, a last-ditch effort at glamour before autumn winds stripped them bare. We could feel the tips of icicles in the wind that crept down our collars and up our sleeves. It was time to go. As we started back up the slope in the almost-dark, I tried to spell out my anxieties.

Monica's reaction to Colin seemed a good place to start – but Sonny only argued that an antipathy to Colin was a point in Monica's favour. 'I've told you before, I just don't buy that country-yokel act. All "yes, miss, no, miss" and "whatever you say". There's something about that fellow, an anger that doesn't quite square with his amiable image. I bet that's what Monica picked up on.'

We had been through this before. 'Sonny, you're so unfair to Colin. Just because you have this deep-seated competitive streak, you think that every decent man must have one. And it worries you – yes, it does, don't try to deny it—' Sonny looked as if he would interrupt, but I held his arm more tightly and marched him on. 'It worries you that it is Polly who holds the franchise for the village shop and Post Office. You would be embarrassed if you were the husband in that kind of set-up, so you think Colin must be seething with resentment, too. Well, it's a load of old codswallop. And sexist too.'

We rehearsed this familiar argument for a minute or two, then returned by mutual consent to the subject of Monica. 'I can't make head nor tail of her mood-shifts. Sometimes she does the sweetest things.' I told Sonny about finding a vivid pencil sketch of Wildfell – with a caption at the bottom saying, *I love it here, Monica.* – in the Saab when I set off for home on Sunday evening.

Sonny produced an infuriating so-what's-the-problem shrug. I launched in again without letting him speak.

'But that's just it! Why should such an attractive woman be so blatantly in need of companionship? So unsure of herself – so vulnerable? Do you know, Sonny, when I'm curled up by the fire at Wildfell, I feel completely secure. It reminds me of Friday evenings when I was a little girl, after Dad had returned from a long-distance haul to Edinburgh or Strasbourg: Dorothy and Paul and Hugo and me, all safely together again. Mum would tell us stories about snowdrift winters in Saskatchewan, where she grew up, Dad would describe the European cities he had passed through, and we'd all breathe a sigh of relief to be safely together in Bristol.'

'From what you've told me,' Sonny said, brushing a shock of blond hair back from his forehead with his free hand, 'it isn't at all like that for Monica.' The wind immediately blew the hair forward again.

'No, just the opposite. Monica sits by the fire with her ears pricked up for danger. As if she hears the footfalls of predators stalking just at the perimeter of the fireglow.'

Sonny's teasing manner had disappeared at last. Some of my concern was breaking down his stubborn insistence on looking on the bright side. 'Sonnyanna', I once called him in a fit of pique. Still, no great fan of Norfolk himself, he reminded me that the cottage took a little getting used to.

I acknowledged that there was something to this. The night sounds had startled me too, when I first visited Clare at Burnham St Stephens. But that wasn't the whole story. 'I still think that Monica is abnormally skittish – as if she lives in a different psychological world. I wish I could understand what makes her tick, *and* what makes me feel so uneasy about sharing Wildfell with her. Have you got any ideas?'

'Mmm, I've certainly got ideas,' Sonny affirmed, 'but they don't have very much to do with your new tenant.' He nuzzled the side of my neck, and for a moment I was distracted from the question of Monica Harcourt. But not for nothing have I earned the reputation of being a very determined lady.

'You're not going to get out of it that easily, Sonny. I need your advice, not your hot breath down my cold neck, or at least not first.' I turned him to face me. 'Help me with this,' I commanded. '*Please*.' And smiled.

He ran his finger fondly down the side of my nose, punctuated the motion with a little tap, and began. I could tell by the didactic tone he assumed, not at all the usual Sonny, that he didn't feel comfortable.

'I can think of two possibilities, Laura, but you're not going to like either of them. First: perhaps you have an over-developed sense of balance. You put the case for Monica very well to Helen initially. In fact, she was extremely wary, and it was you who invoked her sense of adventure and got her to consider Monica seriously. It was only *after* Helen became committed to Monica that you began to see the flaws in the very scheme you had proposed. Could it be that as Helen took up position as Monica's chief advocate, you simply assumed her former role as the reluctant partner to the scheme? That's Theory Number One.'

'That's all very well, but it makes me sound as if I'm merely a pawn in some absurd structural game, doomed to position myself in opposition to Helen. You don't really believe that hogwash, do you?'

I knew by the way he grinned at me that he didn't. 'No, of course I don't. Darling Laura, I can't see you as anyone's pawn. But you may like the other possibility, Theory Number Two, even less.'

'Being?' I lifted my chin defiantly.

'Being that you are dead jealous. That no matter how she tries to win you over, you find it impossible to really like this woman. The idea of sharing the *cottage* with Monica was OK in the abstract. What you can't bear is the reality of sharing *Helen*.'

I was silent for a minute, listening to the sober sound of our footsteps crunching their way across the woody floor of the Heath. How to weigh the balance between thought and intuition, when my own complicated feelings kept threatening the integrity of the scales?

'In one sense you're right,' I said quietly. 'It's true, I do feel threatened by Monica – by the way that Helen has taken to her so completely, without reservations. I guess after so many years I'm used to being Helen's confidante, her emotional port of call. Best friends,' I said, smiling up at Sonny. He had always teased me about this phrase, claiming that Helen and I were still like schoolgirls in some ways. I had never minded the comparison before. 'So I was a little unprepared to find Helen and Monica chumming together in a way that left me on the margins.'

Inside the pocket of the greatcoat, Sonny squeezed my hand in sympathy. He's sophisticated enough to know that jealousy isn't an emotion reserved for sexual partners.

'But that isn't all that's happening here,' I continued, feeling more sure of my ground now that I had made my confession. 'There's something not quite right about Monica. She's hiding something, and I have the damnedest feeling that it's something that matters. I can't feel happy about her moving into Wildfell until I know precisely what it is.'

At the car park, we agreed to make our separate ways to Sonny's flat in Camden Town, just a quarter of a mile from the office. I wanted to keep my car with me. I didn't fancy a trek out to the Heath to pick it up in the morning. Sonny volunteered to provide dinner, in the form of a luxury platter from an Eastern restaurant.

Driving through the winding streets of Hampstead, I

remembered just in time that Sonny wasn't the only one who had some shopping to do. Over the seven years that he and I have been together, we have arrived at a very amicable division of labour: I purchase the condoms, and Sonny wears them. I much prefer embarrassment in the chemist's to the risks of the pill. I pulled the Saab up in front of a late-opening chemist and dashed inside. Emerging three minutes later, I caught a glimpse of someone who looked familiar, wearing a remarkably short skirt: Mina Harrison was just coming out of a bistro across the way. She was accompanied by a solid-looking man in his mid-fifties, who took her arm in a gallant fashion as he steered her down the street. She looked happy, perhaps a little tipsy, and very smitten.

I watched quietly from the doorway of the chemist's while they nudged themselves into the back seat of a waiting limousine, and departed. Then I approached the restaurant and manoeuvred a brief exchange with the headwaiter. There is no reason to think he bought my story of plans to join my friend Ms Harrison at her table to meet her new fiancé and of delays – my ankle boots and leggings were not exactly *de rigueur* for dinner in this part of town. But he saw no harm in telling me that 'the fiancé', a regular of the restaurant, was none other than il Signor Gianfranco Permatelli. This information was worth every penny of the £10 note that I slipped into his pocket.

As I drove away from Hampstead, my thoughts focused upon Ceresa Nazionale: to be specific, how to break the news to them that their star interpreter, newly vetted by Laura Principal, was stepping out with Gianfranco Permatelli. They wouldn't need a detective to tell them that Permatelli is the director of Eccole, nor that Eccole is the stiffest competitor Ceresa faces this side of the River Tiber. I hoped that the messenger who brought the news of Mina Harrison's misdemeanours wouldn't also carry the blame . . .

By the time I reached Camden, Sonny's Cavalier was already in place outside the flat. Quietly I let myself in, draped my scarf and coat over a hook, and tiptoed down the hallway to the sitting room. On the large low coffee table in front of the sofa was an open bottle of sparkling wine, two bowls, chopsticks, paper napkins, and a massive oval platter of food. Someone had arranged the food in pretty concentric circles, lettuce rolls fanning the outer edge, a carrot sculpture in the centre. No sign, however, of that someone. I laid a speculative forefinger on one delicate pink sesame prawn. Close enough to piping hot to be distinctly appetising.

I loosened the laces on my ankle boots, kicked them off and let my cold toes enjoy a moment of freedom. Then with the platter balanced on the palm of one hand, and a glass of white wine in the other, I headed for the bathroom. Sure enough, Sonny was stretched out in the tub with his eyes closed, the bubbles on his chest moving slowly up and down. I set the platter gently on the side table where Sonny's glass rested within his reach. When I bent over to wake him with a kiss, a hand shot out of the steaming bathwater, encircled the back of my neck and almost tipped me over into the tub. My wine splashed into the bath. I fetched the wine bottle, refilled our glasses, threw off my leggings and jumper and *etceteras*, and slid into the big white cast-iron tub beside Sonny. It was crowded. It was cosy. And the sesame prawns were not the only thing that was delicious. As we ate, Sonny proposed a household resolution that Singaporean food should only be consumed on cold nights in the bath. I was looking forward to a chilly winter.

CHAPTER 5

I needn't have worried about the reaction of Ceresa Nazionale to the bad news concerning Mina Harrison. The deputy chief took it like – well, he took it like he already knew all about it.

Part of me admired his self-possession. The other part speculated on whether I had been set up. I had a distinct feeling that it was my credentials that were under scrutiny last week, rather than Mina Harrison's. I put this possibility to him.

'My dear Ms Principal,' the deputy demurred. His gestures indicated how pained he was to be suspected of subterfuge.

In the discussion that followed, he didn't so much allay my suspicions as persuade me that they were irrelevant. He offered me a retainer for the next two years, on condition that I would take on cases for Ceresa Nazionale at short notice. I pointed out that I couldn't always guarantee to handle this work myself, but that the firm included a very experienced partner and two skilled operators. One of them would certainly be available, and I would supervise. We shook on it. A substantial cheque went a long way towards ensuring that I parted from Ceresa Nazionale on amicable terms.

The pleasure of the cheque from Ceresa Nazionale, and the security that it implied, cast a mellow glow over the next few days. Sonny had missed me (actively) during his vacation in the Orkneys, and he spent much of the following week energetically making that absence up to me. We toasted our new client more often, perhaps, than custom allows. I pursued Loizou family affairs, plugged some holes in the company accounts, and scarcely thought of Monica.

But by Friday, the old apprehension about our new tenant returned in full. During the drive to Norfolk, scenes from my friendship with Helen played through my mind like fragile images from an old film. As I approached Burnham St Stephens, I had to force myself to concentrate on the road.

It seemed appropriate to my mood that the entrance to Wildfell should be temporarily blocked. As I started to accelerate around the last curve in the drive, the way was barred by a ramshackle wooden gate. I halted the Saab, swung myself up and out into the road. Since Helen and I don't keep any livestock, the gate has rarely been in use. Years of inattention have strained the massive hinges and allowed the gate to droop. As I pushed it open, it scraped a semi-circular channel in the gravel. Though I have been a determined rower since my undergraduate days, and have the shoulders to prove it, the gate was difficult to budge. I was surprised that the village children, a wiry but under-sized bunch, had managed to shut it.

Childish intervention was visible also in a posy of late autumn flowers, propped against the fence in a battered tin vase. An exuberantly colourful branch of winter jasmine overhung the delicate white flowers and fuzzy green leaves of alpine cyclamen. The children often visited on weekends, sometimes doing small chores in exchange for pocket money that they spent at the village shop. They occasionally brought fruit or vegetables, the surplus from their parents' gardens. Touched by this prettier offering, I commandeered the flowers for our dining table, and made the last small lap of my journey home.

Helen and Ginny were only a few moments behind. Ginny raced in with an enthusiastic hug, then insisted on my standing ABSOLUTELY STILL while she dug in her case for a new sweatshirt, slipped it on, and modelled it for me. I thought, of course, that she looked great. I was experienced enough to keep the 'of course' to myself.

Helen was bubbling, too. One of her pet hates is the sentimentalising of the family – you know the kind of thing, someone harking back nostalgically, uncritically, to the days when traditional families (read 'patriarchs') went

35

unchallenged. Well, she had found grounds for complaint that very Friday morning in the news story that graced the front page of the *Independent*. Amidst denouncements about the behaviour of 'young people today', about 'soaring numbers of fatherless families', about 'drug abuse and homosexuality', Teresa St James, the elegant and unusually outspoken wife of the Prime Minister, had announced the launching of a new 'initiative for the family'. The Campaign for Family Revival promised a moral platform for the regeneration of traditional responsibilities. A moral platform, indeed!

I tuned out Helen's indignation, my attention arrested by the beautifully-lit photo that accompanied the story. It had been taken on a wide flight of stone steps, quite probably at the sumptuous country home that Steven St James, while still an aspiring politician with little distinction other than his aristocratic name, had inherited from his father-in-law. The stately figure of his wife dominated the photo. I drew Ginny's attention to a taller, younger woman standing in the corner of the photograph, her head turned a quarter pivot away, as if to distance herself from the proceedings. 'That's Elinor, the PM's youngest daughter,' I told her. 'Any guesses as to what makes her so uncomfortable?'

'Could be,' suggested Ginny, with a ten-year-old's insight, 'that she doesn't like her mum going on about the "behaviour of young people today".'

Our speculations were cut short by Helen's announcement that anyone who wanted to share in the eating, would have to pitch in with the making. I think that was how she put it! Thanks to her, we managed to have the cottage tidy, the fire blazing, and chicken satay ready at six o'clock when Monica drove up.

Our guest arrived in a breathless state. You might have imagined she had cycled all the way from Cambridge, but her condition turned out to be due to high spirits and a dose of nerves. Helen and I had promised to move cautiously in discussing the future of the cottage. For Monica, there was no such hesitation.

'Do you believe in omens?' she blurted out, as soon as we had all settled with drinks and food in front of the fire.

I looked sceptical. The supernatural has never been my strong point.

'Portents,' Monica insisted. 'You know, signs. As in prescience, foresight, prophecy. Reading the runes. Well, never mind,' she soothed, seeing our perplexed looks, 'just listen to this.' And she proceeded to describe, in a manner I found rather touching, the doubts and anxieties that had troubled her after the previous weekend at Wildfell. It wasn't that she didn't like us, she hurried to assure. On the contrary, she loved the cottage and she longed to be included in our little circle. What she doubted was her own capacity to fit in, to be the kind of person she thought we wanted. But – and here was where the omen came in – her doubts had been banished towards the end of the week.

'So what happened, Monica? Did you have a dream or something?' Helen asked. She leaned forward in her chair, her eyes fixed on the other woman's face. I felt, not for the first time, a pang of something very akin to pain. I reached across the sofa and stroked Ginny's hair.

Monica paused for a moment to force some morsels of chicken off a bamboo stick with the tip of her fork. One tiny segment flew to the floor and Ginny retrieved it for the neighbour's cat, which was perched on the back of the sofa. We all watched as Ginny enticed the cat onto the polished floor. Then Monica returned to Helen's question with a smile.

'No, better than a dream, *much* better. A painting! I suppose it sounds silly, but there it is. In the Thursday landscape studio, one of my students showed me a painting, a wonderfully accomplished piece of work, the kind of thing teachers always hope their students will produce. But here's the amazing part. This painting reminded me of Wildfell! In fact, it could have *been* Wildfell. The composition had the shape, the mood, the character of this cottage, and of the woods and the landscape round about. In the painting, the sky looked all dark and thundery, but for me it was just as if the sun had come out from behind a cloud. I knew then that everything will be all right.' Monica took a deep breath before launching her final plea. 'If only, if only, you'll have me.'

Monica looked directly at me, nervously, appealingly. And

I had no power to resist. What could I possibly say? That this stuff about paintings and prescience is altogether too fanciful? That I feel uncomfortable around an adult woman who allows herself to be so openly vulnerable? That – and here I could be honest – that Sonny was partly right, and I wasn't sure I could handle the new dynamics between Helen, Monica, Ginny and me? I smiled, Monica smiled back, and the moment for speaking out was gone.

After that, practical issues of rent and so forth were resolved in a flash. Monica wanted to bring a few bits of furniture down the following weekend, if we had no objections. I had none; I even offered to deliver a key to her flat on Friday evening and go over final details then. So it was settled. Helen looked excited. Monica looked radiant. Ginny looked bored. The conversation settled onto more mundane ground and I gradually felt reassured.

Ginny had secured our agreement to a basketball challenge match, two on two, after supper, and even she was impressed that 'a woman from Newcastle' could handle the ball so well. Monica's reaction to the newspaper cutting about the Campaign for Family Revival – a derisive snort and a few choice words about Richard Dolby, the spokesperson for the Pro-Life Campaign who also featured in the photograph – further endeared her to Helen. More relaxed now that a decision had been reached, Monica fitted in good-naturedly with our routines. In spite of my continuing reluctance, I was forced to admit that Monica might just prove to be our kind of person.

We had planned a tromp through the woods for Saturday morning. Growing up in Bristol, one of my most cherished autumn pastimes was the game of conkers. My big brother Hugo was the neighbourhood champion three years in a row, and from him I had learned how to select the most promising horse chestnuts, how to dry them and pierce them with string, how to grip the string so that it wouldn't fly away at the moment of impact and precisely where to hit your opponent's conker so as to inflict maximum damage. Damp autumn days always bring back to me a memory of Hugo at nine years old, black curls breaking out of his woolly cap, strolling down the alley behind our house where the neighbourhood children congregated. Hoping to achieve an air of nonchalance, Hugo would place his hands carelessly in the pockets of his flannel trousers, but I knew and he knew I knew that actually he was clutching his No. 1 conker, his Kingmaker, infusing it with strength for the match ahead.

Ginny, I'm pleased to say, had not outgrown her own interest in conkers. She and I vied for the best, as we did every autumn, using underhand stratagems to divert one another away from promising sources. Monica, however, outmanoeuvred us both. Her capacity to spot a spiky green jacket among yellowing leaves at the base of a bush demonstrated the value of an artist's eye. Only a sudden shower of rain cut short our adventures. We dashed for home. Half an hour later, armoured by hot chocolate and wellies, we set out to chart the depths of the puddles between Wildfell and the stream.

After lunch, while one end of a rainbow tucked itself absurdly behind the Saab, Monica studied Ordnance Survey maps of the local area. Holkham Bay, she explained, was likely to be perfect for some of her current work on seascapes. She had had the idea for this work years ago, on a six-mile stretch of sandy beach in Oregon. Ahead of her, as she described it, was nothing but the Pacific Ocean all the way to Japan; behind her, the dignity and silence of the forests. She had been working as an au pair for a family in Portland, spending the summer before her art foundation course abroad. But she hadn't been prepared for the splendour of the Pacific, for this sense of being on the edge of the world. And ever since, she had pondered the possibility of a series of paintings that would capture that feeling. Over the intervening decade, she had also been struck by the very different attractions of the Wash, by the homeliness of some of the seascapes in this part of the world, and the more measured sense of peace that they can invoke. What she aimed for, as I understood it, was a comparison, not of coastlines but of different dimensions of life – of passion and serenity, of challenge and security, of isolation and community.

So, in the early afternoon, Monica set off for the beach. She was armed not with towel and suncream, but with tripod and camera. She had targeted an isolated stretch of Holkham Bay where her view would be framed by pine trees and where the sea meandered rather than plunged towards the shore.

To see her come back three hours later, you would have thought she had found Treasure Island. Her wide, low-lidded eyes were bright with excitement. She made an elaborate show of spreading out the Ordnance Survey map and tapping a section of shoreline with her finger. We suspected of course that Monica had seen something more engaging than shoreline through the camera lens.

'No, not a word,' she backed off laughing when pressed. 'As soon as this film is developed, you'll see for yourselves. Then I'll need your help to decide what to do.'

Over that second weekend together, was there any sign of what was to come? Most of the time, I would have to say 'no'. Monica seemed so engaged, so full of mischief, so willing to be one of the gang.

And yet, although she was familiar with the cottage this time round, and although she knew Helen and me a great deal better, Monica seemed even more edgy than before.

Take what happened at breakfast that Saturday morning. Monica and Ginny were chatting in an animated way about a children's exhibition at the Arnolfini Gallery in Bristol. As they talked, Monica traced with her finger the delicate shape of the cyclamen petals. When she passed some remark about the flower, I explained how the posy had been left in a rough tin vase, a secret offering from the village children. Monica froze. She looked at the branch of jasmine with distaste, then snatched her finger away, excused herself from the table and disappeared upstairs without a backward glance. Not until we coaxed her out for a walk, half an hour later, did she reappear. But even then she seemed withdrawn, her sense of fun dampened by anxieties she made no attempt to share.

Sunday morning brought an even more dramatic – or perhaps I should say *melo*dramatic – example. We returned from mushroom-picking in the woods at about half-past eleven, feeling refreshed and exhilarated. Monica went upstairs to take a shower. As I prepared the salad for lunch, I could hear her la-la-ing her way through the melody of *Bright, bright sunshiney day*. A few minutes later, I was pulled up with alarm by her appearance in the kitchen doorway. Her face was pinched and white. She demanded to know, in a voice that caught in her throat, if I had been in her room. I assured her that I hadn't. She made a small apologetic gesture with her hand, and rushed to the sitting room, where I heard her confront Helen and Ginny with the same question. Their denials sounded, as well they might, bewildered. I joined them in the sitting room, and asked Monica, more gently than my feelings commanded, for an explanation.

Monica took a deep, raggedy breath. Then she produced a paperback novel and set it down with a snap on the table. The direct gaze of Kate Delafield stared out at us from the collage on the cover of *Murder at the Nightwood Bar*.

'Someone's moved my bookmark. I left it at Chapter 17 – look, you can see that the book falls open there – and now it's inside the back cover. Someone's been going through my things.' I suppressed a thought of The Three Bears.

'But Monica, perhaps you placed your bookmark at the back while you were reading. Maybe you just forgot and left it there.' This was Ginny. Fools and children rush in.

Monica shook her head vehemently. 'I wouldn't forget something like that,' she said rather shrilly. 'No, someone's been in my room while we were out.'

'Sorr-*ee*,' muttered Ginny, and trailed out of the room. Helen decided on a conciliatory approach. She prepared tea, and drew Monica out about the position of the book.

Meanwhile I inspected our visitor's bedroom. There was, as I had expected, nothing to see. The room was spare and light, just as it had been when I had seen it last. It was tidy – the coverlet of the bed pulled neatly up, the wardrobe door closed. The only signs of Monica's occupation were an alarm clock on the bedside cabinet, and a blue lambswool cardigan draped across the end of the bed.

Later, Monica raised the subject of the book again. I was tired and definitely not in the mood for histrionics. But this time, her comments were light-hearted.

'Sorry,' she said with a brilliant smile, directed primarily at me. 'I do seem to attract this kind of thing. Footsteps in the night, heavy breathing on my answerphone, peculiar messages in my pigeonhole. I've even started to keep a diary. A book of weird events.'

She glanced at me again, an embarrassed, self-deprecating look. 'They don't really mean anything very much. I guess sometimes I overreact. But this thing today shocked me because, well, this is the first time as far as I know that anyone has come right inside my room.' She looked pleadingly, first at me and then, when I hesitated, at Helen. Helen, of course, made reassuring noises. I tried to steady myself, though I had an unpleasant feeling of foreboding. And I began to develop a theory about Monica Harcourt.

'What do you make of it all?' Helen asked me on the Sunday evening, while we were packing up what was left of the groceries.

'A textbook case of "the evil eye",' I pronounced. 'Here is Monica, brimming over with goodwill. She feels she is fortunate, perhaps compared to other people she knows, unfairly so. She's healthy, bright and beautiful, she has the job she wants, she loves her work. And now on top of all that, it looks as if she will get the chance to pursue a long-cherished project.'

'So?' Scepticism roughened the edges of Helen's voice. 'This hardly sounds like a problem.'

'So,' I retorted, 'it is precisely the fact that things *are* going well that constitutes the problem. It's success that makes Monica uneasy. Being fortunate, so conspicuously fortunate, invites the evil eye.'

'I've heard,' Helen mused, 'that in parts of India, it is very bad form to comment upon the good looks or the health of a newborn baby, because to draw attention to the parents' happiness is asking for trouble. Is that the sort of thing you mean by the evil eye?'

'How about a more psychological reading? Projection, maybe. Monica imagines that if things go well for her, she'll become the target for other people's resentment and envy. The more obvious her good luck, the greater the misfortune to come.'

Helen considered. 'Do you think that has something to do with her ambivalence about Oregon?' she asked.

Something, indeed. Monica had a specific time-frame in mind for her seascapes project. She was perched on the edge of a sabbatical this coming year, to finish her paintings on the Pacific Coast. She had applied for, virtually been promised, a grant from an arts council in Oregon, and all she needed now was agreement from the University authorities here for the time off. Monica had left us with no doubt that she longed to go to Oregon, intended to go, expected to go.

And yet, curiously, the mere mention of the grant seemed to trouble her. She paced up and down the room, protesting that she hadn't pinned her hopes on getting leave. She proclaimed – in complete contradistinction to her comments of the previous five minutes – that it was probably a silly project anyway. Helen and I couldn't make head nor tail of this shift of emphasis. 'An example of the evil eye in operation?' Helen asked again.

'A classic example,' I concurred. 'I suppose, for someone inclined to the psychology of the evil eye, even our offer of a room at Wildfell will accentuate the sense of threat. Anxiety, fears, sudden mood changes – all projections of the envy that Monica fears other people harbour towards her.'

Proving yet again that though I am a passable musician, a strong athlete and a good detective, as a psychologist I have an awful lot to learn.

In Cambridge a week later, on the Friday evening, I saw for the first time the flat where Monica lived. That evening is as unforgettable to me as Monica herself.

Her back parlour riveted my attention, in part because it was so palpably an artist's studio. A scarred oak dining table, very old and probably valuable, sprawled across one side of the large square room. Much of the table's surface was covered by a white sheet with idiosyncratic speckles, which clearly performed as a paint-rag. The cloth was secured to the table by tubes of oil paint, books, nails, screws and brushes. Tin cans with their labels removed held chopsticks and palette knives and other instruments, many of which had been pressed away from kitchen duty into the service of art. No trace here of the ladylike water colourist with creamy smock and delicate still life. This table exposed a more professional activity. Or perhaps, a more desperate one – urgent, pragmatic, tough-minded, leaving the niceties of words like 'sensitive' and 'artistic' outside the door. My ignorance humbled me. I hadn't known this was what Monica meant by painting.

The second wall of the room was taken up by generously-proportioned French doors. It was easy to see how the sunlight would dance in and fill the room on a bright day. But now, the glass panels of the doors blankly reflected back the light of an unshaded bulb. Pressing my damp forehead against the glass, I could just make out the ghostly shapes of shrubs lining the path outside. Above the doors, a blind of narrow bamboo strips, obviously rarely used, was tied crookedly into a roll.

A third wall was lined with paintings. Canvases, most of them large, spilled out of the alcoves on either side of the chimney, filled the shelves above, and rested precariously on sections of floor.

The room contained only three other pieces of furniture. An oak stool, high and every bit as pitted as the table, with a china mug upon it. Another stool, with a slide projector, aimed towards the whitewashed surface of the chimney breast. And an old pine rocking chair, splashed with blood and sheltering Monica's body.

From the moment of my arrival at Monica's front door this evening, key to the cottage, list of instructions and draft contract in hand, I had sensed something was wrong. 'Do you mind coming late on Friday evening?' Monica had asked. 'When I finish work, say ten p.m.? We could have a drink, a little signing ceremony.' It suited me. But when I reached her front door, there was no response. The lights were on; there was a crack of warm yellow from the front room, where the heavy linen curtains met, and a faint buzz of radio voices from inside, but no response to my knock. The crack-crack of the brass knocker was unmissable in a small house like Monica's. Enough to waken the dead.

I hung around outside the front door for a few minutes in

case she had stepped out for some fresh air. Then I pursued the path that ran between the houses, treading carefully in the dark. I reached the back of Monica's house feeling very much like an intruder, but driven on by a sense of alarm. Blinds were drawn in what I assumed was the kitchen, but the French doors in the back parlour were uncurtained, light flooding out onto the meagre lawn. One glimpse was enough. I set off on foot for the nearby constabulary, returning shortly afterwards with two police officers, doubtful but stalwart, in tow. They broke a kitchen window, and the three of us stepped gingerly into the home of the late Monica Harcourt.

I stood in Monica's studio for a long while, perhaps five minutes, before I could gaze upon her body. Until I had glanced through the French doors that Friday evening, I had considered murder only in a detached, professional context. I had been at the edges of two murder investigations, both of the victims men who had made a living and found a death through illicit drugs. And though these deaths were shocking in their way, there is enough of the Puritan in me that I am somehow unsurprised when people who live by the sword die by the sword.

Monica's death was different. Her body brought a bleak sense of unfinished business, of the brutality of the intrusion into the fabric of another person's life. And it wasn't squeamishness that held me back from looking at her, or horror, or even grief. It was acute awareness of the discourtesy of the gaze. In the initial fraction of a second between glimpsing her and jerking my head away, I knew it was Monica. I knew also that she was very dead. It seemed disrespectful to live and breathe so palpably in her presence; that I should glance at her, when she no longer had the power to glance back, to hunch her body against my gaze, to challenge me with a defiant look, or simply to walk away. It seemed shocking that, silenced by her death, I should nevertheless be already edging towards the next issue; that her death should become, so quickly, not an overwhelming fact that obliterated all others, but a platform for questions, explorations, enquiries, preparations – actions that would affirm my life as much as they confirmed Monica's death.

I made myself stand near, within two feet of the rocking chair. I compelled myself to look.

Monica's body was tied into the chair. There were ropes around her wrists, and another around her neck. Her head fell sideways, and just above her left ear a great bitter gash of blood and bone and some soft grey substance obliterated her tangled curls of reddish hair. On the same side, her cheek was swollen and discoloured. Her jaw hung slackly open. Her upper body was a mass of wounds, her jumper torn, her arms nicked and sliced as if she had been in a fight with a tiger. I reached out and touched her cold, blood-streaked fingers, but the WPC gently took my hand and replaced it against my waist.

The Sergeant asked me a great many questions. Why had I come to see Ms Harcourt so late in the day? Did she usually work in the evenings? Was her door normally kept locked? Did she have any rope in her flat? Was she on close terms with the neighbours? Was anything missing? Had any of her things been moved?

I didn't know, of course. I had to tell them so, again and again. Yes, this was my first visit to Monica's home. I didn't really know her very well.

'And yet,' the Sergeant enquired, 'you say you were planning to share with her your home in Norfolk?'

'Yes,' I said.

CHAPTER 6

Normally, I am an early riser. To me, the hours before breakfast are the most desirable part of the day – the time when the river is smoothest for rowing, the traffic is sparsest for driving, the telephone is least intrusive. At six a.m. I enjoy the illusion that I'm getting ahead with the things I have to do.

But the shock of Monica's death had silenced my internal alarm clock. When I awoke in my bed in Cambridge that Saturday morning, it was half-past ten. A knocking on the door, muted but insistent, echoed in my brain. Heavy-hearted, I think, is the term for people weighed down by sadness. In my case, heavy-headed might be more apt.

Reluctantly I swung my legs over the side of the bed and encased them in a pair of jeans. My wrinkled T-shirt would do for the moment; it was unlikely that the visitor was anyone more imposing than the milkman.

It wasn't the milkman. Helen was standing on the doorstep. Clearly the events of the past thirty-six hours had told on her too. She was uncharacteristically crumpled, her face pale and anxious. But she was obviously relieved to find me in, and her smile was lop-sided but composed.

It was none too warm in the house. I pulled on a jumper over the T-shirt, and made a pot of Earl Grey tea. Helen and I sat on the cushions on the carpeted floor, the tea tray between us, and spoke of everyday things. Helen asked after Sonny, and I after Ginny. I reported that Colin had rung from Wildfell to say that the wheelbarrow had gone missing; we touched on the possibility of security locks for the shed and the cottage. All this was ritual. We recreated our movements

47

over the past couple of days, skirting carefully around the event on which the active parts of our minds were most tenaciously fixed. Neither of us referred directly to the fact that Monica had been killed on Thursday evening. Nor to the uncomfortable fact that her body had lain there in isolation for twenty-four hours before I showed up.

Helen, it seemed, had locked up the library at nine o'clock on Thursday evening. Normally, after prising Ginny away from her friend Karen, with whom she hung out when Helen had a late shift, they would have gone straight home. But Friday was a staff development day at Ginny's school, so the pupils were free. Helen had whisked her daughter off to London for two glamorous nights in a small hotel. Friday evening, replete with stalls for a musical, lived up to expectations, but was punctuated around midnight by my call. I hated breaking the bad news by telephone, but didn't want Helen to learn of Monica's death from the police on her arrival home. Helen and Ginny slept fitfully. The next morning, this morning, Saturday morning – murder plays hell with your sense of time – Helen put Ginny on the first train bound for Bristol to spend a few days with her dad. Then she hightailed it back to Cambridge and to me.

Helen cleared her throat. 'What are your plans for today?' she asked. I recognised the additional unspoken question.

'I've got a ticket for the match this afternoon,' I reminded her. Helen didn't share my love of football, and I suspect that she had barely registered that Cambridge United were in fighting form. 'But I'm really not in the mood. So if you're willing to wait while I shower and brush my teeth, I'll come over to your place with you and you can make me breakfast.'

Helen's look of relief told me that I'd got the unspoken question right. At Wildfell, Helen is fearless, but in Cambridge, ever since the time James disappeared, she experiences something near panic at the prospect of arriving home alone to an empty house.

Helen made a token gesture of demurral. I waved it aside. 'Look, the things in your kitchen are bound to be more edible than the things in mine. After breakfast, we'll plan the rest of the day.' It would only take me an hour to settle her in, and then I could get down to the business that had been taking shape in my mind as we talked.

Helen lives about five minutes' drive away from Clare Street, in a quiet corner of Newnham near the meadow. Her house, not quite at the end of the terrace, is small and perhaps a little shabby. The paint on the stonework around the bay window is mottled and scraped; the tiny front garden, bounded by a shapeless hedge, is cluttered with leggy shrubs.

But the inside is a little haven, a retreat. The small front parlour is pure Victoriana, right down to the delicate white cloth whose lace border overhangs the black marble mantelpiece. And once the coals are glowing in the grate, there's no cosier room in Cambridge.

Now she retreated to the kitchen. We called companionable comments back and forth while she defrosted home-made cheese scones and squeezed orange juice into a frosty jug. Even with her eyes red-rimmed from tears, even with a sense of shock colouring her tone, Helen couldn't abandon the habit of hospitality. There's something to be said for domesticity.

I stacked the kindling and set about lighting the fire. When the flames caught, I flexed my back and straightened. In the mirror above the fireplace I saw that despite sleeping late this morning, there were dark rings below my eyes. Then my glance fell on a large white card propped on top of the mantelcloth. At first sight, it might have been a formal invitation: a college dinner perhaps or a wedding?

Looking closer, I saw that it was an invitation all right, but quite unlike the kind I had at first imagined. The typed message read as follows: *I'm in serious trouble. You must help me – there is no one else. Come to my flat this evening at 10 p.m.* It was signed *Monica*.

Trouble? Helen hadn't mentioned anything about Monica being in trouble. Why would she keep such a thing from me, I wondered, especially now? I sat in the plum-coloured armchair, shivering a little and waiting for her. A moment later she appeared in the doorway, a wooden tray laden with breakfast held out in front of her like a ritual sacrifice.

She halted when she saw my face. 'Laura, whatever's the matter?'

By way of answer, I held the invitation towards her at arm's length. Helen looked puzzled. She set the tray down on a sidetable, then took the card from my hand and read it, once and again, with an air of deliberation.

'Good lord, Laura. Where did you get this?'

I pointed in the direction of the fire. 'From your mantelpiece,' I replied drily. 'Surely you haven't forgotten it was there?'

Puzzlement changed to astonishment so deeply etched that no one could doubt its authenticity. *'Forgotten?'* she repeated. 'Don't forget, Laura, I've only just got back from London. The last time I was in this sitting room was Thursday morning. I've never seen this note before.'

Once we had recovered from sheer surprise, we began talking so rapidly that we had to remind ourselves to eat the scones. The invitation from Monica must have reached Helen's house some time *after* eight-thirty a.m. on Thursday, when she had already left for work. The first post had arrived before breakfast as usual that day, and among the bills and magazines there was certainly nothing from Monica. If Monica herself had brought the note over to Newnham, it must have arrived during the morning or afternoon on Thursday. If, on the other hand, Monica had put it in the post, the invitation might have been in transit when she died and might even have reached Helen's house on Friday morning after Monica's death.

That macabre thought made Helen distinctly uncomfortable. 'But it's not likely,' I argued, thinking aloud. 'If you had sent an invitation – well, "summons" really, as the tone is quite imperative – by post, it wouldn't do at all to say, "this evening at 10 p.m.", when the note would be unlikely to arrive until the following day. Altogether too ambiguous.'

'So you think Monica hand-delivered this note?'

I nodded. 'Or someone else did so on her behalf. She probably expected you to come home after work on Thursday, as you usually do. You hadn't told her you planned to go to London?'

Helen shook her head. 'I only decided myself the evening before. But there's another problem with this theory. If Monica wanted to get hold of me urgently, why didn't she try to contact me at the University? She teaches until late afternoon. It would have been damned inconvenient to come all the way over to Newnham to deliver a note, when she could simply have walked across campus.'

'Not just one problem but two,' I intervened. 'Whether the note came by post or by hand, how did it get from the letter box onto your mantelpiece? Don't you think you should give your cleaner, that student, whatshername, a quick ring?'

'Hannah,' Helen reminded me in a reproving tone, but she didn't reject the suggestion.

Hannah was at home, immersed in her books. She confirmed that she had found a typed note tucked through the letter box when she arrived at midday on Thursday. She had propped it up on the mantelpiece. There was no envelope. Hand delivery it was.

So, the invitation had been delivered between 8.30 a.m. and midday on Thursday, possibly by Monica. What kind of serious trouble she might have been in, neither Helen nor I knew. But one thing we both realised: if Helen *had* come straight home from work, as she usually did, on that Thursday, she would have rushed over to Monica's and perhaps prevented Monica's murder. Or perhaps been killed herself. Recalling the body, the amount of sheer hatred that went into that attack, I thought the second possibility was by far the more likely . . .

One of the advantages of having taught adults in a smallish town is that, as your former students become more and more senior, you come to know a fair number of people in useful positions. I rang Detective Sergeant Pelletier at Cambridge Police Station, and caught her just as she was about to leave the station. Sure enough, she was on the team established that morning to investigate Monica's murder. And she was more than a little interested when I told her I had turned up fresh information about the victim's state of mind on the day she was killed. I persuaded her to meet me at Monica's flat in an hour.

It was with some misgivings that I parted from Helen. The sight of the invitation had thoroughly shaken her. During our conversation, she became more and more frenetic, laughing inappropriately and fretting over silly things, like the dry cleaning. But she would have no truck with my suggestions for her welfare. No, she didn't want to visit friends, thank you, and she certainly had no intention of spending the rest of the day in bed. I could see her casting about for something to do that would feel sufficiently safe, and yet be sufficiently distracting. Eventually she settled on a workout followed by a sauna and a swim – on her own. Having focused her mind on this, Helen became adamant, so I dropped her off at the Leisure Club in Impington, insisting she should call me if she needed company. She waved me off and marched resolutely through the automatic doors.

Then it was back to Clare Street, where I handed my ticket for the Cambridge United match over to neighbours. Olwyn and her younger brother never miss a match. They assured me they had a schoolfriend who would be only too pleased to take my usual place in the stands.

It wasn't easy to find a parking spot in the area adjoining Mill Road, where Monica had lived. I tried Covent Garden and Cross Street without success, and finally found an opening on Mawson Road around the corner from Monica's flat. I hung about on the pavement outside for ten minutes until an unmarked police car came to a halt on double yellow lines and Nicole Pelletier bounded towards me, keys in hand.

Nicole is a large handsome woman with olive skin and hair that approaches that blue-black colour you rarely see on Europeans. She applies to policework the same kind of fierce energy that she reserved for netball when I was her history tutor at Eastern U.

'I suppose you know the rules,' the Detective Sergeant warned as she unlocked the front door. 'Eyes only, no touching, and any information I give you will be strictly between us.' So much for the remnants of my academic authority.

She scrutinised a studio bed in the front room before plonking herself down on it and directing me to a chair. I was glad she avoided the back parlour where Monica used to work. A uniformed Police Constable stood nearby with a steno-

grapher's notebook and pencil in hand. I tried to introduce
the issue of the invitation, but Nicole refused to relinquish the
initiative.

'The first thing I want to know is why you insisted on seeing
me at the scene of the crime,' she began. 'For most people,
one look would be enough.'

The account I gave about Monica and Helen and me seemed
for the moment to satisfy Nicole: how, after only two visits,
Monica already seemed a part of our life at Wildfell Cottage.
How we became committed to her. How we regretted now not
only her death, but also being robbed of the chance to know
her well. And I told Nicole, most importantly, about the need
to find the film . . .

It wasn't until I awoke this morning that I recalled the
photographs – the ones Monica had taken near Holkham
Beach. I had two reasons for wanting to see that film. For
one, it represented the best side of Monica as we briefly knew
her – intense, laughing, in love with the sea. But beyond that,
it represented a loose end. Monica had wanted to share with
us an observation, something she found amusing and notable.
And it seemed appropriate that we *should* share it.

I don't know how much of my account Nicole believed but
she did instruct her colleague, an older man with remarkably
fine posture, to have a skim around for a film or for the
camera. She motioned me to stay where I was. 'First,' she
insisted, 'I want the lowdown on Monica. All the feelings and
impressions and just-maybes that didn't come up in your
interview last night.'

So I told her nearly everything. About Monica's past life –
the little I had gleaned – and about her plans to go to America.
About her changeable moods. About her dedication as a
teacher, her professionalism as a painter. Her warmth. I
finished by recalling Monica's fear. Someone had been after
Monica – and she had known it.

What I kept from Nicole was the fact that Monica had been
surrounded by sceptics: that Helen and I, for instance, had
bracketed the reality behind her questions about safety and
risk, the glances over her shoulder, the stories of footsteps in
the night. That although we hadn't said as much, we suspected

these were neurotic symptoms – the product perhaps of overwork or isolation, or of the recent death of her mother. That, in short, we didn't believe.

I had left academic work partly because I wanted to feel that what I did made a concrete difference in people's lives. I sure as hell had failed to make a difference to Monica.

Throughout my account, Nicole listened attentively. She let me set the agenda, let me wander where I wanted in describing Monica. If she discounted some parts of my story, she didn't say so. She asked few questions. Were there any relatives? Any boyfriends? Had the deceased ever been married? Who did she hang out with at work? The most striking thing about my answers was how uninformative they were.

Meanwhile, the upright Constable had returned from the kitchen area with an Olympus camera, one of the fancy kind with an integral zoom lens. There was a film inside. 'We'll have this developed right away,' Nicole stated. 'I'll let you know if anything interesting turns up.'

I countered. 'Interesting or not, I'd like to see those photos.' I pulled the invitation from my jacket pocket. 'And before you rush off, maybe *you'd* like to have a closer look at this.'

The note to Helen asking her to visit Monica on the night of her death created a sensation. Detective Sergeant Pelletier was unconvincing in her attempt to look cool, but it has to be said in her favour that she didn't allow excitement to dull her efficiency.

After transcribing the typed message onto a yellow legal pad, she then secured the original card in a clear plastic evidence bag. She radioed Murder Headquarters to make certain that Superintendent Neill was on the premises. Then she instructed me – I bridled at the tone – to ride with her in the police car. It wasn't that she had me pegged as a dangerous criminal, set to flee the country. As far as I could figure, she merely wanted to ensure that it would be she who ushered me into Neill's presence. Nicole wanted there to be no doubt about who should get the kudos for turning up the invitation. I flashed her a warning look, the one Sonny refers to as my 'shot across the bows' look and, to her credit, she backed off.

'I'd appreciate it,' she said.

We entered the Police Station from the parking lot at the rear. Nicole handed the film to a uniformed Constable with instructions to retrieve the developed prints as quickly as possible. Meanwhile, I was escorted to a small interview room and left on my own. It was much like the ones painted battleship grey in countless police dramas, the only distinguishing feature being a publicity poster for the Cambridge Festival pinned on the back of the door. Since there was a mackintosh draped over it, I had to conclude that the poster was not there for aesthetic reasons. Perhaps it was part of someone's campaign to bring culture to the Constabulary. I closed my eyes and rested.

When Nicole returned, she was preceded through the door by a tall heavyset man whom she introduced as Superintendent Neill. Nicole was much as she had been at Monica's flat, focused and brusque, but there was an added watchfulness about her which owed much, I supposed, to the presence of her governor. After an hour with them, I began to think that it was he who should be watchful. In spite of his bluster and habit of command, Neill gave the impression of coasting, while even through her deference to rank, Nicole's demeanour rang out sharp and hungry.

Neill picked up the transcription of the note, frowned as he read it, then passed it to Nicole. 'So,' he said, addressing me, 'a note from the dead girl. How did you come by this?'

'Monica,' I corrected him. 'The dead girl's name was Monica Harcourt.' I explained how Monica had recently come to know Helen and me, and that Helen had been absent from home for a couple of days. 'So it's only this morning that she found the invitation. Monica must have put this note through Helen's letter box on Thursday, the day she died. Or at least, that's how it looks.'

Neill wasn't interested in the implication that how it looked might be different from how it actually was.

'So why isn't this Helen with us? Why didn't *she* bring the note?' Neill's glance was irritable, scanning the room for a target. 'No, wait a minute.' He turned to a weary-looking Detective Constable, who was trying hard not to slouch against the Cambridge Festival poster. 'Do we know where to locate this woman? Have we got an address?'

The Constable managed to look blank and anxious at the same time. Nicole flipped through a file and indicated with a vigorous thumbs-up that the answer to Neill's question was affirmative.

Neill continued: 'Right, send someone over there and bring her down to the station. Right away. I won't settle for this kind of thirdhand statement.' The reprimand was delivered with a severe glance at Nicole.

Should I let him know that Helen wouldn't be found at home? I considered whether to interrupt Neill's impatient instruction, but a warning glance from Nicole made me hesitate. Besides, Helen wouldn't be too keen on being called on by the police while she was washing away her sorrows in the sauna. So I let the Constable go.

By now, Neill had relayed the plastic evidence bag, held gingerly between his stout fingers, back to Nicole. He caught her eye, and she began asking the questions.

She went over with me how Helen had found the note, how she had reacted, why I had volunteered to bring it down to the station instead of her. As to what lay behind the note, I couldn't help at all. I had no idea what trouble Monica was in. And I was certain that Helen was just as bewildered.

CHAPTER 7

Superintendent Neill, Detective Sergeant Pelletier and I wasted far too much of the day going over a few simple matters. Finally Neill left, having conferred with his lieutenant first in the corridor outside the interview room. It was well past the lunch-hour, and the nourishing impact of Helen's cheese scones was wearing off. I thought of asking for a sandwich, but decided that I'd rather wait to eat in a more congenial atmosphere.

By the time Nicole came back, I was napping. She brought me a styrofoam cup of tea, but it did little to revive me. Enough was clearly enough: I needed to be out of there. 'Nicole, my good citizen routine is wearing a bit thin. Any sign of those photographs yet?'

Without a word, she reached in her bag and extracted a glossy Kodak envelope. There were only a dozen or so prints. I raised an eyebrow.

'Unexposed,' Nicole explained. 'This is all there was. Monica was only halfway through the film.'

I spread them out on the table, in sequence. The first three prints offered simple views from the front of Wildfell Cottage, two of the cottage itself, with Helen waving absurdly as I stood sedately by. Another looked outward from the cottage towards the meadow. From under the branches of the apple tree you could see my car insinuating its bonnet into the edge of the picture. I explained all this to Nicole. I also explained that Monica had used an earlier reel of film that weekend during her trek to Holkham Bay. It wasn't at her flat, I was told. Where the hell could it be then? Nicole agreed to assign someone from her team to make enquiries at shops in town that processed film, on the assumption that Monica had dropped off the first complete reel for developing.

Then we returned our attention to the remaining shots. They consisted of portraits – informal studies of a very handsome face. A man in his early thirties, black-skinned, with a strong forehead and exuberant hair. In some poses he looked rather petulant, in others mischievous and relaxed. I had not the faintest idea who he might be.

'A boyfriend?' Nicole was studying my face closely.

'Perhaps. Monica mentioned a relationship in London, a serious one, that lasted a number of years. It finished shortly after she moved to Cambridge, apparently. She never gave us the impression there was anyone special in her life now. In fact, she explicitly said that she anticipated being on her own. That's one of the reasons she was keen on the cottage. She liked the idea of having longstanding companions to share part of her life.'

'So she split up with someone shortly after she arrived in Cambridge,' Nicole recapitulated for the benefit of the Detective Constable, who looked more alert now that he was taking notes. 'When was that?'

'September or October, the year before last. Before that, she was artist-in-residence at Keele University.'

'So was this fellow she talked about from Keele?'

I had to think for a few seconds. 'No. No, I'm sure he wasn't.' My mind's eye recreated that Saturday evening by the fire, when our conversation had focused on relationships. Helen described some of her difficulties with Ginny's father, and Monica joined in about her former boyfriend, wondering in a light-hearted way whether men were worth the trouble.

'Monica said that she used to travel down from Keele to see him most weekends at his place. I'm pretty sure she said London. I have an image of her strolling through West London, you know, somewhere in the region of Holland Park.'

'You don't have an address for him, then?' I shook my head, not for the first time during this interview. 'And what did he do, this boyfriend of hers? Did he have a name, by the way?'

I swallowed the impulse to say of course he had a name. Though I was inclined to like Nicole for old times' sake, this style of questioning was getting right up my nose.

'She did mention his name, but I can't recall what she said. It was an unusual name, something rather pretty.' I ignored the raised eyebrow. The Detective Constable definitely wasn't slouching now. 'He was a writer of some kind, fairly successful.'

'So do you think he could have been the fellow in those pictures?'

I shrugged. 'No way of knowing, but I don't see why not.'

Nicole sighed heavily and asked in an exasperated tone, 'But did she say he was black?'

'She didn't mention it. She said he was kind, affectionate, that sort of thing. That's about it.'

Sitting with Helen this morning, experiencing the hollowness left by Monica's death, I had realised that until Monica's life and death could be put in perspective, Helen and I would be unable to go back to how we were before. So although I wasn't able to tell Nicole much that was concrete about Monica's relationship to the boyfriend, I did my best. After all, I wanted to catch up with this fellow as much as she did, and Nicole had a lot more labour-power at her command. It would pay me to invest, so to speak, in the official enquiry.

So I dived in, collating snippets from several separate conversations as I went along. 'I know that Monica and the boyfriend had been together a long time. She attended art college in London, and there had been a close relationship for years. He was older, more sophisticated, and she may have felt she needed a bit of space, a bit of distance from the relationship. That seemed to be part of her motivation for going to Keele. Though it didn't really work; according to Monica, she spent half her time in London anyway.'

Nicole nodded, mistrust warring with interest in her features. 'You seem to have learned quite a lot in two meetings,' she said grudgingly.

'Like I told you before, Monica was really wound up, ready to talk. Sometimes, we could hardly stop her.'

'So did she say she had any problems with this guy? Was

he ever violent, for instance?' Nicole threw in the 'for instance' casually, as if a question about violence had no particular significance in a murder enquiry.

I shook my head. 'Not violent, not that she mentioned.' I paused to recall the various comments Monica had made about the boyfriend. 'From her description, I got the impression that the boyfriend was a lovely bloke, cheerful and good-natured most of the time, except when he was drinking. Then – sometimes when his writing wasn't going well, other times for no apparent reason – he would go on a bender. For days at a time. Monica would search everywhere for him, check with his friends, ring the hospitals. She'd be anxious and alone. And then he would just show up, looking like a vagrant, covered in muck and guilt. The tension left her anxious and depressed for weeks afterwards. She hinted that the split came because she couldn't take it any more. She needed peace, she said, if she was going to be a proper painter. Hence the break-up.'

'So *she* split up with him?' I caught the glance that Nicole tossed at her Constable companion, and it brought me up short. This wasn't just a trip down Memory Lane, it was an interview. And anything you said could be taken down and used in evidence. I owed it to Monica to get this right.

'Monica said it was an *amicable* split,' I told them, 'though more her idea than his, yes. Still, she referred to him in the present tense, as a friend.'

Nicole scrutinised the prints on the table once more. 'So these pictures of the boyfriend, if it is him, could have been taken last weekend at the cottage?'

'Not a chance,' I replied, relieved to return to solid ground. 'Look at the negatives. The three shots at the cottage are the first on the reel. Monica took them just as she was leaving.'

Suddenly I could see in vivid detail Monica and Helen leaving Wildfell last Sunday afternoon, walking side by side, arms around each other's waists. 'I'm so happy,' Monica had exclaimed, and she'd hugged Helen, as if Helen herself was the source of this joy. Then she had pulled away, swung the camera off her shoulder, and taken three quick final shots.

'These are for the noticeboard in my office – to comfort me

when I'm collapsing under the confidences of endless under-graduates,' Monica declaimed in ringing tones. Then she was off.

I blinked hard to shake off the image, and waited for Nicole to draw the inference.

She did. 'So whoever this man is, Monica spent time with him this very week. For all we know,' she mused, 'these photos could even have been taken on the evening she was killed.'

I picked up a couple of sandwiches on my way back to the car, and drove down to Riverside to share them with the ducks. It was the perfect antidote to the frustration that had settled in at Police Headquarters.

Rivers have a way of turning you away from your shopping list of anxieties. Sitting on the river wall, my feet dangling above the bows of a dilapidated houseboat, I was sorely tempted to call it a day, and spend the rest of the afternoon rowing in the region of Bait's Bite lock.

Duty prevailed. Only two days had passed since Monica's death, but already there were pressing issues to attend to. On the road to London, I concentrated my mind once more on the problem presented by Michael Loizou.

It's curious. When I worked as an academic, my whole thought process was tied to the act of writing. I required a pristine pad of paper and a sharp pencil on a tidy desk in order to draft an article for a history journal; I needed them even to plan my movements for the following day. My shoulder bag forever overflowed with wrinkled scraps of paper and outdated jottings.

Investigative work put paid to all that. After only one week in this job I realised that if analysing and planning depended on being in a position to write, if it had to wait until I was back in my office or sitting on a bench, or – worse still, until I was equipped with a laptop – I might as well kiss detective work goodbye. Instead, I learned to use all the dross periods of the working week – all that time spent in surveillance, when I had other targets for my eyes than a piece of paper, all those hours driving or walking or waiting to see clients – for reviewing cases and planning ahead. While the rest of me follows a target's movements or manoeuvres through the crowds, another part of my brain will be focused on something else entirely.

This time the something else was Michael Loizou. It was almost two weeks now since I had visited Bedford Prison. During that fortnight, on time charged up to Loizou's account, I had posed as the acquisitions agent for a large property company, as a prospective home-buyer in Wimbledon, and as an acquaintance of Sonia Loizou. I had visited estate agents in the West End of London and also in the vicinity of Sonia's home. What I had learned tended to confirm Michael Loizou's suspicions. But mere suspicions didn't do a guy in prison a lot of good, and I wanted more facts and details before visiting him again.

The eyes of my West End estate agent had lit up when, decked out again in my best business suit, I announced that I wanted to acquire a substantial Soho property as an investment for a corporate client. Or proper*ties*, I amended, at which his eyes positively glittered. Since the property slump of 1988, estate agents have been touting for business without much success. Property isn't selling, offices aren't renting, commisions are at rock-bottom level. Lots of these ambitious young men who thought in the mid-1980s that an estate agent's board and public school manners were the key to a yuppie lifestyle, are now working evenings at other jobs to pay the mortgage on the flat. So it wasn't difficult to persuade him to make some enquiries, on my behalf, about the Soho properties owned by Sonia and Dmitri Loizou.

At Dmitri's nightclub, the estate agent found Dmitri Loizou arguing about invoices with his chief bartender. Dmitri didn't want to talk. Even when my fellow held out the bait of a solid corporate purchase, Loizou remained indifferent. He had the bartender escort the man firmly to the door. By the time I saw him again, the agent's eyes had lost some of their lustre.

Poor thing. I, on the other hand, found the description of this encounter deeply interesting. If Dmitri was on the level, if he hadn't already sold the nightclub on the quiet, then it seemed to me he would have had at the very least a question or two to put, like who is this potential purchaser? Does he want to keep a nightclub on this site? What kind of offer does he have in mind? These are the things any property owner would want to know if someone came sniffing around in these hard times, wanting to buy their capital out from under them. But from Dmitri, not so much as an enquiring look. I could think of only one really good explanation for this: I would lay odds on that Dmitri had *already* sold.

Enquiries at the two buildings owned by Dmitri's sister-in-law made me confident that I was on to a winner. Not that there was a sign of Sonia Loizou in the area. Unlike Dmitri, she merely received the rents. She didn't sully herself by appearing on the Soho premises. However, as it happened, her caretaker was in a chatty mood that day, and he revealed to my estate agent that he was wasting his time chasing the lady to sell. Mrs Loizou had exchanged contracts on both her buildings the week before. Signed and sealed on the dotted line.

I sent the agent on his way, declaring sternly that no other properties in London would meet my clients' needs. His disappointment was so tangible that it almost formed a fog in the room. I found myself feeling sorry for him. After he left, I spent a moment or two worrying that compassion might erode my longstanding prejudice against estate agents.

My next step was to find out whether Sonia was ridding herself of investment properties only, or whether she had decided that a family home was too much of an encumbrance too.

Diana Murcott had described herself as the Loizou family solicitor. Since Michael had commissioned me to act on his behalf, she had no qualms about telling me that Sonia had, shortly after Michael went to prison, moved all the Loizou property files from Diana's office to her home safe. She wanted to put their affairs in order, she had said. And yes, Diana confirmed, the family home was in Sonia's name. Michael was a prudent man and a loving husband. He worried that something might happen to him in prison, and he didn't want Sonia to have trouble inheriting his worldly goods.

I drove to Wimbledon and took a glance at the large

detached family home on respectable Nightingale Avenue. It was registered in sole ownership to Sonia Loizou and worth, I reckoned, around £400,000 at current prices, if it could be sold. There was no board up outside, of course: there wouldn't be. Sonia wouldn't put the house on open listing, and take the risk that an acquaintance of Michael's might see it and mention the fact to him. So I did the rounds of estate agents in the area, looking for one who might have handled a sale discreetly. The sixth one I visited, a pleasant-mannered fellow with massive jowls, revealed that Sonia was no longer living on Nightingale Avenue. Moreover, the final selling price had exceeded my estimate by almost ten per cent.

The new occupants in their turn were very obliging, but they were unable to supply a forwarding address. All of Mrs Loizou's mail was sent to a Post Office Box in nearby Richmond. Yes, they assured me, she had taken her old phone number with her. The loving husband Michael could call Sonia from prison as usual, unaware that he was not getting through to the house he thought of as home.

That was where things had stood on Friday, before I learned of Monica's death. Sonia Loizou was certainly not playing straight with her absent mate. I needed now to know whether she was playing alone, and where she thought the game was headed.

First stop in London, the office of Aardvark Investigations. No, no, Sonny and I don't have a partner by the name of Aardvark. Sonny selected this name when he started up the business, as a way of ensuring that he had the top listing under *Detective Agency* in the *Yellow Pages*, and now we're stuck with it. It doesn't sound very impressive, but none of our clients seem to mind.

I slipped the car into its usual spot behind the Satay Palace, cut through the alley to the High Street and, as usual, pushed myself to run up the three flights of stairs. I don't do this sort of thing for the exercise. After all, such intermittent high intensity output can play havoc with the heart. No, this is the recurring test I set myself of fitness. Any time I find myself gasping for breath at the top, I know it is time either to step up the rowing or to step down the wine.

Stevie, my right-hand woman, was in the office making some telephone enquiries. She grinned as I panted in the door. 'Sounds like you'll be teetotal for the next week or so,' she teased. 'What *have* you been doing?'

I told her as gently as I could about Monica. I explained that I would be spending a lot of time in Cambridge over the next couple of weeks, and together we perused the case files, establishing priorities and arranging to put some routine investigations on hold. Stevie was already doing overtime on her current case for Customs & Excise, but apparently Dee was available for freelance work. I had just put the phone down from yet another encounter with Sonny's answerphone – my third this afternoon – when Dee herself appeared in the doorway.

'Hi, Desiree.' I'm probably the only person who calls her by her proper name. I like the rhythm. 'Take off your coat and sit down. Are you on sugar or off it today?' I asked, pouring her out a mug of coffee.

'Black, please,' Dee replied. 'You'll see why when you hear my news. I've landed the part of Jo in a new production of *Little Women* at the Hampstead Theatre. Rehearsals begin in four weeks flat.'

Dee received the exclamations of congratulations from Stevie and me with a solemnly upraised hand.

'The bad news,' she continued, 'is that I have to lose half a stone before opening night. No one envisages tomboy Jo as a tubby. So let's hope the job you've got for me is suitably physical. How about chasing bad guys down dark alleys? That'd put paid to the puppy fat!'

I remarked drily that I hoped it wouldn't come to that. Indeed, I'd be rather alarmed if it did. I described the current state of play in the Loizou case. Desiree's job was to find out more about Dmitri Loizou and any plans he might have for the nightclub. We agreed on a simple approach: Dee would apply for work as a hostess at the club. If she failed to turn up any information that way, she would hang out for a few evenings in the nightclub (with, I emphasised, a *modest* expense account for drinks) and see what she could learn from the staff. Desiree was as ardent in her interest in the case as her name suggests. When I went into my own little office and closed the door, she was busily consulting Stevie about what she should wear in her role as a job applicant. The detective as thespian.

This time Sonny answered his phone on the first ring. 'Me in the flesh,' he announced. 'I'm sorry, Laura, I got tied up with a client. Are you all right? Are you coming home?'

When I'd rung him last night with the stark news of Monica's death, Sonny's voice had resonated with the shock that I had been trying to keep at bay. This afternoon he still sounded churned up. I wished I could see him immediately, but I had a couple of hours' more work to do. We arranged to meet in the West End. Long before my plans changed, before Monica was killed, before I had made up my mind to spend the rest of the weekend in London, Sonny and his friend Jess had organised Saturday evening around a Japanese meal and a film. He was sure that neither the restaurant nor Jess would object to adding me to the party.

So I ended up on Saturday evening discussing bloodstains and mysterious invitations over the sushi. I laid out as impassively as I could what was known at the moment about the circumstances of Monica's death. Jess picked up on what was not known.

'So, this man in the photograph may or may not be Monica's former lover,' he summarised. 'He may or may not be the last person to have seen her alive. And he may or may not be her killer.'

'In a nutshell,' I confirmed. 'And we know that Monica took those photographs of him some time between leaving Wildfell on Sunday afternoon, and her death on Thursday evening.'

'Any guesses as to where the photos were taken?' Sonny kicked in.

'They're all close-ups, you can't see much of the background. But myself, I would be surprised if Monica had travelled outside Cambridge in those few days. She had a busy week planned and she is – was – very disciplined about

66

working. So whoever this man is, my guess is he was probably with her in Cambridge.'

Jess looked excited. 'Are you going to search for him, then?'

I shook my head emphatically. 'No point,' I said. 'He shouldn't be too hard to track down, if he is a successful writer as Monica said. I'll leave it to the police. They can flash his photo at every publisher in London in the space of a day. And anyway,' I added, with a wary glance at Sonny, 'I have other plans.'

The way that Sonny clutched the noodles with his chopsticks conveyed disapproval. He had strong views about the need to separate investigative work from personal concerns, but he is also perceptive enough to see that I wouldn't be budged on this one. 'Such as?' he asked in a defeated tone.

'Two such ases,' I replied. 'First, I've got to find some missing photos. The pics of the maybe-boyfriend were taken *after* Monica left Wildfell Cottage. Before that, she took a camera to Holkham Beach and was kind of secretive and excited about the results. There is sure to be something on that film worth seeing, but, in spite of the best efforts of the Cambridge boys and girls in blue, it hasn't turned up yet.'

'And the second such as?' Sonny probed.

'Do you remember that Monica mentioned serious trouble in her note to Helen? Maybe something from her past had caught up with her; maybe someone was threatening her – I don't know. But whatever it was, there's a strong chance that it has something to do with her death. So I've got some digging to do on that score.'

We chewed it over a while more, and then Jess took a raincheck on the cinema. He claimed he was sleepy and needed an early night. I knew Jess well enough to suppose that it was tact, rather than fatigue, that sent him home. I would find a way to thank him. If he suspected that Monica's death had left me frayed at the edges, if he guessed that I was longing to spend some time alone with Sonny, he was right. And yet Sonny's disapproval weighed me down and we left the restaurant in an uneasy state. We pushed through the crowds towards Piccadilly, avoiding conversation.

Finally Sonny broke the silence. 'Are you sure you want to

do this, Laura? You're damn good at investigative work, but you don't know much about murder. And when a friend is involved, it's hard to be detached – which you need to be if you are going to make the right decisions. *And* if you are going to stay safe . . .'

He was right, of course. But it didn't change anything. 'Sonny, I can't do anything else.' I pulled at his arm and brought him to a halt on the edge of the pavement, turning him to face me so that I could watch his eyes. 'You've got to understand, Sonny. All those fears – Monica as much as told me that she was in danger. And what did I do? *Zilch.* Produced a theory about the evil eye. How can I be a detective when I can't even hear an outright plea for help?'

Sonny put his arms around me. For the first time since Monica's death, I cried. Piccadilly Circus might not have been the place I would have chosen, but Sonny definitely is the person I would have chosen to be with. After a while, I raised my head and blew my nose on his enormous cotton handkerchief.

'Besides,' I continued, 'even if I don't learn anything that leads to her killer, I just want to find out more about Monica. When I came out of the police station this afternoon, I felt so angry. I can't bear to have her reduced by Neill to "that dead girl".'

'OK,' Sonny said. 'You're going to breathe life into "this dead girl". Figure out why she was so vulnerable. Surround her with people and places, plans and projects. I understand: you're going to make her real.'

He was right again. But it was even more than that. If I succeeded – well, maybe then I'd feel less guilty about the grudgingness with which I had allowed Monica to walk into the fringes of my life.

'And what can I do to help you?' Sonny asked.

'Two things,' I replied. 'One, keep an eye on the office for me for a few days. Especially on Dee with this Loizou thing.'

'You got it,' Sonny shot back. 'And the second?'

'Let's skip the film,' I whispered.

And we did.

CHAPTER 8

———

Sonny was burrowed under the duvet on Sunday morning when I set out for Cambridge. Thanks to the ever-open corner shop, I was able to leave him an affectionate note and a huge bunch of yellow chrysanthemums. Not as good as waking up to me, of course, but (as my dad Paul used to say) better than a kick in the teeth.

The drive passed quickly. On a Sunday morning in autumn, with the lanes near-empty and the brown fields on either side dusted with frost, the M11 looks almost romantic. I extracted my sunglasses from the leather pouch on the door of the Saab, put a Johnnie Johnson disc on the CD player, and enjoyed the drive home.

The journey gave me just the opportunity I needed to make plans. I set three goals for the week: find out what Monica saw at Holkham Beach; track down friends or acquaintances who might have additional information about her background; identify the trouble referred to in Monica's note to Helen.

The place to begin was back at Monica's home. Her studio flat, as she described it to me, actually consisted of the ground floor of a Victorian terraced house in a cul-de-sac about a mile from the centre of Cambridge. I had understood Detective Sergeant Pelletier to say that the upstairs was also occupied as a flat. The top floor of Monica's house was joined to the top floor of its neighbour on the right, but at ground level the two houses were divided by a small bricked path that afforded access to the gardens at the rear. It was down this path that I had stumbled on Friday night, like an intruder, drawn uneasily towards the light that spilled from Monica's window. In the dark, I hadn't noticed that the upstairs flat could also be reached from this passage. By the light of day, the entrance, with its white plastic buzzer like those that punctuate the front of student houses, was unmissable. I pressed the buzzer. Sunday morning might not be a very English time to go calling, but seemed a likely time to find people at home.

The woman who answered the door didn't look much like a student, but she did look like my sort of person. She was tall and rangy, with long strong feet and expressive hands. From the neck down, in oversized shirt and dark green leggings, she could have been a teenager. Her face, also long and rangy, was wry and intelligent, with a generous mouth. The face marked her as in her late thirties. Her hair was roughly pinned on top of her head, and a few renegade grey curly strands added another decade to her age. From her distracted look I imagined that I had interrupted her at some vital task, but when I introduced myself as a friend of Monica's, the distant look vanished. Surprise was quickly smoothed off her face by pleasure and something that resembled relief.

'Do come in, please,' she said. 'I'm Margaret Powers. But you'll probably know that?' I shook my head in the negative, and then shook her hand. She drew me into a cream-coloured sitting room with little furniture but extravagant masses of flowers. Chrysanthemums again. Margaret saw me eyeing them. 'To cheer me up,' she said defensively. I made soothing noises. Within two minutes Margaret Powers was launched into a stream of reminiscence about Monica.

'I haven't met any of her other friends, you see,' she interjected by way of explanation. 'I don't want to sound off to people who never met her. It always seems so melodramatic when people do that, as if they are capitalising on a death to get attention. Do you know what I mean?'

I did know. And I could understand when she asked me to stay for a while and talk.

'Don't rush away,' she pleaded.

I promised not to, and made myself comfortable on a pile of oversized cushions against the wall of the sitting room. Margaret arranged herself opposite me, her straight back suggesting more than a passing acquaintance with yoga. We talked about Wildfell, about Monica's excitement at the prospect of sharing. And about what it was like to be Monica's neighbour.

Margaret and Monica had known each other for eighteen months. Since Monica arrived in Cambridge and moved into the flat below, they had become what Margaret called 'domestic friends' – a necessity, she said, if you choose to live alone. A domestic friend is, apparently, someone nearby who will listen to your latest news, or bring you shopping when you're in bed with the flu, pop out to the cinema with you on the spur of the moment, or henna your hair. Like Helen and me, I affirmed to myself.

'The way sisters are supposed to be,' Margaret continued. 'Only I never had a sister, and neither did Monica, not really.'

I told her about the man in the photograph. 'Did Monica ever mention a male friend or a lover who was black?'

Not that Margaret could recall. She knew about the former boyfriend – even knew his first name, Angell, but she had never met him and had no idea what he looked like. He and Monica had been seeing each other at weekends from time to time, but the traffic was Cambridge to London, not the other way around.

Margaret was slightly better informed when it came to Monica's family. 'Only the bare bones, though,' she warned. 'Monica came from Newcastle, from a fairly ordinary sort of middle-class family. Her mother was a social worker, I think, later on in life, and her father was some type of salesman, though he never made as much money as he might because he insisted on getting home to be with his family in the evenings. Monica loved him dearly. He died a few years ago in a car accident, in one of those dense fogs on the A1. His car crashed into the back of a lorry. Then her mum died last year, after several months' struggle with cancer. You can imagine how alone Monica felt. That was what she emphasised most about Wildfell, you know. That it would be like having a home again.'

'So there's no other family?' Margaret was shaking her head emphatically. I misunderstood. 'No cousins she was close to, or aunts or—'

'No, no. You've got it wrong. When I said she didn't have

71

a sister really, I meant not one she was sisterly with. Monica's dad was older than her mother and he had a daughter, I've forgotten her name, from his first marriage. Monica grew up together with her step-sister, though Emma—' Margaret looked quizzically at me before answering her own unspoken question, 'Yes, it was Emma – was eight years older. Monica looked up to her when they were little. But then Emma went off to Australia when Monica was only fifteen, and I got the impression that they don't have much in common now. Emma didn't come back for her stepmother's funeral. Monica was deeply disappointed about that, and said she didn't care if she never saw Emma again.'

Close friends, it turned out, were a rather similar story. The dead woman's friendships had been fragmented by the moves from Newcastle to art college in London and then to Keele. She had been in Cambridge for over a year, and had many acquaintances in the University, but she had been putting enormous amounts of energy into her new job and her painting. That hadn't left much time for developing new relationships. On top of that, during Monica's early months in the city, she had regularly been travelling north at weekends to nurse her mother. Her mother's illness and subsequent death had left Monica emotionally exhausted.

Oddly enough, I wasn't saddened by what Margaret told me. I got an image of Monica as a sturdy convalescent, walking slowly but firmly out of a period of pain. And I was comforted to know that she had chosen to look on Wildfell as home.

Margaret made a pot of coffee, and produced *pain au chocolat* from the local deli. We had both found it a relief to talk about Monica, but had been avoiding the central issue. Now we fell silent for a time, munching our croissants, aware of a blood-stained rocking chair in the room below.

Eventually I reached out and took Margaret's hand. Her long thin fingers were cold. 'We'll have to talk about it,' I said gently. 'I'm sorry, Margaret. Have the police already asked you about Thursday evening?'

She nodded. 'That heavyset man, what's his name?'

'Neill. Superintendent Steven Neill.'

'Oh yes. Well, Superintendent Neill told me that Monica was killed some time on Thursday evening. It's not enough. Information, I mean. Can you tell me anything else?'

I searched her face. She looked miserable, but I thought she was probably strong enough to take it. 'Some things I do know.' I found myself speaking in a quiet voice. 'Monica was attacked with a knife and also with a small hammer. The killer must have taken these away with him, because they're not in the flat, though it is possible that the hammer was something Monica had used in preparing canvases. She was tied up. Given the amount of blood at the site, I'm afraid that she suffered for some time before death. The current estimate is that she died between nine and ten p.m. – probably from a blow to the head. The Coroner hasn't made his final assessment yet.'

Margaret's head was lowered throughout this recital, as if she were seeing with an inner eye. I sat quietly waiting for her reaction. She looked up at me, dully. 'It's not prurience, you know.'

'I know.' I wasn't with Paul when he died, but I'll never forget the nursing staff at Frenchay General, who helped me sketch in the narrative of his last few hours. I waited until Margaret had focused on my face again. 'About Thursday evening, Margaret. Were you home?'

Margaret closed her eyes for a moment, as if trying to shut my question out. Then she lifted her chin and spoke, her voice tainted with misery. 'I'm Communications Officer at Stansted Airport. When I came in from work, the lights were on in Monica's flat, but I didn't see her. I had a Women's Aid meeting at 7 o'clock, so I got straight into the tub with a sandwich, and as soon as I was clean and dressed, I dashed out.' She paused and looked vaguely around the room.

'This is the hard part,' she continued. 'After the meeting, we decided to have a drink at the Black Swan. I was almost out of cash. I don't like to borrow, so I popped home – it's only five minutes on my bike – to get my cashcard, to use at the cash dispenser on Mill Road.'

'What time was that?' I tried to rein in my impatience. No reply. 'Margaret? When did you arrive home?'

'Around nine o'clock.' Margaret was clearly finding this difficult. The pauses were getting longer.

'Were the lights on? Did you see anything or hear anything?' I asked, concerned for Margaret's pain, but not yet ready to give up.

'I saw a man,' she said hollowly. Tears trembled on her bottom lids and ran down the furrows in her cheeks. Suddenly she looked her age. 'He arrived at Monica's door as I came out of the lane. He rang the bell, and then glanced over his shoulder, as if he wanted to be sure no one was watching.'

'So this was around nine o'clock?' No answer. I gave Margaret a nudge. 'Did Monica open the door?'

'Not while I was in earshot. Of course, that didn't surprise me at the time. On weekdays, Monica worked from seven until ten every evening, without fail. She would put her answerphone on and concentrate on nothing but work. Sometimes she would call me at ten, and we would meet up, go for a drink together or have a cup of tea, but I've never known her to have a visitor during evening working hours.'

Margaret rubbed the palms of her hands over her eyes, none too gently, then snapped her head back and looked straight at me for the first time in minutes. 'What upsets me now,' she said, 'is that maybe Monica *did* open the door to this one. Maybe he killed her. And I just cycled away.'

We talked for a while about responsibility – our responsibility for Monica, our involvement in her death. And then I asked about the man again.

Margaret's description was fluent. She had gone over this with the police several times. Medium height, stocky build, well-dressed and healthy-looking. Wearing an expensive camelhair overcoat like the kind you see on company directors. Perhaps fifty-five to sixty years old. Hair, styled probably and more fair than dark. When he raised his hand to the knocker a gold ring, probably a wedding band, gleamed. White. Didn't see him get out of a car or anything like that. Too old for the boyfriend, Angell. Never seen him since. *Would know him anywhere.*

*

First thing Monday morning, I headed for the river. There was not a soul in sight on the grassy bank where I stopped to do my warm-ups. No wonder the office stairs had been difficult to scale. After only a fortnight of idleness, my hamstrings were like piano wire.

But once I was on the river, all stiffness disappeared. I didn't try to think – just concentrated on establishing a steady motion, forward and back, forward and back, forward and back, until the movement had become an autonomous process, like breathing. Then I allowed my mind to register the life of the river. The water was opaque, its surface dark and thick, without reflection. A fine layer of miniature clover-leaves skimmed the surface, clearing where the cool wind slapped an opening, and clustering at the edges of the ripples. My sculler cut through them like the blades of ice-skates through a dusting of snow. Far behind me, the wash of my boat patted the turfed banks of the river. When I flung my head up, I could see a clique of shaggy-footed ponies gossiping where the meadow on the south bank sloped up to a break of trees. I was ready for the week.

I showered, dressed, sorted out the week's schedules with Stevie by telephone and still managed to walk through the front door of Eastern University before nine a.m. I intended to visit the Art Department before the rush of the week reached its peak. The Administrative Office seemed the place to start. A woman in her twenties was preparing a pot of coffee as I came in. Another woman, thinner and older, with a careworn face and tight blue jeans, leaned dispiritedly against the filing cabinet. On the door, a sign designated Mary McKinnon as Departmental Secretary.

'Ms McKinnon?' I asked. The anxious look that passed between the two women gave me some indication of the strain they were under. 'I've come about Monica Harcourt.' Once I had made it clear that I wasn't from the police, that I had known Monica personally and that I was familiar with the circumstances of her death, the thin woman, who turned out to be Mary McKinnon, was only too glad to talk to me.

She had heard the news of Monica's death on local radio on

Saturday afternoon. Two days later, Mary was still distressed. Her thin hand trembled as we spoke. She thought Monica was terrific to work with, one of the best in the University. 'Sensible, serious and conscientious. Not always swanning around, trying to impress with her own importance.' The vehemence with which this was said suggested that these qualities were as valued in the Faculty as they were rare.

Mary described Monica (and this rather surprised me) as quiet and calm. No matter how urgent or how stressful a situation, Monica would weigh it up quietly and then come to a clear decision. No hair-pulling, no anxiety, no histrionics. The job might be demanding, Monica sometimes said, but there was no reason to make it hell.

According to Mary, it was this calm, really, that the students admired. They sensed in her someone centred, someone who had a clear vision of what she was doing. That made them trust her. It meant, too, that in addition to the students she had to see in her capacity as course tutor, she was forever being called upon by other students to comment on work, to listen to their thoughts, to advise them on how to be 'a real artist'. And listen to them she did, in the same unhurried way. Mary sometimes wondered if Monica's patience came from living alone. Mary had occasionally voiced her sympathy aloud when Monica had had a particularly bad day at the beck and call of other people, but then Monica would say, 'Not to worry. When I get home and shut the door, when I turn off the telephone and begin to work, I shall be fine.'

That reminded me of Monica's plans to go abroad. 'What do you know about Monica's application to go to Oregon?' Mary didn't understand what kind of information was wanted, so I prompted: 'Why Oregon, for example? Did she have friends there?'

'If she did,' Mary replied, 'she never mentioned them to me. What Monica talked about was the ocean. There are herds of sea lions, did you know?' She didn't bother to wait for my nod. 'I got the impression that it was the place that attracted Monica. And I know she didn't have anyone to stay with there, because only last week she had got a book about international house exchange and was showing it around the Department. She found it hard to believe that anyone would give up a house by the sea in Oregon for a flat in Cambridge, but the agency assured her that it happened all the time.'

I shifted position to allow some students to pass by. The younger secretary dealt with their enquiries, and Mary motioned me into a tiny side office where we could sit more quietly. I wasn't yet ready to abandon the subject of Monica's application.

'Was her secondment definitely settled, then?'

'No, I'm pretty sure it wasn't,' Mary answered decisively. 'Something funny happened along the way that Monica wouldn't tell me about. I typed her application last Easter and submitted it well in advance of the June meeting of the Secondment Committee. But for some reason it didn't get dealt with at that meeting. Monica went to see various people about it, I guess to chivvy them along. She even went to the Provost once or twice as I recall. It meant ever such a lot to her. I kept telling her that the application was a good one, and that these things always work out in the end. Platitudes, I guess, but I meant them.'

'So Monica was shaken by the delay?'

Mary nodded sadly. 'Shaken's not the word for it. Once she found a note about the application in her pigeonhole, and tore it open eagerly, and then – I swear – she burst into tears.'

And this was the woman Mary had just described as 'calm and centred'. 'Any idea who sent the note?'

'Monica didn't seem to want me to see it, but I had a look at the envelope after she left. Nothing special there – just an internal envelope from the Provost's office. We get them every day. But when she picked it up, for some reason Monica was convinced it concerned her application. And when it wasn't the news that she had been hoping for, she was devastated.'

I got from Mary some more information about Monica's movements – how she spent her days, what her schedule was during the week and so forth. I had less luck on the subject of friends. Monica was well-liked but didn't have close friends on the staff. She generally worked through her lunch-hour –

necessary, she said, if you wanted to have your evenings free for other things.

'Any enemies you know of?' It is impossible to ask this question without sounding both melodramatic and clichéd. I've given up trying. To her credit, although Mary raised a sceptical eyebrow, she answered with a straight face. 'One for sure,' she said. 'Our Senior Lecturer in Printmaking, Ella Grimsby. She disliked Monica with a vengeance. Took every opportunity to be horrid to her, and about her, behind her back. Go ahead and talk to Ella – you'll see her for what she is, a vindictive little cow.'

'And why is she vindictive?'

'Because she's jealous. Monica is – was – a better teacher than her. The students queued up to work with Monica, while they always treated classes with Ella as a chore. Monica was a better artist, too. She had had two good exhibitions – one in London and one in Norwich – just in the brief time she was here, while Ella practically has to pay local galleries to take samples of her work. And most of all, she hated her because Monica was appointed to be Course Tutor over Ella's head. She had been Acting Course Tutor for a year after Simon Jackson left, and just assumed she would be reappointed. Ella was stunned. I felt sorry for her at first; it did seem hard on her, when she had done the job for a year. But I soon stopped feeling sorry because she was so damned awful to Monica!'

I recalled an evening at Wildfell, when Monica had puzzled over her desertion by a young student painter whom she had taken under her wing.

'But Ella can't be so universally despised. Wasn't there one of Monica's tutees who asked to switch to Ella's jurisdiction?'

'Oh, you mean Samantha Nicholson.' Like many administrative secretaries, Mary had an astonishingly well-stocked mental filing cabinet. 'I guess you'd call her the exception that proved the rule. Samantha is a lost little soul. Monica did everything for her; she was kindness itself. Without Monica, I think that Sam would have dropped out of University before she even got going. So don't ask me to explain why Sam should be the only student ever to hand in a request asking to transfer to Ella's tutorial group.'

'Was Monica unhappy about it?'

'She sure was. She was hurt, you could see that, even though she appeared to shrug it off. I tried to get to the bottom of it, but when I stopped Sam later in the corridor to talk about her decision, she went completely tongue-tied, mumbled something unconvincing, blushed like mad and rushed away. She seemed pretty wound up, but I'll be damned if I know what could have brought on that reaction.'

The pot of coffee was coming to an end. I made a move to go, but Mary detained me for a moment longer. 'Look,' she said, 'I don't know if it's fair to ask you this, but I have no idea what to do with some of Monica's things. The memos and work-related materials I'm just tossing out or returning to sender with a brief explanation. But there are other things – more personal items. Could you take them, and perhaps pass them on to friends?'

I agreed. After all, I was hoping that my investigation would turn up one or two people to whom Monica was really close. And I offered to return to help clear out Monica's desk and filing cabinet.

While Mary returned to her work, I took advantage of the departmental phone to ring the office in London again. There were three messages for me. One was a query about an invoice. The second was a complicated set of instructions from Sonny relating to arrangements for the coming weekend. And the third was a request from Helen to meet her at Wildfell, where she had fled for a few days' R and R. She sounded, according to Stevie, quite badly in need of support.

When I hung up, Mary was busy at the word processor. I made a writing motion on the palm of my hand, and pointed first to an electric typewriter perched on a low shelf and then to myself. By way of answer, Mary leaned over and flipped the 'on' switch of the typewriter for me. I picked up two pieces of University notepaper. On one I typed the details of the message from Sonny, folded it, and stuck it in my pocket. On the other, I typed the word THANKS. I set this sheet on the keyboard in front of Mary, waved and left the office.

CHAPTER 9

I only managed a few brisk steps away from the Departmental Office before a group of young women and men detached themselves from the wall and formed a circle around me. Most of them looked down at their feet. I guess it would be more accurate to say that they cast sidelong glances at each other's feet. One girl of about nineteen, with curly brown hair tied back with a piece of lace, and a snub nose, appeared to speak for the rest. 'Is it true that Monica Harcourt is dead?' she asked.

I stalled. 'Was Monica your tutor?'

'She's been my personal tutor for two years now. And she supervised my project. Well, not only mine, most of ours,' she added hurriedly, looking around at the others as if for confirmation of a contentious point.

One of the two young men in the group came to her rescue. 'Yes, Monica supervised my project, too,' he declared, with an authoritative air, as if he were going to say something of great significance. 'She was . . . well, she was a really great supervisor,' he concluded lamely. He acknowledged how inconsequential his remark was with an apologetic smile. 'My name's Gregory Merrick,' he offered tentatively.

The contradictions in Merrick's manner of speaking seemed to match the ones apparent in his physical self: a confident muscular body, a narrow anxious face, and a voice that hadn't quite settled down to manhood yet. I was glad to be not-so-young.

He took the initiative with introductions. 'That's Ruby, by the way,' indicating the girl with the snub nose, 'and this is Amjud. All of us were supervised by Monica.' Gathering

80

confidence, he directed an enquiring glance at the last member of the circle. 'And, well, she was *supposed* to supervise your project, wasn't she?' Gregory asked. 'Samantha Nicholson,' he finished, nodding in her direction, and then relinquished the floor.

Sam, a slender girl whose close-cropped hair was bleached almost white, blushed and looked away. This must be the student who had transferred her project to Ella. There was a pause, during which all of the students turned to face me. I couldn't delay any longer.

In a far more formal manner than I'd intended, I said, 'I'm afraid Monica Harcourt died on Thursday evening. She was killed, I mean. The police are investigating her death.'

They looked at each other's feet again. Clearly they had learned this much already. I didn't know what else to say. Although I had spent several years dealing with undergraduates, in these circumstances I didn't feel able to handle their anxiety. Their feelings were fresher than mine, not honed by decades of use. These emotions seemed plastic to me, too new, too consciously-adopted to be authentic. I wanted desperately to get away. 'Shall I buy you all a cup of tea?' I asked.

A basement tea room with no natural light and bright squares of coloured formica on the wall is not an encouraging ambience for discussions of the recently dead, but as it turned out, dealing with the students' questions – fending off some, answering others – was oddly reassuring. It established my credentials for myself as a person of some importance in Monica's life.

And I felt reassured too by the accounts of the students, as they gradually began to mould their reminiscences of Monica. Her enthusiasm over Amjud's work; the way she talked to Ruby as if she were a fellow artist rather than a student; how Samantha Nicholson and Gregory Merrick were always trailing behind her after painting class, hoping for a chat. (Greg looked uncomfortable with this revelation and Sam blushed furiously, her bright cheeks in startling contrast with the pale hair.) How Monica had teased them in the week before her death, saying, 'When I'm in Oregon, living by the sea . . .' and how flattered they had felt when she asked them to help her choose a house for exchange from the catalogue. I couldn't help but like them, this côterie of students, this little group thrown together by common timetables and a shared fondness for their tutor. I did what I could to help, then left them to comfort each other in their own doubtless more appropriate ways.

But as I stood up to leave the tea room, I saw Mary McKinnon in the doorway, looking shortsightedly about. It turned out she was looking for me. 'Thanks for agreeing to help with Monica's things,' she said warmly. 'I've got something to give you right away. This package was delivered by the technician late on Thursday afternoon, after Monica had gone home.'

The package, a heavy oblong about four inches by six, set off bells of excitement. I tore off the paper, and fumbled rapidly through a stack of photographs. At last: the pictures that had been missing from Monica's flat. No wonder Nicole's officers had turned up nothing when they checked local film-processing agencies. The photos had been here in the University all along.

There were numerous photographs of Helen, Ginny, Monica and me, a powerful record of a brief friendship. Perhaps Monica had sensed its brevity, felt compelled to capture it somehow? And there were the seascapes of Holkham Bay, marvellous, bright and brooding, some of them edged by pine forests. None of the photographs, however, answered the question of what Monica had wanted to share with us from her foray to the beach. None of them clarified why she had come back from the Bay in such a state of excitement the weekend before her death. I did my best to conceal my disappointment not only from Mary McKinnon, but also from myself.

A quick call to Wildfell confirmed Stevie's view: Helen was in no condition to be alone. In fact, she sounded terrible. Her voice was raw, from crying I suppose. There was no lift to it, no lilt. It seemed that the very act of speaking required an effort of will. And she sounded nervous as well. She reported that Miranda had been banging around the shed again. It didn't seem to be a joke.

I wasted no time in setting off for Norfolk, with some vague idea of fetching Helen back to Cambridge where I could keep an eye on her. I arrived at the cottage in record time, but getting in was harder than I expected. The back door was locked – unusual enough during the day when either of us was in residence. Even more unusual, my key wouldn't go all the way in. So Helen had already had the locks changed. Quick work, for this part of the country.

After several knocks, my friend appeared at the door, dressed in a dirty Aran sweater and an old pair of jeans. Although it was a springlike day, the cottage smelled as if it had been closed for months. I insisted on opening the windows and letting in some fresh air. We made our way to the patio. In the sunshine, Helen thawed. I held her hand and twittered on about this and that – Sonia Loizou, rowing on the river, Dee's part in *Little Women* – until the hard edges rounded down and my old Helen appeared again.

There was no doubt that she wanted me to stay. Quite why she was avoiding Cambridge wasn't clear to me, but it seemed to have something to do with putting a distance between herself and the site of Monica's death. My mind flashed to a harshly-lit parlour, uncurtained windows, an old pine rocking chair. I knew a little of what she felt, but I had to get back. For me, the only way to fight this malaise was to find out how and why Monica had died.

At last, Helen asked me what I'd learned. In answer, I led her into the dining room, and laid on the old oak table the message I'd typed that morning in Mary McKinnon's office. 'Compare,' I commanded, passing her a photocopy of the invitation that had been addressed to Helen. She scrutinised first one, then the other.

'Look,' she said, with the first sign of animation that I'd seen on her face since I arrived, 'the tails of the low-hanging letters are faint on both these sheets. Look at that *p*. And see the *g*s in *going*. It's the same typewriter – or at least, it seems to be!' She looked up at me with excitement. 'What do you think, Laura?'

'Same as you. We'll have to wait for the police expert for a final decision, but it looks as if the invitation that we found on your mantelpiece was typed in the departmental office. And the Secretary confirms that Monica did often use that typewriter when she was in the University. She used to lug it down to her office when she had a lot of memos to do, and type them up herself. On the other hand,' I warned, before Helen got too excited, 'lots of other people could have used that typewriter, too. Mary McKinnon, for instance – she's the Administrative Secretary, have you met her?' Helen gave a throwaway nod, indicating yes, she knew her, but no, not well. 'Or the other secretary. Or other tutors besides Monica. Even passers-by might type a quick note, as I did this morning. So there's no guarantee that that letter you received was prepared by Monica.'

Helen conceded the point, and added: 'And what else have you found out? Did you manage to speak to Monica's neighbour?'

I described in detail the visit to Margaret Powers. Helen was appalled at the possibility that Margaret had actually seen the killer, the man in the camelhair coat, arriving at Monica's flat. 'If it is him,' she mused, 'do you think that Margaret herself could be in danger? We're talking here about an incredibly violent man. What would he do if he thought there was a witness?'

I had been concerned about the same thing, but Margaret wouldn't hear of the idea of leaving her flat. She had, however, promised to be cautious. She said that her experience working with Women's Aid had made her cautious anyway. Battering husbands are not the most forgiving of men, and she wasn't the sort to take chances over safety. I hoped she wasn't kidding herself.

While we were going over the investigation, it had become dark in the room and through the French doors we could see a soot-coloured sky heavy with rain. I stepped across the room to switch on the lamps by the fireplace, and the phone rang. Helen answered it. My back was to her, so I registered the odd cadence of the tinny noise from the telephone a few seconds before I turned and saw Helen's bleached and stricken face.

In three strides I had crossed the room and snatched the

phone from her hand. What I heard was a woman's voice. She was sobbing, the sound loud and hysterical. Then she said, as clearly as can be: 'Let me alone! *No* . . .' The rest was a scream. I've rarely heard, outside the cinema, anything more horrible. Then there was a click, followed by the intrusive silence that marks the breaking of a telephone connection. I waited a few seconds, then hung up, and dialled the operator. No, nothing could be traced.

I sat Helen down on the sofa, and folded her in my arms, as much for my own comfort as for hers. 'What did she say, Helen? Before I took the phone from you?' I asked urgently. 'Could you make out the words?'

'Oh yes. She said—,' and here Helen burst into tears again, '—she said, "*Oh God help me. I didn't mean to hurt you*" and "*No, no, no*" over and over again. And she sobbed, as if she was out of control.'

'And was it—?'

Helen answered before I could complete the question. 'It was – I know it was – Monica.'

I nodded agreement. Even through the tones of terror, I, too, had recognised that voice: Monica, screaming for help from beyond the grave.

'What does it mean, Laura?' Helen begged. 'How can it be?'

'Come with me.' Instead of answering, I drew Helen roughly out of the cottage to the Saab. I lifted the hatchback, and there in the corner of the luggage compartment, nestling in a soft bed of cotton inside a shoebag, was my gun. I slipped it into the pocket of my jacket, and once inside the kitchen, I loaded a cartridge into the chamber. While I did so, one part of my mind surveyed the cottage from the outside – the open windows (my doing), the patio doors, the shed. It took four minutes of fast movement to secure everything. Then I returned to Helen's question.

'It means,' I replied, choosing my words with care, 'that someone made a tape recording of Monica's last moments. It means that whoever that person is, he knows we're here at Wildfell. It means that Monica's killer is even more danger- ous, even more sadistic, than we thought before.'

★

Colin and Polly were wonderful. They helped me to persuade Helen to return to Cambridge. She seemed more than merely frightened. She was deflated, almost paralysed, unable to rouse herself to do anything beyond reflecting dully on the horror of Monica's death. Polly whispered to me in an aside that it was a good thing Ginny was away with her father for half-term; it wouldn't have been very easy for the child to see her mother in this state. I put the opposite case, that Ginny's presence would probably have jolted Helen into normality more readily than anything Polly or I could do. Still, there were issues of safety to consider. I made a mental note to ring through to Ginny's father in Bristol and explain the situation to him. If someone had it in for us, it was better that Ginny should be far away.

Helping Helen pack proved to be a slow process, since she had difficulty with even the simplest decision. Polly concentrated on whether the mackintosh should go or stay, while Colin and I did business downstairs. He volunteered to engage a local carpenter on our behalf to construct shutters for the downstairs windows and the French doors. We agreed that the shutters on the local vicarage could serve as a model and that Colin would ring me in Cambridge with a quote. Anything reasonable, I said, so long as the job could be done quickly.

When the packing was done, Polly took Helen over to her house for a bite to eat. I watched them go out of sight across the meadow, then stepped back into the cottage to the sound of a recurrent bleep from inside my briefcase. It was the mobile phone. I responded, shoulders tensed against potential shock.

'Where the hell are you?' Michael Loizou demanded to know. 'That's the fourteenth ring – and I'm only allowed ten minutes on the telephone a day!'

I flexed my shoulders and relaxed. 'You're lucky you reached me at all. I'm in the heart of the North Norfolk countryside, in a village no one outside the county has ever heard of.'

'I used to holiday near Holkham with my gran every summer. Try me,' my prisoner-client cajoled.

'Don't tell me you know Wildfell Cottage, formerly the Old Barn, Burnham St Stephens?'

'Is it on the stream side or the church side of the High Street?' Michael asked smugly.

'The stream runs through our property. The turn-off to Wildfell is just beyond the post office, opposite the Unicorn.'

'Not a bad location,' Michael declared, the faintest hint of surprise in his tone. 'The detecting business must be profitable if you can afford a home in that neck of the woods.'

'Whoah, don't get the wrong idea. I'm not as well off as all that.'

The down-to-earthness of the call helped to shake off the mood created by hearing Monica's voice. And so we fell to discussing business. Apparently, Sonia Loizou had just logged in to visit Michael at Bedford the next day, and he was therefore keen to know whether I had made any progress in the case. If I told Michael what I knew about Sonia and Dmitri, he would probably spill the beans to his wife tomorrow, whereupon she would hightail it for parts unknown with all of his money, and there was not a damn thing I would be able to to do to prevent it. I stalled for time, and Michael accepted my excuses with surprisingly good grace. Maybe prison teaches a person patience.

When he had rung off, I took a deep breath and dialled the number of the Cambridge Police. After an initial exchange with a lowly Constable servicing the Murder Squad, I was treated to attention from Superintendent Neill himself, who listened to my account in a silence that couldn't be described as friendly.

His first question reminded me of why neither Sonny nor I ever hire ex-police officers in spite of their technical skills. 'What makes you think it was the dead girl's voice?' he asked, disbelief dripping down the line.

'Instant recognition,' I responded sharply.

But Neill wasn't persuaded. 'It's not easy at the best of times to identify someone who's screaming. On the telephone, when it comes at you unexpectedly, I'd say it was impossible.' A strong word. Was he calling me a liar?

'Look,' I insisted, 'I didn't put a name to the voice

afterwards, making my memory of Monica fit the sound I'd heard. I recognised her immediately, do you understand that? And so did Helen Cochrane.'

I gathered as the conversation went on that Neill favoured the theory that the call was a hoax – maybe even a hoax unrelated to Monica's death.

'Are you serious?' I asked, letting my voice express the depth of my disdain. 'On Thursday, our friend, Monica Harcourt, is brutally murdered. The following Monday, we are contacted by telephone. Someone on the other end of the line appears to be being tortured. The voice is identical to that of Monica.' I paused, pushing my anger down. 'And you really believe that this could be a mere coincidence?'

'No offence,' Neill replied with a hint of alarm in his voice. Perhaps he belatedly recalled that police work constitutes a service to the public. 'What I meant is, the call might be a hoax triggered by the publicity around Monica's death. See, someone could have read about all this in the papers, some freak who gets turned on by women's fear. He fakes a tape of a woman being tortured. Maybe he even edits it from a horror video, who knows? And then he calls you up to hear your reaction. Whoever the little bastard is, he's probably thrilled to bits right now. But the chances are, you'll never hear from him again. These guys that get their kicks from phone calls, they're too scared to do anything real. Take it from me, you're probably in the clear.'

'Superintendent Neill, it sounds to me as if you have your own fixed line of enquiry, and you're not going to let any events in the real world mess up your approach.'

I paused, took a deep breath, and then plunged on. 'I have just three things more to say, and then I'll leave you to return to your version of your job. First, the voice on the line *was* Monica's. No hoaxer could do that – only the killer. Second, someone reading about the murder in the paper wouldn't know anything about this cottage. It wasn't mentioned in the news. This points to your "hoaxer" being someone who knew a great deal about Monica, and who knows about Helen and me. And finally, since the police rarely bother to pursue the makers of threatening phone calls, you can have no possible grounds for concluding that the people who make them aren't harmful.'

Then I hung up. I felt better for getting all that off my chest, even if it hadn't done much to improve my relations with the police.

CHAPTER 10

Once I had delivered Helen safely back into the hands of friends in Cambridge, and made my own arrangements for her protection, I was relieved to get away. Her lassitude was wearing. I needed to focus on gaps in the investigation, and Helen in her current state was enough to dull anyone's resolve. My first priority was to have a talk with the only person who had been tipped as an enemy of Monica.

Ella Grimsby's tiny office, tucked away behind the north studio, could have passed as a teenager's workroom. Her door was plastered with sketches, cuttings from the newspaper and faded postcards. I was propelled back to the 1980s by a cruel Scarfe caricature of Margaret Thatcher lecturing Ronald Reagan on the need for vigilance in the White House. The door opened before I could survey the rest, and Ella beckoned me in.

Ella Grimsby was not as severe-looking as her name suggests. In fact, there was something rather buxom about her, in spite of her advancing age and her diminutive height. I introduced myself as a private investigator, looking into Monica's death, and as a friend. If Ella was struggling to disguise her shock at the violent death of a colleague, she was certainly giving a world-class performance. She cleared some papers off a ladderback chair so as to reveal a hand-embroidered cushion, motioned me towards it and seated herself in a relaxed fashion behind the desk.

For a moment or two we chatted about this and that. Ella G. had a good line in social trivia – and I don't mean that in a patronising way. I admire people who can immediately make others feel at ease, who can pluck a common thread out of thin air and begin to weave relationships with it. Eventually, though, it was time to shift gear. I began the real conversation by asking Ella whether she knew Monica well. Her generous brown eyebrows shot upwards to an astonishing height. I did my best to refrain from watching them for further signs of life.

'The only people who knew her *well*,' she replied, emphasising the last word, 'were men.' The tone was one of unashamed sarcasm. So this was Mary McKinnon's vindictive little cow.

'You're going to have to explain that,' I remarked. My tone was mild. I had no illusions. Ella Grimsby was not the sort to knuckle under to aggression.

Ella's laugh was rather malicious. 'If you were, as you claim, a friend of Monica's, then surely you would know what I mean. Monica was a competent painter. She was an amicable colleague. She was probably a well-intentioned teacher, though not all students benefited from her attentions. But the most striking thing about Monica was her good looks – and the way she was prepared to use them to get what she wanted.'

'Give me an example,' I interjected.

'No problem,' Ella returned. 'How do you imagine Monica manipulated her way into the job here? I was well past fifty and no great beauty when the Course Tutor, Simon Jackson, resigned. I had done his job – and done it well, I might say – for the previous ten months, while Simon was on sick leave. The course was new – I sweated my guts out to make it work. Then Monica showed up. She had virtually no administrative experience, you realise, and a narrower teaching range. But she was thirty and she had that amazing hair. The Provost was obviously smitten. Not only did he appoint her, but it now emerges that he promised her time off as well to go to her precious California.'

'Oregon,' I interrupted.

Ella acknowledged the correction with an indifferent shrug of her eyebrows, the only person I had ever seen who could do that. 'If you say so. And,' she asked with a challenging look, 'guess who would have been asked to take over the course again when she was gone?'

I didn't need to guess. Nor did I need to pretend to be shocked. I *was* shocked. This was a new and uncomfortable image of Monica. A flirt? Intentionally using sexuality to get preferment? From Ella's point of view, there was every reason to be upset. The force of her anger created an almost physical tension in the room. Could she be violent, I wondered?

Ella and I talked some more about Monica and the course, on more neutral ground. Her descriptions of some aspects of college life (of, for example, the shower of memos that pour out of Personnel) showed a woman sharply observant and rather tolerant in her dealings with others. Only when we returned to the subject of Monica – to the students who, according to Ella, mooned after her, and to her habit of working *incommunicado* in the evenings, a habit that Ella found irritatingly self-indulgent – did her malicious side resurface.

'You see,' she explained, sensing my pulling away again, 'I can take almost anything from people – bigotry, small-mindedness, vanity – you name it, there's a lot of it in academic life. And usually I can manage to see past it to the person beyond. But the thing I *can't* abide is cheating. Your Monica was a cheat.'

'In what sense?' I asked, perplexed by this use of the word. 'Are you saying that she cheated you out of the tutorship?'

Ella rocked back and forth in her chair, elbows akimbo, fingers laced together behind her neck. She looked at me intently, as if considering whether to confide in me or not. She decided against it.

'You really don't know, do you?' she concluded. 'Well, I won't be the one to explain. Ms Detective Nancy Drew or whatever your name is, you're going to have to figure this one out for yourself.'

There wasn't anything more to say. We parted soon afterwards. Under other circumstances, I might have been amused by Ella Grimsby, might even have been pleased to include her among my acquaintances, but I knew it wouldn't happen now. Whatever else she thought of me, my partisanship for Monica would be intolerable to Ella. And whatever else I thought of her, her bitterness towards Monica touched too many uncomfortable chords, not only *vis à vis* Monica herself but also in relation to all we younger women who are fortunate enough to have a few friendly female colleagues with whom to share our professional lives.

The woman behind the uncluttered desk certainly looked like a director's Personal Assistant. I don't know if her typing was more accurate or her shorthand faster, but her clothes were definitely a touch more expensive than those worn by other secretaries in the University, and her heels were a shade higher. I wondered whether the Provost would also be better-dressed than the Dean, his aftershave a trifle more enticing.

There would be no chance to answer that question without an appointment, and appointments, I suspected, were not readily extended to nonentities such as myself. But Miss Trina Thompson, as the PA's nameplate identified her, responded in a kindly way once she knew that I had been a friend of Monica.

'Poor thing,' she exclaimed. 'You know, when I first saw her, so pretty with all that hair and clever as well, I thought she was so lucky. Here she had a good job, and people respected her as an artist, and she had no ties, no responsibilities, outside of her work. I thought she had it made – and she was so nice as well. But Cambridge didn't really work out for her.'

Did she mean the murder?

'Was her experience in Cambridge generally a negative one, then?' I asked.

Suddenly Trina looked rather nervous. 'Well, I got the impression,' she said carefully, 'that the University wasn't quite what she expected. And she didn't really have anyone to confide in, not anyone from the academic staff.'

'Did she particularly need anyone to confide in?' I asked casually.

Trina shook her head. 'Everyone needs someone to confide in,' she replied, looking me in the eye. Clever woman. Her back was straight, but the nervousness hadn't gone.

I held her gaze, and smiled. I made another attempt. 'Look, I'm trying to trace any friends or relatives Monica might have had. I thought perhaps she knew people in Oregon, she was so keen on spending time there. Did she ever say anything about friends in the States?'

'No, nothing. As far as I knew it was the landscape that drew her, or rather the ocean views.'

'Well, perhaps I could find a clue among the things she wrote about Oregon. Do you have a copy of her application for secondment?'

Trina nodded assent, and moved smoothly to a pale blue filing cabinet. In a moment she had located a file and handed it to me. 'These are confidential,' she said, 'but I see no reason now why you shouldn't have a look. Under the circumstances.'

The manila file contained a small package of different items. A curriculum vitae, attractively laid out, listing exhibitions and reproductions of her work as well as jobs and publications. An outline of the work she intended to do in Oregon. A letter from the state university in Eugene Oregon, confirming that they would like to offer her a visiting fellowship. Two references, including one from the Dean. A report from the Research and Grants Committee. And, on the front, an official blue form that obviously acted as a progress chaser.

Trina gave me permission to take a photocopy of the cv. I also made a note of the name of the Head of Department in Oregon who had invited Monica to visit. But what interested me most was the blue progress form. I moved cautiously. 'So how long does it usually take to get a request for secondment approved?' I asked.

'Oh, if the application comes in in good shape, with all the appropriate references for example, we can usually guarantee a decision within two months. People need to know quickly if they are going to make plans.'

'But Monica's took a little longer?'

Trina glanced at me anxiously. 'I don't know what you've heard,' she said, 'from people in Monica's department. There's always one person who is going to be a bit jealous of someone like Monica. But whatever you've heard, it wasn't true. Monica was straight. She was decent, and she went about things the right way. Nothing that happened was her fault.'

'And what did happen?' I asked her gently.

Trina shook her head. 'Don't ask me,' she pleaded. Her makeup glistened ominously. I left.

I picked up some *spanakopitte* from Peppercorns on Mill Road, and returned to Clare Street to reflect on what I'd learned. The spinach and cheese stuffing had just a hint of sharpness: it stimulated my brain as well as my tastebuds. Suddenly I remembered the photographs from Holkham Bay, the ones that Mary McKinnon had produced. I had hustled down to the cottage after only a brief glance at them, and the events with Helen had chased them out of my mind. There they were, still in the sidepocket of my briefcase.

I poured myself a glass of Aqua Libra and spread the photos, all twenty-four of them, out on the desk. Scenes of seaspray and sky and pinewoods obliterated the unanswered post that had accumulated since Friday. I couldn't raise even a glimmer of concern.

The shading of the photos was evocative. Something about that grey-blue silvery light recalled the extraordinary sensations of being on the beach on a wintry day. The sense of being very big, a target for the buffeting wind, and at the same time very tiny. Of being cocooned by the rhythm of the sea. I felt momentarily closer to Monica.

I surveyed the photos in sequence, trying to scan as Monica might have scanned. She had begun with the sweep of the bay. The first photo offered a panoramic view of the elongated curve of land that began to the west of the path by which Monica must have entered, and swept in a pine-tipped point out to sea. There was a series re-covering the same sweep in more detailed, overlapping chunks, like large pieces of an adult jigsaw puzzle. Three shots focused on an opening in the trees about five hundred yards inland from the tip of the peninsula. Each was at a different focal length, bringing the opening progressively closer. I turned on my desk lamp and examined the third picture with care. Yes, standing downwind of the opening in the trees, facing towards the sea, were two small figures. The zoom lens revealed in miniature profile a man and a woman. His arm was around her shoulders, while her head was bowed in an attitude that could be contemplation or grief. Perhaps she was merely protecting her face from the wind. So – Monica had not been alone on the beach that day . . .

I set aside the photos of Helen, Ginny and me without the luxury of a closer look. Instead I shook the envelope. Out fell the negatives. My fingers fumbled as I tried to lift the strips without touching the surfaces. Here they were: 1/1a to 5, and 6 to 10, 16 to 20 and 21 to 24. I rustled the envelope again. Empty. Twenty-four prints, but only twenty negatives. No sign of 11 to 15.

Mary McKinnon answered on the first ring. The photos had come to Monica's pigeonhole, she explained, through the internal post. She assumed they had been developed by a technician in the photography section named Martin who had done private work for Monica before.

Before I could dial the photography section, my own telephone rang, bringing me back from the beach with a jolt. It was Nicole, Detective Sergeant Pelletier, with information for me. She thought I'd like to know, and indeed I did. The police had found the boyfriend.

Nicole saw me in a small interview room at the back of the police station. She produced some coffee in plastic cups, and I must say, she looked as if she needed it. Her dark eyes were strained, a small muscle twitching below the rim. She must be going all out on this case. Today she had pulled her springy blue-black hair back severely from her face and attempted to secure it with an elasticated hairband that obviously wasn't up to the job. A large clump of hair had worked itself free above her right ear, giving her a lopsided air. Nicole tilted her head to the left, as if to compensate.

Sternly, she warned me that much of what she was going to say was confidential. The boyfriend was voluntarily in police custody ('helping the police with their enquiries') and she was breaking regulations by letting me know the content of their interviews. I gave what reassurance I could, and Nicole filled me in on the details.

'You put us on to this bloke's background, and what with him being a writer and all, it didn't take long to come up with a likely name and an address. But there was no one home. We located him eventually in a pub on the Holloway Road, in North London. He was pretty drunk. Looks like he has been drinking for days.'

'Did he know about Monica?'

Nicole nodded vigorously. The twist of black hair bobbed up and down. 'No doubt about it. The first thing he said, when the PC approached him, was "You've come about Monica." And then he cried. Non-stop, for the best part of a quarter of an hour. The PC tried to calm him down, got him a cup of coffee, but he was really out of it. Kept shaking his head and saying, "It's all my fault".'

'What did he mean by that?'

'Don't jump to conclusions,' Nicole interrupted. 'We're not. People often blame themselves when someone close to them is injured. And "It's all my fault" is not the same as "I did it".'

Of course she's dead right about that. One of the negative things about having a useful contact like Nicole is that you have to put up with being lectured at from time to time.

'So what now?'

Nicole perched on the corner of the table, and I could tell from the change in her expression what was coming. 'Well, that's the rub,' she replied. 'We're interrogating him now, or trying to. Most of all, we're trying to sober him up. The barmaid in the London pub said that when a television news report announced the murder of Monica Harcourt in Cambridge, he looked suddenly distraught. He had been already over the limit, and he had three double whiskies in quick succession after that. The police surgeon has seen him. It's going to be at least twenty-four hours before he's in a state to give us any detailed information.'

Nicole smiled at me, a cajoling kind of smile. It didn't suit her. 'But we thought it might be a good idea if someone could talk to him in the meantime, someone he might open up to.

He doesn't like us much, you see. Someone who knew Monica.'

I didn't take her up on that. 'What's he like?' I asked. 'Besides drunk.'

'Well,' Nicole looked again at her notebook, more out of habit than necessity, 'he's a black male, aged thirty-six, probably cleanshaven when he's not drinking, right now looks like he needs a bath and a shave. Medium height. Bloody good-looking, if you ask me.'

I hadn't. 'No, I mean what kind of a man is he? Can you see him as the killer?'

Nicole looked scathing. 'Don't tell me you want to know whether he's the type.' Half the hair on the right-hand side had now escaped from the hairband, giving her a manic look. I contemplated advising her to make for the Ladies before her boss showed up, but decided against it. Discretion and all that. I had no intention of asking whether the man in custody was the type, as she put it, but Nicole saw another opportunity for a lecture, and seized it. She must have really hated being a student. She was the teacher now, I the impractical academic. 'Any man could kill someone, in the right circumstances – you should know that. He doesn't have an air of violence about him, if that's what you mean. Seems a rather gentle bloke, well-spoken, mild-mannered, but you shouldn't take these details too seriously. Not many killers look like Freddy Krueger.'

So – the police watch adolescent horror films. Or maybe Nicole had a misspent youth.

She consulted her notebook and went on: 'Look, we know precious little about him though we have people out checking with his neighbours, and we'll soon have more. What we do know is this.' She consulted her notebook again, and launched into a concise description that would have earned praise in an undergraduate seminar. Perhaps police training had done her some good after all.

'His name is Angell Rideau,' she began. 'He was born in Mauritius, of a Mauritian father and a Sengalese mother. Quite a wealthy family. Moved to Europe in the mid-sixties. Studied Eng. Lit. at Oxford University, graduated with a

Double First. One of these counterculture types, refused to cash in on his success. He began teaching something called Media Studies in a college in London and devoted as much time as he could to writing poetry. Had quite a success with his first two volumes of poetry, is well thought of in literary circles, though I don't imagine he makes any money from it. Still, he has a legacy from his family, as well as his teaching income, and from what our boys in London say, he lives quite well. Has a small Georgian terraced house on the boundary between Holland Park and Notting Hill.'

Nicole paused for breath, and I managed to refrain from congratulating her on the lucidity of her précis. She shifted position again, flipped her notebook closed with a snappy gesture that made the hair bounce, and looked straight at me. 'That's all we know. What we need now is more about his relationship with Monica. How he felt about the break-up and so on.'

As I thought. 'And that's where I come in?'

'Uh huh.' Nicole waited for me to say something. I thought I'd let her make her pitch. I studied my fingernails, and after only ten seconds she launched forth. 'Just a chat, Laura – nothing heavy. He's beginning to sober up and he feels awful. But he really does want to talk about Monica, only not to us. To you, he would probably open up, talk about the relationship. How he heard about the murder, how often he has seen Monica over the past few weeks – that sort of thing. And you could fill us in on the details.'

Great! A drunken fellow, full of remorse, maybe a murderer, and I should chat to him casually about my friend who has just been murdered. *Maybe by him.* Or, just as bad, Monica's long-term lover, who was closer to her and mourns her more than I, and I am supposed to set him up for the police. A no-win scenario.

On the other hand, I found myself wanting to meet this Angell Rideau. He was the only person I'd come across so far who had some shared history with Monica that went back further than eighteen months. Surely I could spare half an hour?

I locked eyes with Nicole, willing myself not to look at

those wayward strands of hair. 'You know me, Nicole,' I said, flashing my most dazzling smile. 'Always ready to help the police. And perhaps,' I added, nodding in the direction of the pathologist's report, 'perhaps you might just lighten your load by leaving that folder on the table while you fetch M. Rideau.'

My ex-pupil's eyes narrowed alarmingly, but after two seconds' hesitation she stood up and without a glance in my direction, placed the folder on the farther edge of the table and walked out. Like most members of the University netball team, Nicole always did have a strong sense of fair play.

I reckoned I could allow myself three minutes at the most. It was more than enough. The salient points jumped off the sheet. On 18 November, Monica Harcourt was viciously attacked. A short-bladed knife, almost certainly a Stanley knife, was repeatedly used. The pathologist counted over sixty separate wounds, most of them to the neck, hands and upper torso. Most were superficial, but two to the chest had done substantial damage, one of them piercing a lung. Monica would have had difficulty breathing before that anyway; the rope around her neck had been tightened so that she had suffered partial strangulation before she died. She had also suffered three severe blows to the head, delivered by a small hard implement, probably a small metal hammer. One of these blows had penetrated the brain, and almost certainly was the cause of death. There were no signs of sexual interference. No precise estimate of the time of death could be made, given that it was a full twenty-four hours before the body was found, but from the contents of Monica's stomach it was clear that at least two hours – and possibly as many as four – had elapsed between her six o'clock supper and her death.

At the sound of approaching footsteps, I replaced the folder and leaned back in my chair, trying hard to look as if I hadn't just been immersed in a nightmare.

CHAPTER 11

Angell wasn't crying when Nicole showed him in, but he had been. He looked deeply distressed, harrowed, drawn. But he stood upright and appeared composed. In fact, he seemed at least as much in command of himself and the situation as I did. Nicole ushered in a police officer ('to accompany you') and left without another word. Angell kept his eyes fixed intently on my face. He appeared not to notice Nicole's departure.

I introduced myself, rather awkwardly. 'Detective Sergeant Pelletier said you would be willing to talk to someone who knew Monica Harcourt. I knew her – not well, but enough to admire her. My name is Laura Principal.'

'Ah, so it's you.' Angell's welcoming smile spared me further embarrassment. 'It was one of the nicest things that happened to Monica in years, getting to know you and your friend Helen. She was elated about the cottage,' he said.

He looked challengingly at me. 'I should tell you, I couldn't help being jealous.' There was a dignity about the way he said this that persisted in spite of the dishevelled state of his clothes and his unshaven face. Apart from the bloodshot whites of his hazel eyes, there was little sign of a hangover.

'I had loved Monica for years,' he continued. 'When she decided to split up with me, I wasn't happy about it, but I could understand her reasons. I thought at that stage that at least she would continue to lean on me as her closest friend. When she told me about the arrangements with you and Helen, even that was in doubt. It's hard to watch while someone you love moves eagerly towards separation – and even expects you to be proud of them for it.'

I needed some background, and told Angell so. His step-by-step explanation made a lot of things clear, and brought Monica more into focus.

They had met years ago, when Monica was at art college in London. She had attended a reading of his poetry, and afterwards he had stopped to speak to an acquaintance who was seated at her table. He had found her endearing – her enthusiasm, her simplicity and even her uncertainty distinguished her from all the other blasé and bored characters around. And she had seemed to be entranced by him. She thought him oh, so sophisticated. She admired his confidence in his writing, his rejection of a conventional career, and what she saw as his kindness to her.

After a time, they fell in love. She probably gave more to the relationship than he did in those early years. After all, she based her home in London in what was initially his patch, she became part of his circle. Although she was very serious about her painting, she always had to struggle against feeling a dilettante compared to Angell, whose seriousness as an artist was validated by books of poetry and a small measure of fame. And how seriously do others take the efforts of a struggling woman painter who lives not in a garret, not in a bed-sit funded by late-night shifts of waitressing, but in a fine Georgian house, the property of her lover? The more Monica tried to overcome her sense of indebtedness by being a hostess and organising his domestic life, the more illegitimate seemed to her (and to some others) her claim to the title of painter.

But the crunch came with the drinking. Angell managed to avoid either shame or self-pity as he explained that he had struggled with a drinking problem for the past ten years. Not every day, but every so often – perhaps three or four times a year – something would take him a certain way and he would be off. He had tried therapy to sort out what it was that drove him to it, but he gave that up when the emotional drain of therapy prevented him from writing. For himself, he was prepared to accept the occasional bouts of drunkenness as the price he had to pay for a full existence. For Monica, they were disastrous. She had constructed a life around his stable presence, and these sudden disappearances completely undermined her. She was paralysed by anxiety, for his safety and for herself. All her work went to pieces, she could do nothing until he returned. And not only was this painful and disruptive for her, it represented an intolerable symbol of her own dependence upon Angell, of what she saw as her lack of centre.

And there was something else. Monica had wanted a child. Three years ago, she had become pregnant. Though it wasn't planned, they had both been delighted. Four months into the pregnancy, with no warning, Angell had gone off on one of his benders. While he was away, Monica fell down the stairs. With no one there to help her, she miscarried. A neighbour found her in time to get her to hospital, but this experience had bled something more than a baby out of Monica. Though she and Angell grieved together, and though for a time the tragedy brought them closer, Monica eventually decided that she wanted a life in which the fixed point came from inside herself and not from someone else.

Angell had recounted for me the pattern of their life in a straightforward way that I found touching. There was no element of special pleading, no attempt to undermine the authenticity of Monica's need to get away. He had loved her, shared his life with her, and, as best he could, protected her. But he wasn't able to give her the kind of security that would make her trust herself.

As he recounted this, Angell sat, composed, in a small wooden armchair. I had no difficulty in seeing why Nicole thought him good-looking. With his strong forehead and planed cheeks, his full mouth and nose, he was something near to beautiful. It was easy to imagine him compelling attention at a poetry reading. Easy to imagine a young girl falling under his spell. Or an old girl, for that matter. I believed him, every word. But we still had a way to go.

'I've seen you before,' I said. 'In snapshots. Monica took some photos of you last week.'

'She was always doing that,' he said, and some of the pain smoothed off his face. 'Portraits weren't her thing at all. When it came to painting, it was landscapes that said what she wanted to say. But when we were together – and this carried on after we split up – she was always composing photos around me, snapping away. Even when she was out of film, she would hold up the camera and look and look and look. I used to tease her by saying that it was her way of reducing me to manageable proportions.'

'So when did Monica take these particular photos?' I asked. Angell's look told me he knew that this was for real, no longer a conversation but an interview.

He didn't seem to mind. 'Don't worry about it – ask your questions. I would rather by far speak to you than the police, especially that uptight WPC.'

I squirmed inwardly, this time for my disloyalty to Nicole. 'Detective Sergeant,' I corrected.

Angell returned to the earlier question. 'Monica rang me on the Sunday evening before her death. She was over the moon, full of news about Wildfell. I drove up to see her in Cambridge on the Monday afternoon and we had a walk by the river – that's where she took the photos of me – and then a little supper at Brown's. I dropped her back at her flat shortly after seven. She was very disciplined about working in the evenings, you know.'

I nodded. 'And you didn't see her or talk to her since?'

'No, I didn't see her again.' For the first time during this discussion, Angell's face crumpled, and I had a glimpse of the agony that drove him on. 'But we did talk on the phone on Wednesday. You see, Monica was eager to move into the cottage as quickly as possible. She wanted to make her mark on it, I guess. She rang me to say that the cottage was going to be empty that coming weekend, but that it was all right with Helen and Laura – with you, I mean – if she went down there by herself and took a few of her things. I think she said that someone was bringing her a set of keys on Friday evening.'

'Me. That's what I was doing at Monica's place on Friday when I found her like that.' I usually don't like euphemisms, but I couldn't bring myself to say 'when I found the body'. After a moment's silence, I prompted Angell: 'So Monica rang to tell you all about it?'

He seemed to recall himself to the present. Or rather, to my presence. 'Yes. Actually, she wanted a small favour. She had borrowed a van from the University, and she wanted me to help her load it with some of her things. Not the easel and so forth, that she could handle on her own, but there's an oak bookcase she wanted to put in the cottage bedroom that was far too heavy for her to move alone. Monica wanted me to come up to Cambridge on the Friday evening, help her load the van, and then stay over and make the trip to Burnham St Stephens with her on Saturday. She wanted me to share her first morning in her new home.'

'You turned her down.' It was a statement, not a question.

'I turned her down,' Angell repeated. 'Not at first. At first I said I'd try to come. But I phoned the next day and left a message on Monica's answerphone telling her I was too busy after all.'

'That was Thursday? The day she died?'

'I guess so. The police haven't told me yet exactly when she died. When I rang Monica, it was late Thursday afternoon. You don't suppose. . .?'

He didn't need to finish the question. 'No,' I cut in quickly. 'If you placed the call late Thursday afternoon, then Monica would still be in her landscape class. We know that she didn't leave the University until half-past six. But what I don't understand is why you cancelled the arrangement to meet on Friday.'

Angell shook his head ruefully. 'To tell you the truth, I chickened out. I had been doing such a good job in the previous weeks of re-orienting myself to the fact that our relationship was over. I had rearranged the house so Monica's absence was less striking; I had found a new routine in the evenings that left less time for missing her; I had even had a small flirtation with a woman I know who lives in Notting Hill. But seeing Monica on Monday all excited about the cottage just cut me up. I started feeling sorry for myself again. I didn't want to face her until I'd got a grip on myself.'

'So what did you do on Thursday evening after you left the message for Monica? Did you go out with the new flirtation?'

'Nope. And this is where I'm going to have to get myself a good lawyer, Laura. Because what I did instead was drink.

And I did it so successfully and so unyieldingly that I can't even tell you where or when.'

There were only about a dozen of us at Monica's funeral service. St Paul's Church echoed to our footsteps and we huddled together in the front pews for emotional warmth. Trina Thompson was there, and Mary McKinnon; two of Monica's students, looking painfully ill at ease; and some of her colleagues from the Art Department – though not, of course, Ella Grimsby. Nicole escorted Angell. He appeared dignified but withdrawn in what I assumed was a hired suit. It didn't really fit, even though Angell looked like the sort of man who was accustomed to well-cut clothes. I tried to introduce him to Helen but she didn't want to know. Margaret Powers, the woman whose flat had been above Monica's, was more open, taking his hand in both her own and whispering, 'I loved her, too.'

Sonny isn't one for funerals, but he was waiting outside the church on Hills Road when I emerged, and walked with me in thoughtful silence to Brown's. Over cappuccino, Sonny made a valiant attempt to persuade me to return with him to London. His plea made quite an impression; part of me longed just to return to the old routine and the familiar comfort of our shared life. That's what Helen was doing: she had gone straight from the cemetery to the library, pausing only to wipe away her tears before plunging herself back into work.

Part of me needed the bustle of London, but the other part needed some more definitive answer than a funeral could provide to the unfinished business of Monica. And Helen needed me here, in Cambridge. I had issued a solemn promise to meet her and Margaret Powers for lunch, ostensibly to bring them up to date with the investigation but actually to help ensure that Helen's brave face would stay in place for the whole of the working day.

Helen, Margaret and I met at one o'clock in the University restaurant, where lack of chic is compensated for by surprisingly good food. The room is laid out with round tables graced with impractical white tablecloths. Since academics fail to concentrate on their eating, these table coverings require changing at frequent intervals. The formal act of peeling off the cloth and laying another is performed by self-conscious apprentices on work experience programmes from the nearby Further Education college. They also take the orders, full of anxiety in case someone asks them to explain what's in the sauce, and they relay the main course from the kitchen to our table. Soup and starters, sweets and coffee, by contrast, are picked up from the buffet table at the end of the room, where plump pleasant-voiced women in their late forties serve the customers fondly and indifferently, as if they are all dear but troublesome grandchildren.

We edged our way through the crowded restaurant, past tables of grey or navy-suited men (the managers), and clumps of men in blue or checked shirts and crumpled jackets of brown and beige (the male academics). An occasional woman, sometimes informal in her dress, often colourful, enlivened the room, so that although there was only a smattering of women having lunch they were highly visible.

We found an empty table with a view of the honeysuckle hedge that shielded diners from the car park, and Helen signalled to a willing waiter our intention to go straight into the main course. We all ordered the special: cheese and artichoke pie with aubergine salad. Once the mineral water arrived, I filled Helen and Margaret in on my interview with Angell, knowing full well that my account couldn't help but be contaminated by the liking I had felt for Monica's friend. 'So what do you two make of Angell?' I asked. It wasn't an idle question.

Margaret took the bull by the horns. 'I'm a firm believer in *cherchez l'homme*,' she declared, pushing her chair a few inches away from the table so she could cross her long legs. 'But in this case, I have to confess to a sneaking sense of relief that Angell seems like such a sweetie. To have Monica's former lover as her killer would be . . . well, even more ghastly.'

Helen played the sceptic. 'Of course any boyfriend of Monica's would be charming. That goes without saying. But charm doesn't rule him out as a suspect.' She had been addressing herself to Margaret with a kind of flinty-eyed determination, but now she included me in her glance. 'Just look at the facts. Angell was angry with Monica for ending the relationship, but he kept hoping that he could win her back. Then she comes up with friends who will be there for her in the long-term, and a home. Exactly what she needs to make her independent. The jilted boyfriend realises that he is not going to be needed any more. On his own admission, he was distraught at her enthusiasm over the cottage. So one: we have motive.'

I could see that I was going to have to draw Helen into the *Cluedo*? championship with Sonny, Dominic and Daniel. She had something of the style already. Helen's version of events was having an impact on Margaret, who nodded reluctantly. I rearranged the cutlery to make room for a salad bowl on the fresh white cloth. The food arrived, a palette of golds and browns and purples. After testing the pie, and pronouncing it good, Helen returned to her account.

'Two,' she announced crisply. 'Timing and opportunity. Monica was expecting him on the evening she was killed. He planned to visit Cambridge to help her load furniture into the van.'

Margaret interrupted. 'Has anyone checked whether there is a van, by the way?'

I picked that up. 'Yes, Monica arrived home from University on Wednesday afternoon with a van. The police have been over it with a fine-tooth comb. Nothing. At least, nothing that gives a clue to the killer. But there *is* a wooden bookcase in the back, and a couple of boxes of books.'

'So there you are!' Helen smiled triumphantly, pausing to wipe her fingers on a napkin. 'Angell *did* come after all. He helped her load the bookcase into the van, then they stopped for a drink, and got to talking about their relationship. Angell pleaded with her to abandon the idea of the cottage and re-establish a home in London with him. She refused. He became enraged and killed her.'

Don't you think you're jumping the gun?' Margaret asked. 'After all, Angell told Laura he didn't actually get to Cambridge, he stayed in London. Someone else may have helped her move the bookcase. Don't forget the man that I saw at Monica's door that evening. That certainly wasn't Angell.'

'But Angell has no alibi whatsoever,' Helen persevered. Even though I didn't agree with Helen, I was encouraged to see her energy. Ever since the grisly telephone call at Wildfell, I had been worried about her lack of grip. And now here she was, pale, and with an uncharacteristic tension in the set of her lips, but certainly vigorous. In fact, she was downright adamant.

'Look,' she continued, 'he can't prove he was drinking himself into oblivion in London. He certainly isn't going to produce a set of witnesses who can verify his movements that evening, since he doesn't even remember what his movements were. He says he rang to tell Monica he wasn't coming, but how the hell do we know that's true?'

'I asked about Monica's answerphone,' I interjected. 'It was switched on when she was found, but the only message was from a local bookstore. Apparently that was left on Friday afternoon. So we have three possibilities: Monica heard the message and wiped it; the killer listened and then erased the tape; or Angell is lying. On the other hand, the police have checked with British Telecom, and there *was* a call to Monica's house from Angell's London number on Thursday at 4.03 p.m. At least part of his story fits.'

Helen was pursuing Angell's prosecution so incisively that I left it to her to make the obvious critique. She obliged, but not without first fixing me with a withering glance. 'So Angell called Monica, so what? He might have called to confirm his time of arrival in Cambridge. To ask if he should bring anything. Or even to check that she would be in all evening so that he could carry through on his plan to kill her.'

'Now you're being really far-fetched,' Margaret retorted. 'Angell doesn't seem at all like a cold-blooded killer. If – and I'm not granting anything – but *if* he killed her, surely it would be in a fit of passion, not with malice aforethought.' She tried to enlist my support. 'What do you think, Laura? Passion – or cold blood?'

The distinction was not one that I could subscribe to. Monica's wounds showed real hatred – but the person who inflicted that damage took his time. He didn't just lash out and then recoil, appalled. He had attacked, looked at his handiwork and attacked again. And again. I didn't want to say it, but whoever murdered Monica had had enough of a relationship with her to want to watch her suffer.

I had been pretty quiet for the last few moments, as I didn't have the heart for the adversarial discussion of Angell's guilt that had galvanised Helen and Margaret. But now I introduced a different tack. 'Look, I've met Angell only twice, under unusual circumstances. I have no way of knowing whether he's capable of killing. The very fact that he and Monica had been lovers means that some punters are bound to put their money on him. But there is one person who would probably know whether Angell was dangerous or not, and that's Monica herself. I'm just trying to think – did she ever say anything that might suggest that she was frightened of Angell?'

The consensus around the table was that in recent weeks Monica *had* been frightened. Helen recalled her anxious questions about visitors and telephone calls, her darting glances towards the shadowy parts of the landscape while we walked, her conviction that someone had been in her bedroom.

Margaret fleshed out this fear. Only the week before her death, Monica had referred to footsteps that stopped outside their house in the night. Margaret, who slept at the back of the house, hadn't heard a thing, and Monica had then shrugged it off as foolishness and declined to talk about it further. But the other woman insisted that, however innocent the event, Monica had been genuinely afraid.

'I must say, this tends to let Angell off the hook,' Helen argued, switching sides. Openmindedness was one of her most consistent qualities.

I didn't follow. 'I don't follow,' I said.

'Well, if Monica *was* scared, it certainly wasn't Angell who scared her. After all, she was anxious to establish that the cottage was safe – that there was no one lurking in the bushes, that the noises in the meadow had a rational explanation. But on the other hand, she wanted to bring Angell to see it as quickly as possible. If Angell was the one who threatened her, surely she would have tried to keep him away from the cottage, even to keep him from knowing about it.'

'That's right – but only assuming she knew that the person who threatened her was Angell,' Margaret answered. 'What if she trusted him, but it was actually he who was ringing her up, or standing outside her window at night-time or whatever? Men who are thwarted in love will do very strange things. Ask any of the people at Women's Aid.'

So all we managed to establish was that Monica, who had known Angell intimately for years, didn't see him as a danger.

'But if it wasn't Angell,' Helen blurted out, 'perhaps Monica might have told him who else she was afraid of.'

I had asked, of course. 'No dice. He said that he would be the last person to know something like that. In recent years, Monica had become more and more reluctant to admit to Angell that anything or anyone caused her concern. It was part of her push for self-sufficiency. Actually, Angell was close to tears when he said this.'

'I can understand why. It must be awful,' Margaret mused, 'to realise that because of the nature of your relationship, someone you love refused to confide in you when they were terrified.' Helen and I agreed. It didn't bear thinking about.

We needed a change of mood. Margaret volunteered to fetch coffee for three. She was only halfway to the buffet table, however, when she suddenly turned back. Her eyes had a shocked look, and her walk was unsteady. I stood up to offer support but she shook me off.

'Who is that man? Over there,' she hissed, gesticulating desperately with her eyes. I followed the trajectory to where a group of navy-suited men were strolling companionably towards the door.

'Which one?'

'The second one in the group. The one who's laughing.'

I quickly eased her into a seat. One or two people were looking curiously at Margaret, the significance of the moment betrayed not in her voice, which was close to a whisper, but in her frozen stance.

Helen answered Margaret's question. 'If you mean the first

man through the door, that's Milton Bannister. He's the Provost – top dog at Eastern University.'

'He's the one,' Margaret whispered.

It was a second before the penny dropped with a sharp metallic click. Margaret saw the understanding in my eyes and confirmed: 'Yes, the one who came to Monica's door the night she was killed. The last person apart from her killer to see Monica alive.'

And just maybe, the first person to see her dead.

CHAPTER 12

By the time Margaret recovered her wits, the Provost, Milton Bannister, had retired securely behind the oak double doors of his office. Trina Thompson was sympathetic, but she couldn't let me in. Nor could she supply an appointment, either, unless she could clear it with him first.

This was hardly a time to pussyfoot, even if I had the feet for it. Margaret had agreed to delay going to the police until three o'clock, to give me an opportunity to confront the Provost and gauge his reaction before the police put him on his guard. There wasn't much time.

'Tell Milton Bannister that Laura Principal wants to see him. Say I was a close friend of Monica's – and that if I don't hear from him by three o'clock, I'll be speaking to the police instead.'

'I'll make certain he gets the message, Dr Principal.' Trina's reply was correct and her posture composed, but I fancied for a moment that I saw a trace of satisfaction flicker across her face. I told her where she could reach me. She followed me to the door, a piece of paper in her hand.

'Your enquiry about Monica's application for secondment set me thinking,' she explained. 'It occurred to me that some of our administrative procedures may need looking into, so I checked the applications for the past five years. Monica's wasn't the only delay. There are four cases altogether which took far longer to be processed than expected. Anyway,' she concluded, fixing me with a level look, 'I just wanted to thank you for bringing this to my attention. It is quite clear that an administrative enquiry is called for.'

And any other kind of investigation? I wondered. 'Could I have a copy of that paper?'

'Sorry, it's confidential – I couldn't possibly allow you to have a copy. But I would like to reassure you that Monica's was not the only instance of delay.' As she said this, she held the paper up where I could see it. On an 'outcome' grid, with perhaps fifty names and details of month of application, date of committee meeting and so forth, four names were neatly highlighted in blue. *Mona Anderson*, *Bridget Cullers*, *Kim Shakespeare* and *Jennifer Ward*. I intoned the names again. Mona Anderson, Law; Bridget Cullers, French; Kim Shakespeare, Statistics; Jennifer Ward, English . . . I prayed that years of Beaujolais hadn't cost me too many of the brain cells devoted to memory.

'Good luck with your enquiry, Trina,' I said by way of acknowledgement. 'I'll be in touch.'

Outside the main administrative complex, where the Provost's office occupied the most prestigious corner on the top floor, the sky was a clear, mild blue. Global warming may have had disastrous consequences in other parts of the globe, but in England the immediate effect has been the creation for the first time in human history of a palatable climate. Umbrella manufacturers and makers of raincoats are going out of business right and left, and for the first time ever, fashionable folk dare to wear shoes made of nubuck even in the autumn. I unzipped my toffee-coloured suede jacket, and set off across campus at an aerobic pace.

Before I had even worked up a decent pulse-rate, I arrived at the photography section. If you know anyone who needs convincing that Eastern University is, in terms of resources, light years behind the other University to which Cambridge gave its name, the photography section would be sure to do the trick. It is located in a linked set of huts that might have done duty during World War Two. These are perched on thick temporary foundations which make the huts look bottom-heavy, like a pear-shaped woman with very short hair.

I made my way up a ramp covered with a dingy material that resembled in texture a cross between astroturf and Velcro. The ramp trembled slightly as I walked; the corridors inside trembled too. I wondered if size and weight were criteria for recruitment in the photography section. Only the lightest applicants need apply?

The office was untidy, with stacks of paper obscuring surfaces and protruding from the open doors of cupboards. There was no one there. A handmade mug half-filled with tea on the desk, and an open drawer in one of the filing cabinets with a folder laid across it, gave the room the quality of a clerical *Mary Celeste*.

I waited barely a moment, then moved on. The next two doors in the corridor were locked. I discovered that for myself after receiving no reply to my knock. The third door, around a corner, opened towards me as I approached.

The man who emerged into the low-ceilinged corridor was in his late twenties, tall and round-faced. He looked like an urbanite's idea of a simple country lad. Except, that is, for the fact that he was wearing a white laboratory coat, and that when he spoke, it was with sharp articulation and a streetwise London accent. This was the man I had come to see: Martin, the technician who developed Monica's photographs.

Martin, it turned out, had been away from work for several days. 'Mumps,' he said, with a hint of a blush. Not so streetwise after all, then. He took me back to the office, where the handmade mug was now in the grasp of a frizzy-haired woman sporting outsize spectacles. She was busy with a notebook, checking off entries against a typed list. She ignored Martin, he ignored her. He cleared two folding metal chairs for us to perch on, produced plastic cups and a bottle of mineral water from a cupboard, and finally settled down.

He told me what he knew about Monica. She was a nice woman, he said, and looked as if he really meant it. Her paintings were remarkable. He was sorry she would never finish the seascapes. He had seen her several times in the weeks before she died, as she was coming and going frequently with films to develop.

'Did she seem at all troubled during that period?' I asked. 'Or frightened?'

'I don't know about frightened.' Martin sipped his water thoughtfully. 'She seemed excited, that's for sure. She popped in here one Thursday afternoon, I guess it was a week or so before she died, to tell me about a painting someone had done in her landscape class. Brilliant, she said it was. Apparently it made her think of a cottage in Norfolk she was hoping to share with some other people, and she was over the moon. I think the painting was like a symbol to her, of things going right in the future.'

I had avoided giving Martin the full story about me and Helen and Monica. He seemed willing to talk without it, and I guess I just intended to save time. But now I felt he was owed an explanation.

'That cottage,' I began. 'I'm one of the owners. Monica had decided to come in with us on a house-share. I think you're right, the decision *did* have a strong emotional significance for her.'

We talked that over for a while, and then I steered the conversation back to Monica's mood in the period preceding her death. I told him in outline about the note to Helen, and Monica's claim that she was in serious trouble. 'If we can track down what the trouble was, it may provide some kind of a clue as to why she died. Can you think about it again? Apart from Wildfell, what else did Monica talk about the last time you saw her?'

'Abortion,' replied Martin unexpectedly. I noticed out of the corner of my eye that the woman with the mug still didn't look up. It was almost as if she was alone in the room.

'*Abortion?*' I repeated, stunned. 'Are you saying that Monica was *pregnant?*'

Martin's reply was swift and vehement. 'No, I didn't mean an abortion for Monica. We discussed abortion rights, that's all. You know, the Pro-Choice campaign. And the other side, the Pro-Lifers.' When I still looked puzzled, Martin launched into an explanation, pausing only for a second to imagine a line between his hand and the green metal wastebasket, and to propel his paper cup along that line. I did the same. Two bull's eyes.

'You know this thing that came up recently with that nursery nurse from Walsall, Beverley whatshername?'

I did. The case of Beverley Cattell had dominated the

tabloid press of Britain for at least a week of the previous month. 'Is that what you meant by abortion?' I replied. 'Monica wanted to talk about Richard Dolby's latest dirty tricks campaign?'

Richard Dolby is the MP for a safe Conservative constituency in north-west England, and the chief Parliamentary spokesman for the anti-abortion campaign. Time and again he has introduced Bills designed to reduce women's access to abortion, going further than some of his like-minded colleagues in that he would deny termination even in cases of rape or severe foetal damage. His stand does not endear him to Pro-Choice supporters like Monica. Or me for that matter – nor, apparently, to Martin.

The contempt that many people feel for Richard Dolby is less a result of his political views, however, than for the way in which he promotes them. He selects individual women to humiliate in public. The most recent of these was a pleasant seventeen-year-old girl whose ex-boyfriend had written to Dolby complaining about her intention to terminate her unplanned pregnancy. Dolby turned the case into a crusade. He wrote articles about Beverley for the tabloid press. Her schoolmates and college friends were interviewed, and any scurrilous bit of gossip that could be turned up was paraded in the papers. It was implied that she slept around, that she refused to take precautions, that she didn't care if she became pregnant, and finally, that she had misled the poor boy (in fact a man seven years her senior) into thinking that they had a future together.

The house where Beverley and her parents lived was besieged, first by reporters and then by campaigners from the Society for the Protection of the Unborn Child. Stalwart support from women's groups only added to the din. The girl was followed from home to college and back again. She became the subject, or rather the object, of public debate within her college as well as outside. The last I heard, she had cancelled the operation, and had withdrawn from her course. Her boyfriend, the aggrieved father-to-be, had taken up with someone else. Richard Dolby appeared in the national press and on television the next day, crowing about the 'moral victory' which had ruined a young woman's life.

'So what was Monica's specific interest in the case?' I asked.

'Like most of us,' Martin continued, 'she was angry about what happened to that girl. She said that one of the most cheering things she could imagine was the thought of Richard Dolby getting his comeuppance. We even speculated on a few fates-worse-than-death that might be particularly appropriate for the creep. Seems a bit ironic now, with Monica dead.' Martin looked shamefaced, as if either the levity of his last encounters with Monica or the mention of death was disrespectful.

I changed the subject. 'Did you develop a film for Monica that was shot mainly at Holkham Beach? You know, seascapes, a panorama of the point where the pinewoods meet the beach?'

Martin nodded. 'I did. Just before I got ill. Monica asked me to retain some of the negatives for enlargement.'

'Were they numbers eleven to fifteen?'

'I don't remember. Do you want me to check?'

'No, it's all right. I take it you haven't had a chance to develop them yet. Could you let me know when you do? I need to take a look at those enlargements. Monica said she had seen something of interest on the beach that day. I think I know what it was, but I need the enlargements for confirmation.'

At that moment the telephone rang. The frizzy-haired administrator looked at me for the first time. Behind her outsize spectacles, she had stunning silk-grey eyes. 'Laura Principal?' she asked.

Good old Trina Thompson. She had tracked me down to say that Milton Bannister would fit me in at three o'clock. That gave me just five minutes to dash across campus again and compose myself before confronting him. I thanked Martin for his time and trouble, and turned to leave.

'Just a sec,' he said. 'I'll develop those negatives first thing tomorrow. Where can I get hold of you?'

I gave him a business card with the office number on it for messages, and said I'd pop by mid-morning. I reckoned

Martin would be one of the people who would miss Monica very much indeed.

I could have made the meeting in time, but with a few seconds to spare, a visit to the loo came out better on the cost-benefit scale than a prompt arrival. Let him wait. I would greet Provost Bannister with clean hands, freshly-brushed hair and an empty bladder. As Trina showed me into his office, I noted the time: five minutes past three. Margaret Powers would no doubt be speaking to the Murder Squad by now.

The Provost was sweetness itself. I have never had much time for top management. They had always seemed to me, from a distance, a vainglorious, shallow and self-seeking lot. Forced to co-mingle at a cocktail party, I gravitate away from the blue suits as naturally as a swinging vegetarian avoids a Steak House family restaurant.

But maybe I've been mistaken all these years, for Milton Bannister was charm incarnate. He abandoned his seat behind the massive mahogany desk for an armchair, informally placed in relation to me, and asked me about myself in a manner that was flattering and well-informed. Trina must have shared some details about my academic background. His conversation was urbane, amusing and modest. He shifted easily from talk about trends in historiography to conversation about his children, mingling the public and the private in a way few powerful men (outside the Mafia) are willing to do. I had no trouble imagining him at Governors' meetings, dominating with subtlety and wit.

'So,' he said, when I was well and truly softened up, 'you are a friend of the unfortunate Monica Harcourt. Please accept my condolences. We are all very shaken by this tragedy. Did you want to talk to me about her death?'

'Not exactly. More about some of the projects she was pursuing before her death.' In my mind's eye I could see a sparkling Monica loping back from the beach. I cleared my throat to recall myself to the present.

'Monica had one firm objective for the next three years,' I continued. 'She intended to finish a series of seascapes. As you know, that's why she applied to the research committee

119

here at Eastern for secondment to Oregon. What I need to know are the details of how that application was handled. Specifically, why was it delayed between June and November?'

'Delayed?' repeated Bannister. He was all innocence and concern. He buzzed for Trina, and asked her to bring Monica's file in. After a moment, she placed it in front of him, with a demure glance. He put on a pair of tortoiseshell reading glasses and leafed through the file.

'Ah, yes. Monica's application was due to go to the June meeting of the committee, but I spotted a problem with it. Her statement – what she was planning to do, the value of her work for the University – was far too brief and un-elaborated. I like to have everything ship-shape before it actually goes before the committee. Saves the committee's time, and usually it saves time for the applicant too. So I suggested that she re-submit in the autumn.'

He looked up and smiled, a confidential smile. Between-you-and-me. 'Some members of the committee can be rather philistine, you know. What they understand is a good solid project in management, in accounting, in natural sciences, even in a field like yours, in history. But painting – well.' He shrugged delicately and shook his head.

'And did she do it?' I asked. The charm was wearing a little thin.

'Let me see.' He put his glasses on again. 'Yes. On October the twenty-eighth, the new statement was submitted. I saw her on November the tenth, and was able to reassure her that there was no reason not to present the application to the next meeting of the committee. She seemed,' he commented with a air of self-congratulation, 'very grateful for my help.'

'Just how grateful?' I enquired.

The smile took on a frozen quality, more like a muscle twitch than an expression of cordiality. Behind the blue eyes lurked something watchful. 'I beg your pardon?'

'My question was, just how grateful? Or, to put it differently, just what sort of a relationship did you have with Monica Harcourt? How well did you know each other?' He didn't reply. I prompted again. 'What did you think of her? What did she think of you?'

The Provost was clinging to his composure with difficulty. Any moment now he would order me from his office, and it would be just my bad luck to collide with members of the Murder Squad, arriving to question him about Margaret Powers' identification.

'I thought she was a first-rate appointment, talented and dedicated to her teaching. She never told me what she thought of me. And . . .' here he fixed me with what he obviously hoped was a magisterial look '. . . as for our relationship, as you call it – she was a member of my staff and I was her Provost. I advised her about the secondment process as I am expected to do. Nothing more.'

Nothing more. The image of Margaret staggering across the University restaurant, stunned and alarmed, intruded. 'So why,' I asked, taking a deep breath, 'did you visit Monica's house at nine o'clock on the night of her murder?'

Milton Bannister's face looked rather less urbane with its new purplish hue. He rose from the leather armchair and came towards me, a muscle twitching at the edge of his jawline. I stood up and faced him. He stopped. His voice when he spoke was low, deliberately so. His words were not intended to penetrate the oak doors.

'You little bitch,' he hissed. 'You lesbian bitch. So you were there, with her. Laughing at me. You probably set it up together. You breathe a word of this – to anyone – and you'll regret it.'

I broke for the door. Trina looked up calmly from her monitor. 'Everything all right, Dr Principal?' she enquired sweetly. It appeared she had heard nothing.

'Did you know,' I asked, bending close over her desk, 'that your boss is a dangerous man?'

'I've heard rumours to that effect,' she replied, and returned once more to her typing.

CHAPTER 13

As I turned left out of Trina Thompson's office, I caught a glimpse at the end of the corridor of a uniformed police officer holding open the swing doors for someone following behind. I didn't wait for Superintendent Neill. Questions about what I was doing here would be uncomfortable for Margaret as well as for me.

I nipped into the toilets, taking the precaution of inhabiting a cubicle in case Nicole was one of those women who couldn't resist a passing loo. After waiting for two minutes, I emerged and made for a call box round the corner. The thought of Milton Bannister in the interview room at Cambridge Police Station had focused my mind most effectively on what I had to do next.

My first call was to the office, to catch up with Desiree's progress on the Loizou case. The Skinny Dipper was, according to Dee, a respectable sort of nightclub. The drinks were drinkable, though expensive; all the tattoos and hairy chests were safely tucked away behind neatly buttoned shirts; and the hostesses claimed they were sent home after work in a taxi. Dee's enquiries about work were rebuffed, but a chat with the hostess who brought Dee's 'Blue Lagoon' netted the information that she had been given notice for the end of the month. No explanation why, the hostess complained in a burst of confidence, but there was a bonus on condition that she keep her departure quiet. And she was not the only employee in this revealing situation.

Dee's diet was, apparently, a success. She was marginally slimmer and even more energetic than usual. I gave her a description of Sonia Loizou, with instructions to track Sonia down near the Post Office Box where her mail was delivered, follow her to her new address, and capture her on film. Dee felt less than confident about using the zoom lens on the office camera, but Stevie offered a quick lesson in return for first-night tickets for *Little Women*.

My second call was to an old friend from the jazz circuit who manages the night-shift at the Northampton headquarters of one of the major credit card companies. He chooses to start work at midnight because it enables him to play jazz violin at gigs in the region and still spend time with his children when they get home from school. I've benefited before from the fact that the nightshift is relatively relaxed, with lots of opportunity for Pete to do a favour for an old friend. Yes, he was quite happy to check whether Sonia Loizou appeared on their books, and to make a note of the type of purchases that interested me. In return, I promised to come over to Northampton soon and have Sunday lunch with him and the family. Not a bad exchange.

Just as the deal was struck, a heavyset woman with a Debenham's carrier bag rapped on the glass. I punched another fifty-pence piece into the telephone, indicating with my fingers that I would only be two more minutes.

I was in luck. The switchboard operator at the University was swift, and Kim Shakespeare, the first name I tried from Trina Thompson's list, picked up her extension as soon as the tone sounded.

I introduced myself, and said that there was something I wanted to consult her about. I left the content vague. This was not so much a clever ploy as necessity, borne of the fact that I hadn't yet decided how to approach the issue of the application for secondment. I didn't want to get Trina into trouble for revealing the names of people who had submitted applications. And it seemed unwise to make too direct a link between the application and Monica's murder. But Kim, for all the pertness of her name, obviously wasn't the sort to leave anything to chance.

'On a statistical matter?' she said. 'You'd be better off with one of the consultants. I'm a research officer. I don't advise on applications.'

I had no option but to come clean. Well, cleaner. I identified myself as a friend of Monica Harcourt. The different quality of the silence on the other end of the line at that point told me that Kim knew about Monica. She and Monica, I said, shared some experiences in common, and talking about them might help me to understand what had led to Monica's death. I finished by saying that I thought it was best to say as little as possible over the phone. Kim agreed to meet me in a quarter of an hour for an early supper in the crêperie on Parker's Piece.

As I exited from the call box, I smiled obligingly at the stout woman in the queue. She held her ground just outside the door. Slowing my exit was, I guess, her way of punishing me.

I liberated my car from the Grafton Centre car park, and found a safe spot for it on Warkworth Street, alongside the police station and within spitting distance of Parker's Piece. With my second conspicuous piece of luck that day, I caught a glimpse of Provost Bannister being escorted into the station through the rear door. I felt considerably cheered – even managed a passing feeling of warmth for Superintendent Neill. Milton Bannister had not lost his composure, however. His grooming was impeccable, and he managed to look as if he were out for an early evening stroll.

With these diversions, I arrived at Hobbs Pavilion five minutes after the agreed time. A glance at the other patrons made it obvious that Kim must be the well-groomed woman who was seated at a pine table in the far corner of the restaurant. By the time I had introduced myself and eased into the chair opposite hers, she had already ordered a scallop crêpe. It didn't take a detective to realise that she didn't intend to define this encounter as a social occasion. She gave me an opportunity to relay my order to the waitress, then brushed aside my attempts at getting-to-know-you talk and went straight to the main event.

'So, you suggested on the phone that Monica Harcourt and I had something in common. How about letting me in on the secret?' There was too much delicacy in Kim's manner to merit the word brusque, but there was about her an economy of speech and movement that seemed designed to make others feel profligate, wasteful of time and energy and of emotion as well.

Unintentionally, I began to emulate her crisp air. 'Monica's passion in life was painting,' I began, rather fast. 'She was engaged in a long-term project, one that involved some work on the west coast of America. She had applied for secondment to the University of Oregon for part of next year. I believe that something odd happened while her application was being considered. And I believe that the same thing may have happened to you.'

There was a long silence. Kim Shakespeare stared at me frankly with a look bordering on contempt. 'Laura,' she said at last, 'I work in the Statistics Department of Eastern. Have you ever been down there?' Down? It took me a second to realise that the 'down' must refer to a basement area in which the Department was housed.

I shook my head. 'Should I?'

'There is very little to see for someone outside the field. There are a great many computers. There are applications of various kinds – work on electroscopy, on radio waves, on reflection, on seed distribution. There are no pictures on the walls. There are no Boston ferns in hanging baskets, no cards from students saying thank you. There are a few girl students who pass through on their way to classes, and a mass of men. There are no women except me.'

'It must be lonely.'

'Lonely has nothing to do with it. It's where I work.' Kim picked absentmindedly at a hangnail on her left thumb, and looked for the first time as if she might depart from her script. 'Look, Laura, you wouldn't know this, but my work is good. With colleagues in Stuttgart and Prague, I'm developing a technique for analysing the distribution of certain toxic substances that accompany fallout. We are tracking the effects of Chernobyl. It's not pretty work, and it's not companionable. But it means the world to me.'

The crêpes arrived, with freshly squeezed orange juice for Kim and white wine for me. I was glad of the chance to pause. Kim seemed to be waiting for me to pick up the conversation.

I couldn't do that, though, because I didn't understand what was going on. After what seemed like an eternity of silent supping (to me at least; Kim looked unperturbed) I finally tried again.

'Kim, I'd like to come down and look over the stats labs some time, if you'll show me around.'

She shrugged, a kind of if-you-like-OK.

'And I would like to know more about your research. Was it for this research, perhaps to visit your European colleagues, that you wanted secondment?'

'Finish your meal, Laura,' Kim instructed, 'and drop these questions. Monica and I were both committed to our work. That's what we have – had – in common. That's *all* we had in common. Anything else you may be thinking of is way off beam. Now, if you'll excuse me, I have several things to do this evening. I'll have to eat in rather a rush, and leave you to finish on your own.'

And that's precisely what she did.

I ordered a dish of white chocolate mousse (hold the cream) and considered the question of who had hurt Kim Shakespeare so badly.

The morning began with a summons from Nicole. She reckoned I was holding out on her. From the depths of my duvet, I listened in on the answering machine as she vented her fury about my visit to Bannister the day before. I hadn't realised that Nicole could be quite so immoderate.

Half an hour later there was a loud and authoritative knocking on my door. That may also have been Nicole and her henchmen – I don't know. I was busy munching my way through a bowl of oat-flakes at the time, and it's not good for the digestion to interrupt breakfast.

I fitted in thirty minutes' rowing, tossed my dirty kit in the laundry, and donned a fresh roll-neck, tailored trousers and a neat tweed jacket. If I was spending the morning in the University again, I might as well look the part.

Mary McKinnon greeted me like an old friend. I hadn't forgotten my promise to help her sort out Monica's things, but meanwhile I wanted to use her College Directory for a few

moments. The encounter with Kim Shakespeare had strength-
ened my hunch that Trina's list needed following up, urgently.
One down. Three to go.

When you're tracing people in detective work, you need a
system. Today I tried reverse alphabetical order. The extension for WARD, Dr J. was answered by another member of the
English staff. It seemed that she and Jennifer shared an office.
Jennifer was at a conference in London, apparently, and
couldn't be reached until late afternoon. I left a message, and
looked up Mona Anderson in the Directory. (So much for my
system.) The only M. Anderson turned out to be Mark, a
lecturer in Film Studies. He seemed mildly affronted when I
told him I was looking for a lawyer named Mona. I guess he
imagined that from seeing his entry in the Directory I thought
he looked like a woman. I informed him that John Wayne's
real name was Marion and hung up. CULLERS, B. was likely to
be Bridget, but no one answered that extension. So much for
modern communications.

I shared a cup of coffee with Mary (actually, we had one
each), wrote a brief note, and set off across campus towards
the French Department to deliver the message to Bridget
Cullers' pigeonhole myself.

But even this communication was forestalled. In the external office of the French Department, staff pigeonholes were
conveniently organised in alphabetical order – system again –
so I could see at a glance that no one occupied the space
between ARBUTHNOT and DEACON.

Further down the corridor, I located office number 802 –
the room number that had been attached to CULLERS, B. in the
Directory. Here I learned that Bridget Cullers had left the
college a year ago. Her office and her phone extension had
been inherited by a pair of teaching assistants. They were both
modern poetry specialists (they volunteered this information)
and both red-haired (this I could see for myself). Essays and
photocopied handouts occupied a good three-quarters of the
floor space in the office. Stepping gingerly over student
assessment sheets, one of the pair found me a forwarding
address, but held out little hope that it was currently inhabited
by Dr Cullers.

I imposed on the literary twins for a few more moments. A telephone? They waved me indifferently towards the desk, and by edging my way carefully along the wall I was able to reach it without crushing any undergraduate's hope of a decent average. The address they had provided was in the village of Horningsea, outside Cambridge but, true to form, there was no listing in the telephone directory for a Cullers in that area. In fact, the only Cullers in the entire Cambridge & District listings turned out to be an elderly Yorkshireman. He was convinced, in spite of all disclaimers, that I was a saleswoman employed by a telephone-order firm dealing in fitted kitchens. His persistent questions about workmanship and materials were knowledgeable but, under the circumstances, irritating. I offered him a discount on kitchen cabinets just to get away.

Bridget would have to wait, then, until I could find time for a personal visit to Horningsea. With Nicole Pelletier breathing down my neck, I wasn't sure this was top priority.

Mona Anderson was a lawyer, and the building occupied by Management and Law was my next target. When I raised her name with the Departmental Secretary, I got a reception you wouldn't call warm. 'Are you a friend of hers?' The frosty tones implied either that no one could possibly be a friend of Mona's, or that if anyone was, it would probably be my sort. I played safe, and used the passing-through-looking-her-up-for-a-friend routine.

Mona Anderson, I learned, had worked for the Department for several years on a part-time contract, teaching Family Law. She had disappeared from the Department eighteen months ago, under a cloud, having left the record-keeping and report-writing associated with her work disastrously incomplete. The Departmental Secretary, it seems, had been left with the task of picking up the pieces.

I was not surprised to learn that my quarry had left no forwarding address. She was married when she left the University. Her husband's first name was Jack, but no one could recall ever having heard his last name.

Back in Mary's office, the phrase 'hopeless quest' echoing in my mind, I tried all the M. Andersons and the J. Andersons in the local telephone directory, but none of them led to a

Mona Anderson who used to work at Eastern University. Then I made enquiries at a firm in town which specialises in family law: some luck at last! Yes, Mona Anderson had once handled cases for them on a freelance basis, but she had moved to Birmingham six months ago. No, they didn't have a forwarding address, but what they did have on file was an introduction for her to a firm in the Birmingham area, and they were willing to part with that address. I composed a polite note asking to be put in touch with Mona Anderson, who might have had dealings with their office. Then, with a sense of returning to the real world, I rang Martin in the photography section.

Martin had only a few minutes to spare. We split the difference and met in the middle of campus on a bench overlooking the tennis courts. With a flourish, he produced the enlargements from Holkham Bay.

These enlargements didn't have the aesthetic force of the shots from which they had been made. Gone was the sense of sweep towards the sea, the play of light and shadow. In its place was a bald and uninteresting composition, two people in grainy close-up, the pine woods little more than a blur in the background.

But what the picture lacked in visual beauty it made up for in dramatic power. For the two people in the photographs were known to me, at least by sight. Now at last I knew what Monica had seen on the beach.

'You recognise him?' Martin asked.

No doubt about it. That face familiar from television campaigns, the self-appointed protector of the foetus. No wonder Monica had been interested in the case of Beverley Cattell.

'Richard Dolby, as I live and breathe! Martin, you've helped a lot. I'll keep these if you don't mind, for a week or so anyway.' I stood up, brushed myself off, and prepared to dash.

'But what about – '

The woman? Not so much a public figure. Rarely photographed, insistent on going her own way in spite of her proximity to fame. I would not have recognised her at all, except for the photograph in the *Independent* of three weeks ago, celebrating the launch of the Campaign for Family Revival. This young woman had been standing to the side of a group on the stone steps at her family home, her face lit by a shaft of sunlight. I had noticed her then, and joked about her with Ginny: her air of wanting to be somewhere else, her pretty features, so like those of her mother. The young woman Monica had photographed on Holkham Beach shortly before her death was none other than Elinor St James, the youngest daughter of the Prime Minister.

I was already heading off for the parking lot. 'Tell you later,' I called back, not sure yet who to share this information with, or even what it meant. Martin waved me on my way.

No wonder Monica had been intrigued. What kind of association was this? The genteel daughter of the Head of Government – a Government which campaigned energetically on a family ticket – on a lonely stretch of beach with an older, rabble-rousing Member of Parliament, and a married man at that. Suddenly, something clicked – some old memory from my younger, activist days in the women's movement.

Fortunately, I seldom clear out the inside of the Saab. An Ordnance Survey map of the area near Wildfell was wedged beneath the driving seat. One quick check was all I needed. I raced back to Mary's office and punched out Helen's extension in the library.

'Helen, I need you to come with me. Right away. We'll be gone all day. You'll need your plimsolls and an anorak.'

'Laura? What *are* you talking about? Just a minute here.' I heard Helen suggest to some people nearby that they come back later, then there were scuffling noises and a door closing. She returned to the phone.

'Laura, for heaven's sake, I'm working. It's the first time in ages that I've been able to concentrate, and I have masses of work to catch up on. The library will grind to a halt if I don't put in some extra hours.'

'Nonsense, Helen, you always say that. It's your way of making yourself feel indispensable – not that you aren't,' I added swiftly. 'This is important, though. *Really* important. I know what Monica saw on the beach that day, and it just might have something to do with her death. I need you with me.'

There was a pause. 'Plimsolls and anorak, you said. We're going to Holkham?'

'You guessed it. I'll hang up and cancel my appointments here. I'll give you fifteen minutes to develop a migraine, and then I'll meet you right by the porter's lodge.'

Helen made it in only eleven minutes. For all her hesitation, her cheeks were pink and her eyes were glowing. There was no trace of the wan creature of a few days ago. Whether she managed to convince anyone that she was suffering from a migraine I rather doubt.

We stopped in Newnham to pick up her plimsolls, and at a delicatessen to buy sandwiches and fruit. Then, like out-of-season picnickers, we set off for the beach.

CHAPTER 14

Helen looked doubtful when I let her off at the bottom of the lane leading to Holkham Bay. I watched as she set out gamely. Her shoulders were squared, her anorak hood was pulled up against the drizzle, and Monica's photos were safe and dry in her jacket pocket. We aimed to meet up again in an hour, but in truth I didn't know how long it would take me to do what I had to do.

I returned to the main road and set a course westwards, the direction from which we had come. A quarter of a mile further on, I saw the sign that I had been looking for. Elegant brown lettering on a discreet ivory-coloured board proclaimed: *The Eastings*. A narrow gravel track snaked beyond it in the direction of the sea.

In places, the gravel was worn thin. I edged the car gingerly along the ruts, almost as concerned about my underbody as I was about the coming encounter. A sharp turn right, and The Eastings came into view. Very nice, too. An eighteenth-century manor house, not too large but large enough, it was magnificently proportioned, with two rows of windows evenly spaced along the southern front. Cream-coloured woodwork and stonework complemented a warm red brick façade. Ivies tumbled out from stoneware urns and window boxes, creating a homely air. You could almost imagine that a stout, friendly-looking housekeeper in a white ruched cap would bustle out of the front door in a moment, a basket on her arm.

I parked alongside the Jaguars and BMWs in the gravel drive, straightened my rumpled jacket and moved in. The brass bell set in the wall didn't detain me, since the front door was unlocked. I opened it and entered a high-ceilinged room panelled in wood of a dark golden tone. From behind a desk that looked rather at sea in the vast vestibule, a kindly-looking young woman in nurse's uniform arose. 'Are you a visitor?' she enquired.

'Yes. I've come to see Ellie. Elinor St James. I've brought her some magazines.' I waved furled copies of the *Rowers' Almanac* in her direction.

The nurse frowned slightly. She peered at the clipboard on the corner of her desk, shaking her head as her finger ran down the page. 'No, I'm sorry,' she said. 'We don't appear to have . . .'

I interrupted: 'She came in two weeks ago, but I'm sure she's still here, because she promised to let me know the minute she left. Let's see,' I said, edging over towards the clipboard. 'I know for sure she was here on the fourteenth, so she was probably admitted about the twelfth of this month.'

The nurse set the clipboard down, and pulled a large leather-covered looseleaf file from the top drawer of the desk. She flicked backwards, through it.

'There must be some mistake,' she said. 'There's no St James listed here. There is an Elinor Jameson, but I don't suppose . . .'

'Well, it is possible that Ellie used a different name,' I conceded. 'Anonymity and all that, you understand. Now let me see, what was her gynaecologist's name? That would be one way of checking.'

The young nurse checked the chart again. 'Was it Mr Hawthorn?' she asked helpfully. 'That's the name of Miss Jameson's consultant.'

I nodded vigorously. 'Well, that confirms it. So when did Ellie check out? I'll have to have words with her when I get back to London. But the poor thing, I guess she's been through a lot lately.'

The expression that passed across the nurse's face at these words was one of unalloyed compassion. I hoped some deeply-buried self-protective urge would prevent her from mentioning my visit to Mr Hawthorn. She even offered the date of Elinor's departure. Perhaps later on I would feel guilty about the ease with which all this information was extracted, but for now the pickings were too good to resist.

'Well, if Elinor didn't wait around to see me, at least I hope she had other chums to visit?' I said, trying to seem put out.

The nurse thought for a minute. 'No. I'm sorry, but I don't believe she did. She stayed rather a long time, longer than usual, you see. And after a couple of days, I began to feel really sad for her, she looked so unhappy . . . Oh, I'm sorry, perhaps I shouldn't have told you that,' she gasped, as my face crumpled.

I gave the appearance of rallying bravely, and urged her on. Now that I had been distressed the nurse reckoned that I deserved an explanation.

'Miss Jameson looked as if – well, as if she wasn't really sure about what she was doing. I know for a fact that Mr Caputi – he's the surgeon who owns this clinic – was concerned. He asked her one day right out if she wanted to talk to a counsellor again, but she said there was no point, as she didn't really have any choice. And during all that time, I noticed, no one came to see her. Not even her mother or father or anyone. Poor girl.'

'It's very reassuring to know there was someone here who cared about Elinor. I'm sure she appreciated it.' I looked around at the interior of the vestibule. 'Tell me, if she didn't have any visitors, did she just stay indoors all the time? Or did she manage to get out?'

'Oh yes, she often went out walking. Through the woods, towards the bay. I remember seeing her coming back once, and I thought she might have overtaxed herself because you could tell she had been crying a lot. Anyway, that's all I can recall. I'm sorry you've had a wasted journey.'

'Thank you. You've been very kind. I do appreciate it, Miss . . .'

'Edwards,' she supplied, helpful to the end.

When I stepped outside, the wind had freshened. Rain splashed my face. I tucked my hair up under a tweed cap, tweaked the brim down over my forehead and set out for the woods that encircled the north side of The Eastings. The woods were lovely, dark and deep, but I had to pace their circumference twice to find what I was looking for – a definite route leading to the northeast. Once inside the wood, relatively little rain penetrated. I did a few stretches for form's sake, then set off along the path at a jog.

After several minutes, just as I began to wonder whether I had come the wrong way, the path widened and the light in front of me silvered. I dashed ahead, and careered out onto the headland, almost crashing into someone as I emerged. I stepped back defensively. The light was behind this person, and my eyes had not yet adjusted from the gloom of the woods, so I was relieved to hear a familiar voice, words tumbling out excitedly.

'You were right, Laura, this *is* it – the spot in the photo where the couple appear! That twisted tree trunk is a dead giveaway.' She looked at me impatiently. 'So go on, tell me. Does this path lead to the Clinic? Did they admit to having Elinor as a patient?'

She looked very, very cold. While I had been in the snug vestibule of The Eastings, Helen had been pacing the perimeter of Holkham Bay in the rain. I took her arm and pointed her in the direction of the car. Only then did I confirm that Richard Dolby, ruthless campaigner against a woman's right to choose, had accompanied the Prime Minister's daughter to Norfolk where she had undergone a secret abortion.

'Good lord, Laura, just think of the scandal! What do we do now?'

I hurried up the pace. 'The scandal is one thing. Interesting, I agree, especially in the light of what he did to Beverley Cattell. But for the moment I'm more concerned with how this ties in with Monica's death. Is it only coincidence that Monica had photographic evidence of a liaison between Dolby and St James? Or did Richard Dolby know she'd seen them together at Holkham? Far-fetched as it sounds, did he perhaps take steps to squash any scandal before it could arise?'

Helen and I stopped for a bowl of steamed mussels on the coast before heading back to Cambridge. We were cold and we were tired.

As we re-entered the Saab, the car phone beeped, and I relinquished my plan for an early night. Jennifer Ward, the second person on Trina's mysterious list, had returned from her conference and could see me this evening, if it was urgent. Other than that, she had no time to spare.

The drive back to Cambridge was like a journey from winter into summer. The storm and the rainclouds remained behind us, set on a course across the North Sea. Ahead, the evening sun shone increasingly warm and mellow. By the time we crossed the Elizabeth Way bridge into the heart of the city, we had stripped down to our vests.

I checked that there were no police cars lurking before pulling up on Clare Street in front of my flat. Helen kissed me and trotted off to take advantage of the summery evening by walking the last mile to her home in Newnham. I showered and changed into a pair of pale dungarees and a long-sleeved pink T-shirt. Before leaving, I affixed a note to the front door of the house saying that I had to visit the Police Station. This was literally true. Nicole must be furious that I hadn't yet provided a detailed report of my activities to her.

It didn't take long to reach Jennifer's office. The signs of diligence in Room 44 of the English Department were impressive. Half-past six on the loveliest evening of the autumn, and Jennifer Ward was still hard at work. So were her two colleagues, one of them tapping away on a dirt-streaked word-processor, the other fending off a plaintive student who was challenging the grade he had been given for a project. Not much in the way of privacy.

Jennifer Ward was a cheerful-looking person in her late twenties. She had frosted hair that sprouted like a waterfall from a central point high on the crown. Her thick brown and silver fringe flowed almost to the frame of a stylish pair of glasses. Her brown eyes sought me out as soon as I entered the room.

'Is that you?' I asked, pointing to the colourful poster that announced a forthcoming local production of Caryl Churchill's *Top Girls*, starring Jennifer Ward.

'So perceptive!' she declared, laughing. 'I can sell you tickets, if you're interested?' There was more than a hint of irony in the way she said this.

'Maybe later,' I stalled. I explained my involvement with Monica and proposed that we retire to the river for half-an-hour's quiet conversation in the sunshine.

Jennifer snatched up a cardigan and declared herself ready. I was heartened by the contrast with Kim Shakespeare. Perhaps I would get some information out of this young woman.

On warm evenings, the banks of the River Cam near the Backs teem with tourists and students from the language schools. The beauty of the landscape survives this assault, but the sense of peace that would otherwise be invoked by the graceful sweep of Clare College or the majesty of the chapel at King's is lost as punts drift haphazardly by, full of giggling, splashing, shouting visitors.

Myself, I prefer the place where the River Cam passes through Chesterton. I parked the car near the Pike and Eel pub, and Jennifer and I followed the footpath until we found a warm spot on the grassy bank underneath an overhanging willow. It was quiet here. On the opposite side of the river, near Coldham's Common, a middle-aged man strolled by with a terrier at his heels. An undergraduate rowed past, sweat beading her broad forehead, and a woman with a *Thomas the Tank Engine* lunchbox in her basket and a child perched on the crossbar cycled along the path behind us. But in the main, we were undisturbed. A swan sailed by with its feathers ruffled, but we never did see what had roused its anger. There was a warm stiff breeze. Water lapped at the edge of the bank.

We had finished with our pleasantries on the way over. 'So,' Jennifer enquired simply. 'What can I do to help?'

Once again, as with Kim Shakespeare, I explained my interest in secondment applications. 'Monica was agitated about that process of secondment,' I concluded. 'It seems to me important to find out why.'

Jennifer lifted her knees almost to her chest, embraced them with her arms and gave me a lopsided smile. 'You've come to the right place,' she said. 'I can tell you a thing or two about applications for secondment. Listen up and listen tight.'

Three years before, Jennifer had landed a plum part in a

Brecht production which was being mounted by one of the best amateur companies in the country. She played Pirate Jenny – the worm who turned, the girl whose demure and deferential manner slid away to reveal a sexy, powerful and vengeful woman. Jennifer loved the part, and she knew she was good. One evening they played to a packed house in the University auditorium, and afterwards there was a reception for the cast and crew. Many of the college bigwigs were there, and most, including the Provost, complimented her on the performance.

The following week, Jennifer received an invitation to the Provost's office to discuss something 'that might be to her advantage'. Though an invitation of this kind was decidedly unusual, Milton Bannister received her in a professional manner that put her at ease.

'That charm again?' I interjected cynically.

'Yes. I can well understand his interest in the stage,' said Jennifer, laughing. 'He's quite a little performer himself.'

He had drawn Jennifer's attention to a new initiative that was being financed through the European Arts Council: a summer school for amateur actors from all over Europe, to be held in ('of all marvellous places') Siena, the following summer term. Two productions were to be mounted and toured; there would be masterclasses with top actors and directors; most expenses would be paid by the organisers. It was the chance of a lifetime.

'Well, old Bannister reeled me in,' Jennifer declared jokingly, her eye resting on a fisherman who was collecting up his gear on the opposite bank. 'With my talent and his contacts, he assured me, I had a strong chance of a place. All I needed to do was to make an application for secondment from teaching for the summer term. He would take care of the rest. As you can imagine, I was pretty damned excited when I left his office. That po-faced secretary of his gave me a wodge of forms, and I devoted several hours over the next two weeks to polishing up my cv and writing proposals. And, of course, dreaming of drinking espresso in the Piazza del Campo.' As she said this, Jennifer's good humour suddenly slipped, and for a moment she looked angry with herself.

I shifted uncomfortably, having a pretty good idea of what was to come. 'When did you discover what he was up to?'

Jennifer rested her chin on her knees and spoke softly, looking not towards me but towards the river. 'Two weeks before the date for the committee decision on my application, he called me in. I remember it was first thing on a Wednesday morning, just before my Modern American class. He was all smiles. He plied me with coffee and chit-chat, like two old friends together. He enthused about Siena, and said he had spoken to his colleague in the Arts Council office, who was most impressed with my qualifications. But before the final stage of the application went through, both here and in Brussels, he said, he had to know the answer to one question. He had done a lot for me; what was I planning to do for him?'

Jennifer fumbled in the pocket of her cardigan but didn't seem to find what she was searching for.

'Do you know what hurt most, Laura?' Jennifer asked. I offered her a tissue from the pocket of my dungarees. She had tears in her eyes. 'That he didn't even pretend to affection or friendship. He presented it as a bald exchange – his influence for my body. His power for my soul. Except that the exchange would be loaded. He would retain his power. I would lose my soul.' She touched the tissue to her eyes, and shook her head.

'I told him of course to piss off – to shove Siena and the Arts Council and the Research Committee. But I still didn't feel good. I felt foolish, sullied. You see, he had made me desire something, he had made me long for that opportunity in Siena with all my heart, and I felt tainted by my own longing. As if I was complicit.' She cried openly now, tears dampening her pleated skirt.

I couldn't stop myself from asking, 'But didn't you report it to anyone? Like the Union?'

She cast me a bleak look. I had stirred up a lot of anger, and some of it was transferring onto me.

'Get serious,' she hissed. 'Report it – as if it were a gas leak? I did tell my Head of Department, Ryan Doyle – a clever man, a kindly man, someone I had always thought I could trust. He listened with great sympathy and compassion. He offered me Kleenex and tut-tutted at appropriate places in the story. Then he advised me, for my own good, to avoid parts such as Pirate Jenny, "provocative parts" he called them, in the future. And like the Branch Secretary of the Union – oh yes, I spoke to her too – he expressed relief that there was no harm done.'

No harm done. Astonishing! Some of my colleagues in business, not to mention the police, imagine that the academic world is a place in the grip of feminists and liberals. How would they make sense of the episode that Jennifer had just described?

'No harm done,' I repeated. 'Well, no, I guess not. Not if they ignore the damage to your reputation. To your sense of integrity. To your relationship with the Provost – I bet, among other things, that he acts as the final court of appeal in cases of sexual harassment in the University. Am I right?'

Jennifer nodded forlornly, but I hadn't finished. 'And what about a legitimate opportunity lost? What about your self-confidence? Your capacity to expect that male co-workers will relate to you as a colleague and not as a sexual object?'

I was on a soapbox now. I could have gone on, would have gone on, but Jennifer had clearly had enough. We drove back to the University in silence, all trace of the warm-hearted expansive Jennifer expunged. She was an even better actor than most people realised.

CHAPTER 15

The sunshine of yesterday evening wasn't just a flash in the pan. The sun was asserting itself, bold as brass, again the next morning. I enjoyed the walk to the University, moving in and out of the susurrant shade of chestnut trees as I criss-crossed Jesus Green.

Mary McKinnon had thrown all the windows open in her office in deference to the day. Instead of perching upright in a prim typist's chair as she had been when I first saw her, Mary reclined in a gaily-striped deck chair, her thin ankles resting on the edge of the desk. Work didn't appear to be the main thing on her mind.

She waved in greeting, and tried to entice me to sit down by proffering a cup of coffee. I declined, claiming that I had already had my quota for the day. The truth is, I had hyped myself up for the task of sorting through Monica's private papers, and didn't want to lose the momentum.

So I took a raincheck on the coffee and settled myself into the furnished closet that had passed for Monica's office when she was alive. If Monica had been into cat-swinging, she couldn't have done it here. Her office was six feet by eight feet maximum, and except for the central rectangle of grubby lino, every inch was covered by furniture. There was a sturdy wooden pedestal desk, and bookshelves that looked as if they issued from the same factory. There were two filing cabinets. A gap of perhaps six inches between the cabinets was filled by maroon artists' folders. A metal waste-paper bin and a wooden chair with a flat foam cushion completed the furnishings.

The room was functional. It was also crowded and uninviting. Had this room jarred on Monica as much as it did on me?

Visual pleasure was clearly not a priority for the University authorities. Dull colours became duller by association. The wood of the desk was tinted with reddish hue, intended to emulate the colour of teak, while the stain on the bookcase inclined to a muddy blond shade. One of the filing cabinets presented in institutional grey and the other, rather battered, in institutional green. I suppose the repetition of institutional shades might be some bulk-buying bureaucrat's idea of a co-ordinated colour scheme.

The window in her office – a tall narrow casement that overlooked a section of parking lot – provided the only spot of colour. The blue and green print of its curtains reminded me of something. After a few seconds, I realised that it was the same print as the upholstery on British Rail trains.

I began my task by scanning the contents of the notice board. Nothing there needed to be preserved: two course outlines, some memos, a notice about van hire, an invitation to the winter art exhibition at the Sainsbury Centre. The most intimate note was struck by a cheerful postcard from a student on a backpacking holiday in Nepal.

I turned my attention to the desk drawers and the filing cabinets. Mary had already done much of the legwork (or is it armwork?), re-filing papers concerned with students and courses that Monica had taught. Only the more personal items were left, the kind of things Monica might have taken with her if she had lived long enough to move to another job.

I pulled a chair over to the first filing cabinet and began to examine the files and folders relating to Monica's painting. At the end of two hours, I had nothing to show for my efforts but an ache in my lower back. There was correspondence with other artists, and with exhibitors and suppliers of art materials, folders full of sketches – roughs for future work, and balance sheets for the taxman. Nothing here that shed any light on her death.

I stood up and did a series of stretches to release the tension in my spine. This exercise brought my head down, and that's how I happened to notice something propped at the back of a drawer, behind the last hanging file. Well, well . . . It was a slim hard-backed book, perhaps six inches by ten, the cover marbled in green. A diary! I flipped through the ivory pages, many of them awash with a flowing script. Just to be sure, I compared it with the jottings on a notepad on the desk. Yes, the handwriting was Monica's.

I eased myself into the chair and began to read. The last entry was dated two days before Monica's death.

November 16

It was the absence of sound that woke me last night. I was asleep when he came. I heard someone turn with a deliberate stride from the main road into the cul-de-sac. I registered this in my sleep, just as a mother hears her child shift the blankets for a moment and then be still. I think I would have gone on sleeping, maybe I would have incorporated his footsteps into the rhythm of my dream, except that they suddenly stopped. There was no warning – no change of pace, no scraping of a key in the lock again. The footsteps simply stopped. Outside my door. Again.

I don't know how long he maintained his vigil, silent and alert. I could scarcely breathe, let alone tell the time. I should make a spyhole, to gaze upon him unobserved, to see precisely what he's doing. Some day, perhaps, I'll have the courage. But I dread the image of myself peeling back the corner of the curtain, trying to peer out without being seen, revealed to the world as neurotic. Afraid.

I forced myself to sit up this time, to swing my legs (quietly, quietly) over the edge of the bed. Standing upright, I felt less exposed. I stepped carefully towards the front door, rocking from the outside edges of my feet to the inside. I pressed my body close to the door, listening. I avoided the letter box in case something dreadful might be pressed through.

After long minutes, there was a soft shuffling sound on the pavement outside, then a hint of impact. Maybe he placed a hand on the surface of the door, I don't know. Then a scrape of leather, and a clattering movement back towards the High Street.

I was desperate to prevent him getting away unseen a third time. I fumbled with the doorchain, flung the door open, stumbled out onto the pavement. He was gone. I saw the shifting of a shadow at the entrance to the alleyway, or at least I believe I did. That was all.

You can't hear silence, so they say. I searched my mind for what I had heard, for the echoes of those footsteps. I tried to conjure comfort from them. Perhaps he merely stopped beneath the lamp-post to consult a street map? Perhaps he never got as far as my house, passed by quietly on the other side? Perhaps, after all, he was only a figure in a nightmare . . .

No. I can't convince myself this time, any more than I could before. I would like to believe that he was merely passing by, but I know that's not the case. I know that his footsteps stopped dead outside my house. On purpose. Whatever's going on here, it's directed at me.

Its literary failings didn't prevent me from recognising the diary as the only real find of the day. When we were at Wildfell, Monica had mentioned keeping a record of the many things that went bump in the night for her, so there was a chance that this journal would throw something up about who was harassing her and why. I flicked through the pages, scanning for names, but the only ones that jumped up at me were Helen Cochrane and Laura Principal. A closer analysis could wait until I was back in London.

I collected up the things I intended to take with me. The diary, of course. Correspondence relating to Monica's second-ment, though it was formal and unrevealing. I sealed the papers in a large envelope and placed it on top of the diary. I also decided to keep a pile of materials relating to exhibitions and sales of Monica's work, as well as the roughs of future work. If the police investigations proved Angell innocent, I would give the folder to him. Perhaps one day there would be a retrospective of Monica's work. It's doubtful – you can't exhibit promise – but who knows?

When I returned to the Departmental Office, Mary was busy with a crowd of enquiring students. She caught my eye, and tuned them out for a moment. 'Have you finished already?' She signalled me to slide in closer to her desk. 'Anything of interest?'

'Already? It feels like years!' I corrected her, laughing. 'I didn't expect anything dramatic. The police have already purloined her address and appointment books and anything else of obvious interest, but I did make one little discovery.' I patted the notebook affectionately. 'Tucked away in the back of the filing cabinet I found this – Monica's secret diary. I'll have a good read of it in the office tomorrow, and if it throws out any leads, I'll be sure to let you know.'

'Thanks, Laura. I'm glad to be included.' She smiled self-deprecatingly, but I knew what she meant. Mary glanced over at the students. They were absorbed in the intricacies of a Government form relating to student grants so, for a brief spell, she was off the hook.

'Are you ready for that coffee now? I can probably rustle up some chocolate biscuits.'

'I'd like to, Mary, but this has taken longer than I expected. I'm due in London early this afternoon.' I showed her the things of Monica's that I was taking away. 'Look,' I said, lowering my voice, 'I'd appreciate it if you don't mention the diary to the police until I've had a chance to read it through.'

Mary didn't have a problem with that. I wedged a copy of my business card under her keyboard and underlined the office number. She promised to ring if anything came up. Then I pushed my way between the students, nodding to the ones I recognised, and headed for my car.

I made it to London in record time. Sonny's delight when I appeared was touching. Perhaps if I absented myself from the office more often, my skills as a manager and otherwise would be more appreciated. I brought him up to date with developments in connection with Monica's murder, and let him savour the detention of Milton Bannister. While we waited for Desiree to show, he filled me in on the progress of the cases that pay the rent.

'Old Macdonald's back.'

'You're kidding! What is it this time – security for the Kensington townhouse? Protection for the dog?'

'No, he's gone one better than that. Someone, it seems, is sending him anonymous hate letters. He's getting right scared. Or so he claims.'

Sonny's sceptical tone of voice was not without foundation. Old Macdonald is our name for a rich American rancher who spends a lot of time in England. He first came to us four years ago with a neat little problem that was easily put right and led to satisfaction – his with the solution, ours with the fee – on all sides. But he also ended up fascinated by Stevie. According to him, Stevie is the first Amazon he's ever met, and he hasn't yet made up his mind whether he hates her or loves her.

While trying to decide, Macdonald strove to capture her attention, first by showing off and then through argument. He failed decisively on both counts. Stevie had other things on her mind. Then he took another tack and tried to put her on his payroll. But becoming a bodyguard for an autocratic rancher is not Stevie's idea of a good career move. So he was left with no option but to engage her services through the firm. Which he does, with regularity, on pretexts that look flimsier by the year.

'What does Stevie say?'

'Well, you know Stevie. She says she will fit in his little problem around her current caseload, but only as long as he keeps a respectful distance.'

'And does he?'

Sonny shrugged. 'So far. When Stevie commands someone to back off, they generally comply.' His attitude said he was keeping his options open on this one.

At that moment, the office door swung sharply open, and with a snick-snick of high heels on linoleum, an angry-looking young woman marched towards the desk.

'Hi, Mina,' I greeted her. It's not true, what cowboys used to say in films to the outraged city girl. Anger doesn't make a good-looking woman more so – or at least, not in the case of this particular freelance interpreter. With her face contorted and her body rigid, Mina Harrison looked about as attractive as a wooden puppet.

'Call yourself a private investigator!' she expostulated. Her head shook with indignation. 'You're nothing but a bloody spy. Following me around. You didn't say anything about that to me, did you? You didn't tell me you were going to chase me across London, checking up on my every movement.

How *dare* you! What I do outside office hours is none of your business, none at all. You've lost me the Ceresa contract now, and I want to know what you're going to do about it.'

Sonny was enjoying this. Usually we field the irate customers for each other, but every once in a while he likes to watch me exercise my diplomatic skills. I gave him my wanna-help-out? look, but he refused to respond.

'You're mistaken, Mina,' I answered coolly. 'I didn't tail you. You had the misfortune to cuddle up to Signor Permatelli in his limousine at precisely the moment I happened to walk past. A one in a million chance, and it went against you. Bad luck, I'll grant you. But as for reporting it to Ceresa Nazionale, anything else would have been a dereliction of duty. After all, I had been hired to find out if it was safe to entrust the most delicate secrets of Ceresa's UK strategy to your office, and I found out – by accident, but found out nevertheless – that you were cheek to cheek with the head honcho of Ceresa's chief competitor. Do you actually believe that I should have sat on this information?'

Sonny brandished a chair in her direction. Mina sat down, as much deflated now as angry.

'But I *needed* that contract. Things are difficult right now. And you could have come to me, told me what you knew – given me a chance to break it off with Gian instead of shafting me without a second chance. It's not very . . .' Mina cast around for a strong enough word '. . . sisterly!' she concluded, with a note of triumph.

Sonny cast me a sympathetic glance. I bulged my eyes at him in a way that should have conveyed my urgent need for coffee. He didn't take the hint.

'Do you want some coffee, Mina?' I enquired.

'Thanks,' she muttered, scrabbling in her handbag for a tube of Hermesetas.

'Sonny, would you . . . ?' Sonny looked sourly at me as he shifted out of his chair. I'd pay for this later.

'Mina.' I waited for her to look me in the eye. 'I'm sorry you lost the contract. Especially sorry since you needed it so much.'

At these words of understanding, Mina's shell of indignation began to crack. Her foot tapped furiously a few times in an effort to retain control of herself, and the tube of sweeteners rolled off her lap onto the floor. But I carried on.

'Yes, I am sorry. But don't get the wrong idea about who is the injured party here. I asked you whether there was anything else about your situation that might be relevant to Ceresa. You lied. Like a pro. You gave me a bald-faced "no". All the time you knew full well that there was a conflict of interest between your relationship with Permatelli and your work for Ceresa. Is it really me you are angry with? Or yourself, for screwing up a good job?'

Mina began to cry. Her nose reddened. Within thirty seconds, tears were coursing down her face, turning her subtle make-up into a Hallowe'en mask.

Sonny set the coffee on the edge of the desk, picked up the Hermesetas from the floor, and added one to Mina's cup. 'Here,' he said gently. Like many men, he's a sucker for tears. But at least he doesn't run away.

'I really loved him,' Mina sobbed. 'We had a wonderful time together. Only in October we went to St Lucia for a fortnight, did you know that?' I shook my head. Mina didn't notice. 'I was sure he loved me,' she went on miserably, 'but yesterday he sent – can you believe this? – a *fax* to my office, to say that he was returning to Turin and he thought it better if we terminated our dealings immediately. Dealings! As if I were his bookie.'

Mina had had a raw deal, that's for certain. I felt dead sorry for her. Whether or not Permatelli had known about the Ceresa interest in Mina Harrison, and whether his decision to dump her was linked in any way to my investigation, we'd probably never know. What was familiar – depressingly so – was the way that a love affair between two emotional equals carries greater material costs for the woman than for the man. Mina lost an important client because of her affair with Permatelli; he returned to his executive position in Turin unscathed.

This thought didn't put me in a good mood. Nor did my failure to figure out why, throughout the past half hour, as I looked at Mina I kept thinking of Monica Harcourt's face. What was the connection between them?

Mina's exit from the office a few minutes later was more subdued than her entrance had been. Sonny, chastened by Mina's tears, took the opportunity of our being alone in the office to kiss me tenderly. He looked so serious that I stood on tiptoe to ruffle his hair, hoping to raise a grin. He kissed me again, and this time I could see and feel the beginnings of a smile. The good news is that, when Sonny put on his coat a while later and headed out on a case, he forgot to have a go at me about the coffee.

I wrote a memo to Stevie, suggesting she check whether Old Macdonald could use the services of an experienced Italian interpreter. Just as I finished, Desiree bounced in. Lycra didn't prevent her black leggings from bagging in the thighs.

'Hey, girl!' I exclaimed, 'Jo is not supposed to be tubby, but no one says she has to look like Twiggy. When they say *Little* Women, they don't mean anorexic. When is this dieting going to stop?'

'When I can find time to go home and fix myself a decent salad! There I was, trapped all of yesterday in the car watching Sonia Loizou. After all my promises about dieting, I couldn't resort to Kentucky Fried Chicken – not and hold up my head in this office again. But on the other hand, I had no time to get hold of yummy cottage cheese. So I am fading away in the interests of detective work. But it's worth it – wait till you see my catch.'

'Start at the beginning, OK? How long did you have to stake out the Post Office Box before Sonia showed up?'

'On the second morning, there she was. Neat as a pin. Little precise features, little precise body, slim-fitting well-cut suit. Just as you described her. She drove up in a navy-blue Audi, one of those understated luxury jobs with leather upholstery, and double-parked outside the Post Office. I couldn't really miss her: no one could. If the lady is trying to give her husband and his pals the slip, she has a few things to learn about blending into the background.'

'So you followed her home?'

'I followed her to Waitrose for some groceries. By the look of her shopping bag, the lady eats even less than I do. Then to an off-licence, a chemist, and at last back to her flat.' Dee consulted her notebook, flapping it open in front of her like eager journalists do in 1940s movies. 'Sonia Loizou (or Sonia Lincoln, if you go by the tag on her door) now occupies an undistinguished mansion flat – Number 84, Causley House, to be precise. Didn't really look her style, I thought, but she lives there all right.'

'Maybe not for long,' I interrupted. 'So, go on, tell me about this prolonged period of starvation.'

'Well, having tracked her down to Causley House I didn't want to lose her again, so I decided to sit tight until she emerged. To my dismay – not to mention discomfort – she stayed put all afternoon and evening. Only emerged the next morning, just about the time I woke up from a quick forty winks.'

'Desiree,' I began, irritation colouring my tone. For once, Dee managed to look repentant.

'I know, I know.' She raised her hands in a gesture of submission. 'All-night surveillance only with prior instructions . . . But this one was a work of love! I won't charge overtime, honest. And the crucial thing is, I did catch her coming out. And – wait for it,' she said, brandishing a pair of photos, 'she was accompanied by an athletic-looking guy with a moustache. Sounds familiar?'

I pounced on the photos. 'Well, well – Dmitri, Michael's loving brother. So he spent the night with Sonia. Above and beyond the call of brotherly duty, wouldn't you say? He didn't spot you, did he?'

Desiree looked uncomfortable for a brief moment, and I felt a stab of anxiety, but then she assured me that the Loizous had been concentrating on securing the door when the photo was taken. Dmitri did glance in her direction, but he gave no sign of recognition. And after all, she had only been in the nightclub for a few hours. He wasn't likely to recall her face.

When Desiree had signed out, with a flurry of messages and farewells, I rang my credit card pal in Northampton. I caught him just as he was getting dressed after his daytime sleep. He couldn't spare me long, since he was due soon at the school gates, but he had time enough to tell me what I had expected to hear. Ten days before, Sonia Loizou had made over a voucher for a considerable sum to a travel agent in the West End.

I immediately rang the travel agency concerned, pretending to be investigating a fraudulent use of credit cards. The staff there were only too happy to tell me that someone calling herself Sonia Loizou had recently booked two tickets to South America – one way, for the last day of the month. The second ticket was in the name of Mr Loizou – Dmitri, of course, not Michael.

CHAPTER 16

The Palm Court at the Waldorf is one of the few places in the world that still holds afternoon tea dances. The central floor is a splash of pale polished wood shaped like Nelson's hat, each elongated tail offering access to a pink-washed upper tier. The dance floor is fringed by a forest of parlour palms. Their vibrant foliage owes a lot to greenhouse rest-cures because, although the mirrors that encircle the walls give an impression of light, no sun actually penetrates the tea room.

It seemed to me a suitably artificial atmosphere for the meeting to come. I mounted two shallow steps onto the upper tier, and followed a waiter with an ambiguous European accent towards a corner where a small sofa and armchairs in green brocade nudged up against a marble-topped coffee table. The waiter parted reluctantly with a handwritten menu. I adjusted a satin cushion to support my back, and watched with pleasure as a blushing couple in their sixties glided gracefully onto the dance-floor. She wore a sober navy silk dress with a neat belt, while he was more dashing in a dark green blazer and turquoise tie. The way they danced, taking rhythm from one another's body, suggested they were very much in love. Or can dancers fake that?

My guest was on time. At four o'clock precisely, the hour I had specified in my note, he passed through the main doors and stood on the outer edge of the dance-floor. I had a moment to study his face before he was conducted to my corner.

My visitor might have been quite attractive as a young man, but in his forties that boyish appeal had yielded to a rumpled look. The sagging face lacked definition. The nose was bent, suggesting a rugby injury many years before. His hair was pepper and salt, but a former fairness showed through in startlingly blond eyebrows. The eyes were not unpleasant, pale blue and large, but they were trapped above prominent bags that imparted a look of permanent exhaustion. The effect was clownish. Whatever Elinor St James saw in Richard Dolby, it certainly wasn't good looks.

'Have a seat,' I said. 'I am Laura Principal.'

Since it was four o'clock, I suggested that we have something to eat. Dolby ordered a tuna fish sandwich, while I opted for the full afternoon tea. It would save me having to worry about supper. My guest sat upright in the frivolous chair, no hint of impatience on his features, while the waiter took our order. Clearly Richard Dolby was accustomed to doing private business in public places. Only when the waiter moved discreetly away did he look me in the eye.

'I haven't long,' he stated with a studied coldness of tone. 'In less than an hour I'm due at Westminster. Please tell me precisely what you want.'

'I want, Mr Dolby, to know why you assisted Elinor St James to have an abortion. Was the child yours?'

He may have winced slightly at my provocative use of the word 'child' – a word on which he had been known to insist – but he maintained a stony silence.

'Mr Dolby? I haven't long either. And I must have some answers. Today.' The elderly couple had sat down now, and were looking at the menu. Green blazer had his arm protectively around navy frock's shoulder. For some reason, this generated in me a wave of sympathy for Elinor St James. My voice was loud as well as cold.

'Mr Dolby?'

He seemed to have arrived at a decision. The blue eyes turned their startled gaze on me. He gestured towards my leather shoulder bag, which was snuggled in the corner of the sofa. 'I'll have to ask you to show me the contents of your handbag,' he said, no hint of apology in his tone. 'Whatever we discuss today, our conversation must not be the subject of an unauthorised recording. You understand?'

I passed the bag across the table to him. He peered inside,

rustled the contents about, and passed it back again. I also opened my jacket pockets to his gaze, and lifted the sofa cushions. No recording machinery appeared. But he knew, and he knew that I knew, that his inspection entailed a tacit agreement to cooperate.

'Whether the child was yours or not, Mr Dolby, Elinor St James is not very happy about the abortion. And neither will her mother and father be if it gets out. Didn't you advise her to tell them?'

Two waiters headed in our direction, the second carrying a silver tray. The first waiter moved the floral centrepiece to one side. He lifted the dishes one by one from the tray and placed them on the table, each movement accompanied by a barely perceptible bow. Tuna fish with a flourish. When they retired again, I poured tea for both of us, and tucked resolutely into a cucumber sandwich. It was Dolby's turn to speak. No further prompts.

I had finished my cup of tea before he began. 'You must understand,' he said, with an attempt at dignity, 'that Elinor St James is someone whom I like and admire. I have known her for many years.'

'Since she was a child, then?' I interjected sourly. I'm not above turning the knife on occasion.

Dolby, probably wisely, pretended I hadn't spoken. 'Under other circumstances,' he continued, 'we would certainly consider marriage. But she's young. She has her studies to think about, and I . . .' he managed to look as if it were an afterthought, a minor consideration '. . . I have a family and a career.'

'Like Beverley Cattell?' I asked.

For the first time his composure slipped. Did he really imagine the comparison wouldn't be made?

'That was different,' Dolby snapped. 'She was careless. She didn't give a damn.'

'And you do, I suppose. You care such a goddamn lot.' The businessmen at the next table glanced covertly in my direction. I lowered my voice a notch. 'Especially about keeping it quiet.'

Dolby gets a lot of credit for control. Where *do* they learn it? I reckon expensive boarding schools, no Mummy to cuddle you and no one to depend on but yourself, do have their uses. Especially if you want to bully and bluff your way through a political career. He didn't reply to my outburst. He simply shifted to what he thought was the heart of the matter.

'Ms Principal, please. Let's get on with it. You haven't come here to lecture me.' The voice of reason now – the practical seasoned politician to the fore. 'You want money.' I raised an eyebrow, but let him continue.

'Well, I'm not a rich man by any means. I can't match the kind of prices the tabloid press would pay for your revelations, so I'm loath to give you anything. After all, if I do pay you, what's to stop you from going out afterwards and selling your story to the *Sun*?'

Now *my* composure was in danger of slipping. 'Listen to me carefully,' I said, pausing a moment until his gaze was forced to meet mine. 'Watch my lips. I don't want money – yours or the *Sun*'s. I want to know about The Eastings and Elinor's time there. Every little detail.'

The blue eyes stared at me for several seconds, weighing me up. I'm not sure what tipped the balance, but once Dolby began to speak he was surprisingly candid. Perhaps he reckoned that, without witnesses, his word would carry far more weight than that of a female Private Eye. Or perhaps he thought it was worth spilling the beans in the hope of getting out of this mess lightly.

'I had no idea,' he said, the practical politician replaced by the man of injured innocence, 'that Elinor was unprotected. When she said she was pregnant, that she had had it confirmed in Harley Street, I was shocked to the core. I am very fond of her – we are fond of one another – but I never envisaged anything like this.'

I layered a scone with strawberry preserve and clotted cream for myself, and pondered the word 'unprotected'. I also offered half-heartedly to pour Dolby another cup of tea. The tuna fish sandwich hadn't seen the inside of his mouth yet. He waved the offer aside, and continued. About Elinor's indecision. About her rigid mother, who would surely have insisted on knowing the name of her lover. About staying for three nights at a small hotel in Burnham Market, near Holkham, so that he could visit Elinor regularly in the days following the operation.

'And where did you meet?'

'I beg your pardon?' Dolby looked up at me, puzzled. 'Oh, I see. On the beach. Elinor would make her way along a path from the Clinic at an agreed time, and I met her where the path merged into the beach. Then no one would see us. Or even if they did, they wouldn't connect us with the Clinic.'

'So what about the woman you saw on the beach that day?'

Dolby looked blank. Apart from the eyebrows, his pale broad face reminded me of the side of a slab of halibut. 'What day? I don't know what you're talking about.'

'Are you saying you saw no one else at all during the meetings you had with Elinor?'

He shook his head. 'No, not a soul. We were fortunate in that respect. The weather was uninviting. Sensible people don't venture out onto the beach in weather like that.'

A waiter materialised from behind a palm tree, and glanced enquiringly at the table. I waved him away and focused again upon Richard Dolby.

'But you weren't alone. A woman named Monica Harcourt, a painter, went to the beach one weekend. She saw you there: she recognised you. She even took some photographs. A few days later, she was brutally murdered.'

'*Murdered?* Where, in Holkham? By whom? But I never read about this in the papers!' If he was faking, he was doing a pretty good job.

'Not in Holkham,' I said quietly. 'In her flat in Cambridge, where she lived. And by whom is what I mean to find out.'

'How appalling,' Dolby declared. The conventional expression carried more feeling than it usually does. 'Was she a friend of yours?'

'You could say that.'

There was another brief period of silence, during which the waiter finally cleared the table. I hoped the Waldorf had some useful outlet for second-hand tuna fish sandwiches. Dolby lifted his shirt cuff delicately, and looked at his watch. The apology sounded almost sincere.

'Look, I'm sorry, I've really got to go. What happens now? What are you going to do?'

I looked at him for a minute longer, taking in once again the crooked nose and the straight back. 'I'll let you know.'

He stood up to go. I was relieved that he didn't offer me his hand. Instead, he acknowledged me with a curt nod of his head, his expression a mixture of hope and petulance, and turned on his heel.

'One more thing!' I barked. I waited until he had turned again to face me. 'Until I decide what to do, don't go harassing any more nursery nurses, OK?'

I didn't mind at all that the businessmen at the adjoining table overheard.

It was dark and wet as I drove back to the office. Lights from the shops along the Euston Road reflected luridly in the waves of rain that washed along the edges of the street. Richard Dolby puzzled me. I knew from his public record that he was a nasty piece of work, and nothing I had seen of him today had altered that. On the other hand, I doubted that he had anything to do with Monica's death. His bewilderment at my questions seemed utterly unforced, and he appeared not even to have registered the existence of photographs that would prove his presence near The Eastings. Without an interest in suppressing those photos, he had no motive for murder.

The stairs to my office looked even steeper than usual. Was this the effect, I wondered, of three cream scones in mid-afternoon? Up the stairs I ran, panting like a walrus, thankful that it was past evening now and the office would be empty. No one there to laugh at my gasps for breath.

I unlocked the door, felt for the light switch with my left hand, and stepped inside. My panting must have obscured other noises, because he was almost upon me before I realised there was a man standing behind the door. As I turned, a large figure loomed out of the darkness, pulsating in a series of strobe-like flashes as the fluorescent lights struggled on. I lunged swiftly to the left. A blow that had been aimed for somewhere around the base of my skull missed, and instead a heavy rubber torch struck me a sharp crack on the ear. It hurt like hell and set me off balance. I went with the fall, rolling onto my left shoulder and out of reach.

In the full glare of the lights now, I could see a man clad all in black, his face obscured by a balaclava except for gleaming feral eyes. I didn't wait for a further description. I flipped over onto my back and pulled my knees up to my chest, kicking out powerfully as he dived at me. The soles of my boots connected joltingly with his breastbone, and though he tried to clutch my leg, I managed to throw him onto his side and launch myself upright. He felt behind himself in a panicky way. I hoped that meant that I had broken something serious, but instead he produced a long-bladed hunting knife, and threw himself at me. I retreated round the corner of the desk, never for a second taking my eyes off his right hand. For half a minute we shimmied back and forth around the desk, participants in a frenetic dance. No future in sashaying with this particular partner. I drew a deep breath, cast my eyes right as if I would make a move in that direction, then flung myself onto and across the desk, booted feet first. I managed to deliver a hard kick to his abdomen, but it didn't disarm him. The knife raked my calf, cutting through an artery. We both fell back. There was a tremendous clatter from opposite me, and the door flew open.

'What the hell . . . ?'

I was right in Stevie's line of vision, but how could she miss me anyway? Blood was pumping from my leg. The floor around was slippery with it. As she dashed towards me, my attacker shot out of the door and down the stairs. Stevie looked uncharacteristically nonplussed. She gave chase as far as the first bend in the stairs, then came back. I don't remember her making a tourniquet from the sleeves of her cotton parka and applying it to my leg. I don't remember her dialling 999. I don't remember anything else until I woke up in the Royal Free Hospital, Hampstead.

The room was taller than it was wide, a cavernous expanse of ceiling glooming high above as I lay on the metal bed. Most of the space was bleached by a fluorescent glare, but the area around me was softened by shadows cast from a curtain that screened me on two sides.

The sedative and the transfusion of strangers' blood that had been administered to me on arrival at the hospital had delivered me into a dreamless sleep. I awoke the next morning feeling marvellous. Sure, my leg throbbed, and the back of my hand was uncomfortable where the drip had gone in, but I felt rested for the first time in weeks. What a way to catch up on your sleep.

Sonny found me in high spirits. He smoothed the hair off my temples, and kissed my eyes and my lips in a tender way that revealed how frightening he had found the news of my injury. I returned the kiss with enthusiasm, giving him the opportunity to cast aside his fantasies of death in favour of other, more pleasurable ones.

'So, angel,' he exclaimed a bit later on, stroking the bruise on my hand, 'what have you been doing that's made you a target for assassination?'

Sonny had been allowed to visit my bedside last night when I was flat out and unable to appreciate his presence. He had been consumed throughout the night by that image of me, but this morning, both the Sister's report and my own demeanour confirmed for him that Laura Principal was not in danger. From that moment on, he seemed to take pleasure in my incapacity, demanding more than once to peer under the crisp hospital covers at my bandaged leg, and acting the part of a hospital visitor (What can I get you? Sweets – newspapers – a dressing gown?) with a suspicious degree of enthusiasm. His switch of tack to a discussion of work came just in time to prevent me rising from my bed of pain and throwing him out. Between us, we went over the possibilities.

Possibility one – apparently favoured by the Metropolitan Police, who had joined me earlier in the day for a meagre hospital brunch – was that I had surprised a routine burglar, bent on searching out our safe. The locks on the door had been fiddled by the use of a set of picklocks, usually the mark of a professional, and someone had explored the contents of my desk and my filing cabinet.

Neither Sonny nor I were keen on this explanation. In

Knightsbridge, burglars might go in for the glamour of balaclavas, but in our neighbourhood they prefer the strategy of blending in with the locals. And a hunting knife was hardly standard equipment for thieves in any part of England.

Sonny held stubbornly to a conviction that the knife-wielding intruder was after yours truly. He emphasised the pattern of disruption: 'Your desk drawers, then the filing cabinet in your office. If someone was going for petty cash, they would have tried the other desks. A filing cabinet is scraping the bottom of the barrel.'

'Unless,' I joined in, 'Mr Balaclava was looking for something connected with one of the cases I'm working on. That's got to be it, Sonny. Look, I'm going to be stuck here for another day. Or two,' I appended swiftly as Sonny began to bristle. 'You'll have to check out Dmitri Loizou for me.'

Sonny knew the outlines of the Loizou case. I reminded him how Desiree had tracked Sonia down to her hideaway, and about the photographs she had taken of Michael's wife and brother together. We agreed that Dmitri – or rather, one of his associates – seemed a likely candidate for the partner in my close encounter. Dmitri could well be trying to recover evidence from me before I passed it on to his brother.

'Sonny, you'll have to check that the photos of Sonia and Dmitri are still at Wong's, where I took them to get duplicates. And talk to Dmitri – heavy him a little. But if we're wrong about the break-in, if he doesn't seem to know that we know what he's up to with Sonia, don't give the game away. I'll need to talk to Michael Loizou first. Oh, and check whether Diana Murcott has got me a date to visit Michael in prison again. The sooner the better.'

Like a lamb, Sonny jotted down the details. At my last comment, however, he started to put his notebook away.

'And one other thing, Sonny. The most important.'

'Yes, I know,' he said, bringing the notebook out again. 'Can you give me Dee's address off the top of your head? If Dmitri is our boy, the first thing I'd better do is arrange it so that he can't get to Dee the way he got to you.'

Sometimes Sonny could be such a darling. He leaned a long way over and kissed me again, taking care not to put any weight on my right leg. Such a nice kiss. 'Thanks, love,' I whispered. 'I'll be home soon.'

Before making his way to the door, Sonny produced a copy of the *Cambridge Evening News* from his bag, and pointed out a photo on the inside news page. So, I wasn't the only person who had noticed Milton Bannister being escorted into the station. This picture was taken from the other side of the road, the image of the Provost small but crystal-clear. *A man is helping police with their enquiries.*

I itched to be in on those interviews.

CHAPTER 17

Although I had begun the morning feeling fresh, by midday fatigue had set in again. Partly this was hospital *ennui* – the effect of an overheated room and an understimulated brain. Partly it was the result of entertaining so many visitors. There was Stevie, hard on Sonny's heels, checking that her rescue bid had not been in vain. Then my brother Hugo turned up, dashing in between jobs, with my nephew in tow. The Ward Sister allowed him in for five minutes, and his four-year-old antics provided the first laugh of the day. Finally, Helen hot-footed it in from Cambridge, laden with gifts.

My old friend's eyes were alert, and her dark-blonde hair was cut short in a dashing new style. She looked better than she had since Monica died. But appearances can be deceiving. Helen managed to concentrate on my health for less than a minute before she returned with obsessive intensity to the subject of the murder.

'The worst thing is, Laura, that I can't bear to answer the phone. Every time it rings, I freeze, reminded of that scream – of Monica tied to the chair. How could he do that to her?' she carried on, knowing that we'd been through all this before, not really caring. 'Monica's scream was horrible, but I keep hoping that maybe that's all there was. Maybe just that one moment of terror and then it ended. You saw her, Laura. Did she die quickly, do you think? Or did it go on and on for her, the fear and the pain?'

Helen knew the answer to that already. We'd been over this many times before. Instead of a direct reply, this time I held her hand, the touch bringing uncomfortably to mind Monica's body and her cold, bloodstained fingers.

I twisted around to look at the flowers from Ginny and her dad on my bedside table. The card warned that she wouldn't take a little cut to the leg as an excuse for poor performance at basketball. 'Is Ginny OK in Bristol?'

Helen brightened. 'She's getting bored – fed up with being away from all her friends, I think. But I don't want her home until this is over. Because when the phone rings, the other thing I think of—' and here Helen's voice lowered to a whisper, '—is that bastard on the other end of the line, longing for me to be terrified too.'

She directed a pleading glance at me. 'Is it Bannister, do you think? Is he the one?'

'Well, you know that the police have been on to him for quite a while. They must be building up a decent case by this time. The fact that he visited Monica on the night she died hasn't yet been satisfactorily explained. I'll bet you two to one he was sexually harassing Monica. But did he murder her? I just don't know. There are some things that don't really fit . . .'

But Helen wasn't listening. 'I've got a feeling about this. Do you know, I didn't realise before that I could hate, but now I do. The man who did that to Monica deserves to be hated. If Bannister is the one, I hope they lock him away. I hope they play that tape to him, the tape of Monica screaming, every night for the rest of his life. Bastards like him hardly deserve to live.' The last defiant words came out in a strangled way. Helen began to cry, quietly, hatred yielding to pain.

After she had left, I stared bleakly at the wall for a moment before clambering out of bed and shuffling to the toilet and back. I was exhausted. So many visitors. The room was bursting with blooms, the Sister was bursting with irritation, and I was looking forward to a hospital lunch and a nice long nap.

That was when Angell arrived. There was no trace now of the scruffy man I had talked with in the Police Station in Cambridge. Angell looked – how shall I put it? – *superb*. His striking face glowed with energy, and he carried himself like an athlete on a winning streak. Even the Sister cheered up during the couple of moments that he spoke to her.

In spite of his confident appearance, Angell's approach was diffident. Perhaps he viewed himself as still under suspicion, unsure of his welcome. 'The man in your office told me where you were,' he said, a question in his voice. 'I hope you don't mind me coming.'

'That's my partner, Sonny,' I explained, motioning him to a seat beside the bed. And I didn't mind at all. The nap would wait.

'Good lord,' exclaimed Angell, focusing on the bruising on my temple. 'What exactly happened to you? You don't look like the sort of person who spends much of her life in hospital.'

'As a matter of fact, this is my first time in hospital since my mother Dorothy gave birth to me. But it's not bad here. If they would turn down the heating and turn up the quality of the cuisine, I could even grow to like it.'

'Sonny said you'd had an accident.'

I laughed – the second time that day. Sonny appears gregarious on the surface, but he is also, in his own way, discreet.

'That's a tactful way of putting it. You can call this injury accidental only in the sense that *I* sure as hell didn't intend it! But someone else did. A youngish guy, about five-eleven, fit, with a black balaclava and a large hunting-knife. Ring any bells?'

'A poet's life may be colourful, but I'm glad to say it's not *that* colourful. I don't generally run to acquaintance with armed attackers. How bad are your injuries?'

I showed him the bandage on my leg, and explained how Stevie had got me to Casualty before I lost any more blood. He looked suitably impressed. 'Monica said you were somebody very special. As usual, she got it right.' We paused. That name could still pack a punch.

'Do you mind?' I dislike asking for help, but Angell responded with an ease that made it all right. He plumped the pillow gently, and edged it into position behind my back. I used my left leg to push myself more upright. This little ritual put us both in a better state for talking.

I filled Angell in on my suspicions about Milton Bannister's attempt to cash in on Monica's secondment.

'I knew she was upset,' he affirmed. 'For weeks the fellowship in Oregon was her favourite topic of speculation. I could come and visit her, she promised, in a little wooden house made of pale grey boards near the sea. She would do her best painting ever and I would write a nearly perfect poem. Then all of a sudden she turned sour about the whole business. When I asked her about it, she turned on me as if the mere mention of Oregon was an insult. At the time I hadn't the faintest idea what had gone wrong.'

'Does what I suggested about the Provost and sexual harassment fit? Because the evidence is purely circumstantial, you see. We know for sure that he tried it on with one member of staff, and other cases suggest a similar pattern. But without Monica here to tell us what exactly happened to her it's impossible to be one hundred per cent sure.'

'But it fits.' Angell nodded vigorously. He had no hesitation. 'What else could have turned Monica from delight about the seascape project to despair? And think about her reaction. If the delay in processing her application was just some bureaucratic thing, she would have been frustrated, sure, maybe even pissed off. But she would have told me about it – or other people, don't you think?'

'I think. But her not telling you about Bannister trying to get her into the sack – how can you account for that?'

'The thing you've got to understand is that sometimes our relationship, Monica's and mine, got in the way of her confidence in herself as an artist.' Angell pondered for a moment, a look of deep concentration on his face. 'Let me give you an example. When Monica had her first exhibition, one or two people on the art circuit, jealous I suppose of her success, implied that it was my contacts, rather than her own talent, that got her this opportunity. Well, some artists would just shrug off an accusation like that, but not Monica. There was a core of self-doubt inside her that was ready to believe this sort of thing. That particular incident almost took the shine off the exhibition for her.'

I began to get the picture. 'So you're telling me that the Provost's proposition would just bring the whole issue up again for Monica? The awful thought that she had no talent?

That she simply relied on the patronage of influential men, that sort of thing?'

Angell nodded. 'I guess she'd find it deeply shaming. And in the circumstances, I'm the last person she would have confided in. I could never get her quite to accept that I really believed in her.'

We talked a bit longer, but Angell was starting to fidget. Most visitors to hospital do, after the first quarter of an hour. There's a sense of imprisonment here. Unless you can give in to it and lie back, the urge to escape constantly resurfaces. But suddenly Angell brightened. 'Guess who's turned up?'

I considered for a moment. 'Emma Harcourt?' I ventured. 'Monica's sister?'

Angell looked as surprised as if I had leaped out of bed and done cartwheels down the corridor. 'How did you know?' My engimatic smile (I practise this one for impressing clients) suggested that this foreknowledge was a routine part of the detective's art.

But I spoiled the impression because I couldn't resist a question. 'So where's she been?'

Angell's look of relief told me that he preferred his detectives fallible. 'All over. Travelling. She's spent months on southeast Asia, then India, then the Middle East. Quite an adventurer.'

Margaret Powers mentioned that Monica had been distressed by Emma's absence from her mother's funeral. 'Was she abroad when Monica's mum died?'

'She left New Zealand even before her stepmother fell ill, so she never knew anything about it. That's why she didn't turn up for the funeral.'

'Do the police know about her yet?'

'They will by now. Emma showed up at Margaret Powers' place the night before last, looking for Monica. Margaret had to be the one to break the news. Courageous of her. And very traumatic for Emma. Apparently she couldn't believe it at first. She was reeling anyway with culture shock from the contrast between staid old England and cosmopolitan Cairo. She had expected to surprise Monica, have a happy reunion –

perhaps even stay with her a few weeks. And instead she was greeted by this.'

It was what you might call a bummer of a landing. 'Is she still at Margaret's flat?'

'No, she's staying at my place in London for a week or so. Margaret was terrific, got her through the first stage of shock. Then Emma said she wanted to meet me. She knew about me, you see, from letters and so forth over the years. She even knew about the baby. She said to Margaret that I was like the only remaining person that she might conceivably be able to call "family".'

He paused, considering. 'And it does feel a bit like that. I'm hoping she'll stay for a while. Shall I bring her in to meet you?'

'Whoah!' I exclaimed. 'Some day soon, but not yet. My leg hurts, my head is throbbing and I've got work to do. No new visitors yet. *Please*. Perhaps I could call to see you both next week, assuming I'm out of here and Emma's still in London?'

We fixed it up for Friday.

Before Angell left, he furnished me with one more piece of information – a message from the office. Bridget Cullers, the third of the women from Trina's list, wanted to see me.

Getting out of hospital is not as easy as you might imagine. My Aunt Peggy has been waiting eighteen months for a small operation on her knee joint. She's a living testament to the current shortage of hospital beds in Britain, one of hundreds of thousands, it should be said. Knowing this, I imagined that the Royal Free would be only too happy to wave me goodbye.

No such luck. According to the Sister in charge of the ward, I couldn't leave until the consultant had done his rounds the following day. Would I be physically detained, I asked, if I simply picked up my things and strolled out of the door? No one would stop me, the Sister replied. She added, most persuasively, that my insurance coverage would cease the moment I discharged myself. Now any self-employed person needs to keep up-to-date with insurance against illness or injury, but to void your insurance in my job, where occasional injury is almost guaranteed, would itself be a sign of unfitness for work. I smiled weakly and shuffled off to the washroom to brush my teeth.

It was, in fact, a further twenty-four hours before I could get the medical equivalent of an exit visa. Dr Mukherjee said I should avoid straining my leg for the next couple of weeks, and warned that it would still be painful. He was dead right. By the time I had buh-bumped the momentous journey from Ward G4 to the main entrance, I knew that driving to Cambridge was out of the question. I hailed a taxi to King's Cross station. Thank God for British Rail. By the time I sat down in a carriage bound for Cambridge, even the blue-and-green upholstery looked good.

When the train came to the end of the line seventy minutes later, I hobbled to the pay telephone. Sonny was furious to learn that I was in Cambridge. That is why, of course, I had gone directly there before ringing him.

'But I'm fine, love,' I protested, suppressing a moan about the pain in my leg. 'I just want to have a quick chat with Bridget Cullers, to see what she can tell us about Milton Bannister. Then I'll be back. And I promise you, I'll sit on the sofa with my leg up on cushions and act the part of a proper convalescent. You can wait on me hand and foot for the rest of the week.'

From his tone of voice, I suspected that this angel-of-mercy scenario wasn't exactly what Sonny had in mind. I blew a kiss down the telephone and limped to the taxi rank without so much as a sideways glance at a British Rail sandwich. Such forbearance.

Bridget Cullers lives a few miles outside Cambridge in a pretty village that has sprouted with casual grace on the eastern bank of the Cam. Her house is one of a small row of detached homes backing onto the river. The front of the house is shielded by a line of mature fir trees. The taxi driver agreed to cool his heels in the pub down the road while I kept my appointment.

'Is your mum in?' He was brown-haired, lanky, aged about seven, and he looked at me blankly. 'Or your dad? Are there any grown-ups here?'

'Mum! *Mu-u-um!*' The shout reverberated through the house, and on the heels of the echo a pretty blonde woman appeared, chubby-cheeked. She was, indeed, Bridget Cullers – or at least, that was the name by which she had been known when she lectured at the University. Now she went by her married name, Kennedy. She had left work when she was carrying her youngest, now eleven months old and asleep upstairs. She had never returned. At close quarters, in spite of her girlish appearance, she had a world-weary look. Her eyes were downturned at the corners and puffy underneath.

She offered me a glass of white wine. The bottle was already opened, and not as cold as I would have liked, but I accepted. We sat in a cheerful sunroom behind the kitchen, while the lanky boy watched *Return of the Jedi* on video in an adjoining room. Knowing something of the capacity of children for interruption, I assumed we wouldn't have long to talk.

'I saw his picture in the *Evening News*,' Bridget began. 'Bannister – Milton Bannister. I thought it might help the case against him if someone knew how he treated other members of his staff.'

She had learned about me from Mary McKinnon, with whom she had been in contact yesterday for the first time in a year.

'One of the things I've discovered,' I told her, 'is that you and Monica Harcourt have in common the experience of applying through Bannister for secondment. Anything you can tell me about your application might help me understand what happened to Monica.'

Bridget didn't hesitate for an instant. It was as if she had been waiting – a long time – for someone to enquire.

'I had a marvellous plan for a series of seminars with French writers, especially the political theorists who are best known over here. You should have seen the list of people who were willing to take part – a star-studded cast. My intention was to mount the seminars, and then edit a collection of papers based on the presentations. I had a promise from the French Cultural Attaché for a grant to underwrite the series, two publishers waving contracts for publication under my nose, and the facilities and accommodation more or less mapped out. All I needed was an assurance of time free from teaching to see the thing through.'

Already Bridget's story was painfully familiar. 'I suppose Bannister encouraged you?'

'Encouraged me? He raved about the project! How it would put us on the map, bring prestige to the University, and how it was all my doing. Secondment was his suggestion. In fact, he practically insisted on it. But when all the papers were in for the committee, he suddenly changed his mind. I got a curt note, saying that he wasn't sure this was a good idea after all.'

I had to resist the temptation to reach over and refill my wineglass. I wasn't sure how creatively the wine would mix with the medication still rushing through my system. 'So you went to see him,' I prompted.

'More fool I. Twice. The first time he made a series of objections – the Department couldn't spare me, he didn't know if French was the right priority, and so on. I was bewildered. The committee meeting took place, and still he hemmed and hawed. I couldn't understand what was going on at all. So naïve,' she concluded bitterly. 'Me, not him.'

As if I could mistake her meaning. 'And the second visit?'

'Well, the second time he took a different tack. He had thought it over, he said, and he could see the advantages. He was sorry he had caused a delay. What had lain behind his pessimism, he realised, was anxiety about my going away. Still I didn't twig. "My going away – to Paris? But why?" And, of course, that's when he finally told me about the condition for secondment: what he called a "firmer" relationship with him. At last I realised that the entire thing, from the first time he had called me in, had been a setup. I panicked. Ran out of the office in tears. Well, from then on he hounded me. There's no other way of putting it. There were phone calls, summonses at peculiar times, notes to my Head of Department saying how embarrassing it would be if I fluffed this opportunity.'

She grimaced, as another memory struck. 'One day I ran into him in the staff restaurant. He was with three of his cronies from administration. He spoke to me quite formally – "Dr Cullers, isn't it? From French?" – but he smirked, and I had the uncomfortable feeling that he had said something about me, something untrue, to the other men. They all looked away, kind of embarrassed.

'Well,' she continued, 'to cut a long story short, I couldn't complete the preparations for the seminar. Every time a decision was needed, I would go to pieces. Eventually my Head of Department forced me to hand the arrangements over to two of my colleagues. Most of the work was already done. They were only too pleased to pick up the glory. By then, I was several weeks pregnant with Florence. I think people just blamed my unhappy state on the pregnancy.'

Bridget glanced warily in the direction of the next room. The sounds of intergalactic battle drifted out. She continued, reassured.

'Well, *most* people blamed the pregnancy. Except for Randolph, my husband. He blamed me. He's the only one I told, you see, and he kept asking me if I fancied the Provost. I wouldn't exactly say he was jealous, but he has always admired power, and I think he imagines that everyone else must be turned on by power too. So what with one thing and another, it seemed easier to take maternity leave and just wait for things to calm down.'

Another competent woman disappears from public life. 'Why did you resign?' I asked gently. 'Why not come back after maternity leave?'

'I tried,' she affirmed. She plucked at her jeans with one hand, held the wineglass with the other. 'My plan all along was to get away for a few weeks, forget the Department, immerse myself in the children and then return as if nothing had ever happened. I suppose in a foolish part of my mind I almost hoped that Florence – that's the baby – would cleanse me somehow, make me less vulnerable. But it didn't work like that.' She sighed and refilled her own wineglass in a melancholy unthinking way.

'I drove into the University when Florence was about six weeks old – just a friendly visit, to show the baby off to the women in the office and check the timetables for next term. But I could hardly make it through the door. My knees began to shake; I thought I was going to be sick. I told myself again and again that this was foolish, that he couldn't harm me, that this was *my* workplace and these were *my* colleagues and I wouldn't be chased away. But no amount of pep-talking could change the way I felt.'

Bridget belatedly leaned forward and waved the cool green bottle in my direction. I felt something rather akin to hatred for Milton Bannister. Wine would have helped to soothe this anger, but I placed my hand over my glass and shook my head.

'So you quit,' I stated.

'Yes, I quit. I gave the old motherhood story: wanted to enjoy every minute of my children's early years, couldn't bear to be away from them. I don't think anyone believed me. People who know me, know I love my kids – but they also know that I am a workaholic. I'm never happier than when I have a new project on the go.'

'So what are you doing now?' Not to ask would have been callous.

She looked vaguely around and took another sip of wine. 'Oh, as you see,' she replied, 'I do what needs to be done in the house. I care for the children as best as I can. I read literature. There was never enough time to keep up, even in my own field, when I was working; now there's time in abundance. I did look around for other jobs, but there is a limited amount in my area, and I'm tied here because of Randolph. Besides, I didn't want to go from a senior position, a job where I was in the centre of things, to the kind of marginal work available, say, doing supervisions for Cambridge University. A few hours here, a few hours there, being patronised by everyone, including the students.'

'I understand.' There was a pause.

Bridget looked directly at me. 'Randolph thinks I am a coward for leaving. What do you think?'

'I know who's the coward here, and it isn't you. It's the person who uses his authority to bully and intimidate. Like you, I would like to see Bannister get his comeuppance.'

'Did he murder Monica Harcourt? Do you know?'

'I don't know. Not yet. But I will.'

CHAPTER 18

On my return to town, I had the driver cruise down Warkworth Street past the back of the Police Station. Nicole's Ford
Escort was tucked in a corner of the staff parking lot, hemmed
in between a traffic patrol car and a van with one wheel
removed. The Escort looked as if it hadn't been home in days.

The same thing might be said of Nicole. When she trudged
along the corridor to collect me, discouragement was etched
on her face. The pallor of her skin spoke of long shifts, too
much caffeine, too much tobacco. Her hair was still springy,
but the shine was gone. I hoped my news might bring a glow.

She met my gaze resignedly. I had been out of touch for
days, and was braced for a volley of indignant accusations.
But the sight of my bandages and bruises stayed the attack,
and the story of the balaclava intruder won me time and even,
from Nicole, a gentle approach.

She pursued what was from her perspective the obvious line
of enquiry. 'So, have you considered how Mr Balaclava (we
were all doing it now) might be connected with the dead g—
. . . with Monica's death?'

'I've considered,' I conceded. 'But it goes nowhere. Our
only suspect is Milton Bannister. He was in custody at the
time, keeping you company I assume.'

'Half-five, six o'clock?'

I nodded.

'Still chatting to Neill. The only way he could have attacked
you is by psychic transfer.'

'Nope. The stitches in my leg say it was more material than
that. And I can't buy the idea that whoever killed Monica also
wants me. I'm still convinced that the attack on Monica was

173

specific, not just a random loony who goes for a series of women, but someone who hated Monica herself. Monica might have an enemy I don't know of, but it's dead certain that she and I don't have the same enemy in common.'

'Anything else?' Nicole was taking few notes, not really joining in, just getting me to talk.

'Yeah. If someone sets out to kill me, someone as ruthless as the guy who murdered Monica, he would have done a much better job, planned it better, left me no escape. Besides, there was no way of knowing I would even show up in the office that night. No, the guy with the hunting knife was just looking for something, that's how I see it, and I happened along.'

'And what exactly was he looking for?' There was a bit of colour in Nicole's cheeks now. She looked irritated rather than disconsolate. I'm obviously good for this woman.

'Nothing to do with this case,' I assured her. 'Some other matter I've been dealing with. Wouldn't interest you.'

'Try me,' she said. It was an order.

So I sketched for her the trials and tribulations of a crook who's been taken for a ride by members of his family. I altered the names slightly to protect, as they say, the innocent.

Nicole's conclusion embodied the keen sense of compassion I've come to expect from the police. 'Serves him bloody right,' she declared.

'Ah,' I countered, an image of Michael Loizou in my mind, 'but you haven't seen that heavenly face. And speaking of celestial beings, what happened with Bannister?'

'Well, you know we had to let him go,' Nicole recounted. 'Once Margaret Powers had identified him in a line-up, he retracted his know-nothing account and produced instead a story about the dead girl inviting him around to see her paintings. There's a new one!' she laughed cynically. 'A load of rubbish, of course, but difficult to disprove. He says he arrived there just before nine p.m. On foot. He knocked on the door, received no answer, went away again. He says there were no lights on at the front of the house, so he assumed she had forgotten the arrangement and gone out.'

'Did he produce an alibi for the rest of the evening?'

'No better and no worse than most alibis we get. According to Bannister, he walked back to his car, went for a short drive in the country and then proceeded home. He saw no one until he greeted his wife at half-past ten.'

'And you let him go,' I exclaimed, outrage overriding restraint. 'With a suspicious story like that!'

Nicole's expression left me in no doubt that she shared my disbelief. 'Suspicious it is. Uncommon it isn't. We certainly can't clear him out on the basis of that bit of whimsy but neither, on the other hand, can we hold him. No,' and she staved off my protests with an outstretched palm, 'it *isn't* because he's such an upstanding citizen, whatever the public might think. It's because of the evidence. Look, let's go over it. We have no motive. We have nothing whatsoever to connect him to Monica – apart from the fact that he is her employer, as he is of four hundred other people. We have no forensic evidence to link him with the scene of the crime, though of course the technicians are going over it all again. Nothing really except the fact that he knocked on Monica's door the evening she was murdered. And even that he can explain away. Of course we had to let him go.'

No connection? No motive? Time for me to replay my good citizen role. I advised Nicole to brace herself.

'Just listen to this,' I said. For the first time, I filled her in on Bannister's career in sexual harassment, and about his thwarting of Monica's plans for secondment. I trod a narrative route to Jennifer Ward and Bridget Cullers that left Trina Thompson in the clear. If the police had any sense, they would demand to see her files, but I wasn't going to make a path for them on this one.

Nicole was transfixed. She took copious notes, checked details, asked pointed questions. I was glad to see the lean and hungry look returning to her face.

After I had recounted at length my discussions with Jennifer and Bridget, Nicole asked me whether I believed them.

'Another case of blame the victim?' I enquired coldly. I had seen too many rape cases in which the first word to be doubted was that of the victim of the assault.

'Hold on,' she soothed, before we clashed in earnest. 'If

what these women say is true, and if that creep did away with Monica Harcourt for some reason connected with sexual harassment, then obviously he will deny that he ever put pressure on these girls. If it comes to court, they'll have to testify, and it will be their word against his. It matters not only that they speak the truth, but also that they're credible. And if you have doubts, in a one-to-one interview with them, then the jury will have even bigger doubts. That's all. That's why I need to know if you believe them.'

OK. 'I believe them. Both of them. They've never met, yet they recount the same sequence of events in their dealings with Bannister. Bridget's a broken woman, thanks to that man. She's given up her job, her career, her financial autonomy, and taken a severe blow to her self-esteem. With Jennifer, the fact that she keeps going so impressively makes her account all the more poignant. I believe them. And I believe that Bannister tried the same trick with Monica.'

Nicole frowned. 'There's a problem with his motive, you know.'

'I know.' It had been bothering me all afternoon. Might as well bring it out in the open. 'Say he did make the moves on Monica. That still doesn't mean that he killed her. Jennifer Ward told him in no uncertain terms to get lost, and he didn't lay a hand on her. So why would he attack Monica who, it seems, he was still hoping to get into the sack?'

I didn't know the answer to my own question. Yet. I left Nicole on the telephone, filling her governor in on Bannister's personnel policies. She wanted clearance to make her own visits to Bridget and to Jennifer. And then to bring Bannister in again. Things were looking up.

Outside the main door of the Police Station, there is a billboard hung with photos of missing persons. Against it, to my astonishment, a familiar figure lounged. Stevie held out a piece of paper to me as I approached.

'What the hell are you doing here? What about Old Macdonald?'

'This came through by courier a couple of hours ago,' she said. So Diana Murcott had pulled strings again: a pass to

Bedford Prison. This afternoon. 'Macdonald can wait. I thought you'd like a chauffeur so I came straight here.'

'I owe you,' I said. Again. 'Thanks, friend.' Stevie had brought a long low Mercedes sports car, one of the two older luxury vehicles she maintains herself. She tucked me into the passenger seat, wrapped a rug around my legs and drove so smoothly that I slept all the way to Bedford.

I didn't find it easy to break the news to Michael Loizou. How do you tell a guy in prison that his wife and only brother have conspired to betray him? But I made myself relate the whole sordid story, leaving no details out: the sale of the home on Nightingale Avenue, the exchange of contracts for the nightclub and the office buildings, the forthcoming flight to South America. When I finished, he sat quietly on a plain wooden chair in the visitors' room. His pale hands rested on the table. The fingernails were paint-stained. I know he is a criminal – convicted not once, but several times, of serious offences. Can I help it that he looked angelic at that moment? His head was bowed, and a wisp of light brown hair curled on the side of his slender neck.

But when at last he raised his head, and his eyes met mine, he was smiling. Not a grin, but a definite smile. Of what? Contentment – satisfaction?

'What have I missed here?' I asked.

So he told me. My first image of the Loizous, the happy families story, had never been the real picture. Dmitri and Sonia had always been a team of sorts, excluding Michael, even when the three of them were teenagers together in South London. They had plotted and schemed and lied to little brother Michael as a matter of routine. The marriage was something their fathers arranged; it had never been a love match, and Sonia and Dmitri had seen it as a sort of a joke, a way of keeping Michael in check while remaining close themselves.

'I have wanted them out of my life for years,' Michael concluded. 'And now they're going.' He smiled again, the perfect teeth looking out of place in this dreary prison room. I could place the smile this time: quiet triumph.

'Why do you think I put those properties in their names? I

knew I could never force them to get off my back,' he explained. 'Making me miserable is far too important a part of the dynamic between them. So this seemed the neatest way to dispose of them. As long as they think it's all their idea, as long as they believe I'm furious about the departure, they'll be content. And I'll be free.'

'But the money? Your investments?'

'Don't worry.' Michael turned a look of such sweetness on me that I wondered how Sonia could ever resist him. 'There's plenty more where that came from. Just so long as they are gone for good by the time I get out. My release is set for next week, did I tell you that?'

'Congratulations,' I said automatically. I was too stunned to take it all in.

Michael leaned forward in his chair. 'No, it's me that should congratulate you. You've done a terrific job. No, really. But I'd like it if you did one more thing. I've been a model prisoner while I've been in here this time – even learned to draw. And – this was a surprise to me – I'm quite good at it. One of my efforts won a prize in a national competition for prisoners, and since then it has been selected for the winter exhibition at the Sainsbury Centre in Norwich. I'd like you to see it. Will you come with me to the Preview?'

I have just related to him the news that his wife and brother are betraying him, cheating him out of a fortune, and he wants me to come and see his etchings. How can I possibly refuse?

Stevie drove me the thirty or so miles back to Cambridge, then dropped me off as near to the library at Eastern University as she could. 'No jogging,' she ordered, as she waved me goodbye. Hah, bloody hah. I was in the process of perfecting a rolling sailor's gait, one leg stiff and extended to the side, the other taking most of the weight and doing double service. It looked absurd, it was uncomfortable, but it got me from one place to another.

I had to steel myself before tackling the library stairs. The aluminium railing served as a sort of tow-rope, so I could drag myself up. At the top, outside the main entrance, I lowered myself gingerly onto an empty chair and stretched out the offending limb. The door swung open, spilling out a trio of students and a fresh-faced woman in black leggings and a long pink cashmere sweater. She looked familiar.

'Hey, Laura!' she exclaimed, stopping next to my chair. 'What happened to you?'

I recalled a drinks party in Helen's Victorian parlour a few months ago. This woman, a colleague of hers, had been present. I answered swiftly, to cover the fact that I couldn't remember her name. People seem to fix on 'Laura Principal' like a magnet, but most names drift away from me until the second or third meeting.

'Helen's out,' she said, after hearing a watered-down version of the attack. 'Finance committee. I assume you're looking for her. Do you want to wait in her office? She'll be another half an hour or so.'

I thanked her, but said I'd rather look around the library. With time to kill, it struck me that I could do worse than try to locate some of Monica's students. After all, the group of young people whom I had met before had seen Monica on a regular basis. They claimed that she talked to them and treated them like equals, so there was just a chance that she might have said something to one of them that would give a pattern to the last few hours of her life.

Helen's colleague (Martine? Marina? Maureen?) fetched me a map of the library, pointing out all the areas with cubicles where students could settle down to work. I began at the west corner, feeling conspicuous as I hobbled between study bays. One round of the main floor, I promised myself, and then I'd sit down like a sensible person to wait for Helen.

Of Ruby, Gregory or Amjud, there was no sign, but in a narrow cubicle behind the encyclopaedias, I spotted the unmistakable cropped blonde hair of the girl named Sam. She was chewing her lip. I watched her for a moment working away. She wrote in a hardcover notebook in a laborious hand, much as a seven-year-old concentrates on the momentous task of producing joined-up writing. I was struck by the contrast between the blasé pop star appearance, and the little-girl vulnerability. She looked up at the sound of my approach. It took her a moment to recognise me.

'You've come about Monica,' she guessed, putting her pencil away in a small plastic case. 'I'm glad, actually. I've been feeling so terrible about what happened.'

I was more than a little taken aback. I whisked Sam off to an empty seminar room as fast as my leg would carry me, concerned not to shatter the mood of confession. But when I sat Sam down, she needed no prompting. Her story came tumbling out – not that I could understand it at first. The easy assumption of the young that their world is the only world, that the context of their lives is what 'everyone knows', made parts of what she said unintelligible at first. I was forced to interrupt frequently to clarify who was who and what was what. But it was, in essence, a simple story and a rather pathetic one.

Sam had arrived from Oldham the year before. She felt like a fish out of water in the south and homesick to boot. Her tutors were generally amiable but distant; Monica alone had been kind. Perhaps Monica recognised in Sam the kind of marginality that troubled her own existence. Whatever her motivation, she took the girl under her wing. She showed her around the University, insinuated her gracefully into the most congenial groups of students, and arranged to meet her weekly during the first academic term, until Sam herself, more confident and better integrated, pronounced the arrangement redundant. One particular weekend when Sam was feeling really desperate, Monica even had her round to Sunday lunch.

Sam had responded with gratitude and affection. Monica, she said, was like a big sister. Even when Sam became much more independent, she felt safer just for knowing Monica was there. Until she heard the rumour.

'What rumour?' Funny, I thought, Sam had really warmed to her topic. Her description of Monica was enthusiastic and spontaneous, without a trace of inhibition. But now, suddenly, Sam became the blushing awkward girl I had first seen a couple of weeks ago.

'Come on, Sam, you're going to have to spell it out for me.'

After a few more blushes, and general hesitation, that's exactly what Sam did. 'I didn't know at first that Monica was, you know, a lesbian. She just seemed so friendly, and like I told you, I needed a friend. But then last month I suddenly found out, and I thought that perhaps she had the wrong idea about me. I was really upset – with maybe everyone thinking that I had a relationship with her, and I was the only one who didn't realise.'

You could have knocked me over with a feather. I had heard the same sort of accusation from Milton Bannister, but I had discounted his 'lesbian bitch' as the routine complaint of a man who can't deal with independent women. The professional equivalent of a brickie shouting 'Dyke!' when you decline to smile at him on the street.

'Sam, listen to me. Try not to be embarrassed. The possibility that Monica might have had women lovers is news to me, but it might be important. Please tell me – how did you hear about this? Did Monica herself tell you?'

Sam looked startled. 'You didn't know? But you are a close friend of hers. I thought that maybe you—'

'Think again. Come on – where did you get this information?'

If Sam had blushed before, it was pale in comparison with the crimson flush that showed now, even in the parting of her crisp creamy-coloured hair. 'Well, one day I came into the cafeteria for a doughnut, and all the gang – Amjud, Gillian, Greg, they're the ones you've met – were sitting around the table deep in discussion. They looked embarrassed when I got near. I teased them that it was some new detail of Amjud's love life – he's got a new passion practically every week. But they weren't really laughing. That's when I realised it was something a bit more serious. Most of them made some sort of excuse about classes or something and took off as fast as they could. Gillian stayed behind. She's my best friend. She told me. She said *she* knew that I didn't know anything about it, but maybe it would be better if I stopped hanging around Monica now, because people were getting the wrong idea about me. I was really angry with Monica.'

'So what did Monica say when you mentioned this rumour to her?' Although I tried to keep the irony out of my voice at this point, I doubt if I succeeded.

'Oh no!' You'd think from the vehemence of the response that I had suggested indulging in sado-masochistic sexual practices in the central courtyard. 'No, I couldn't talk to *her* about it! What would I say?'

'How about: "I've heard a rumour, Monica. Is it true?"' Whoops. I certainly wasn't succeeding now.

Well, to cut a long story short, of course Sam hadn't raised the issue with Monica. Instead, she had avoided her from that moment on. She had cancelled her appointments, been too busy to talk, and applied to transfer her project supervision to Ella Grimsby. I recalled Monica's dismay about a student who had suddenly begun avoiding her, and her worry that the young woman concerned might be in need of a friend. The fact that Sam now felt guilty was no consolation.

'Look, Sam, you had known Monica quite well for – how long? – a year and a bit. Had she been a good friend to you in all that time? Had she ever made you feel uncomfortable with her, or threatened? Did she ever ride roughshod over your feelings?' Sam's slow, heavy shaking of the tousled head confirmed all the other things I had known about Monica. 'Or did she behave like someone who cared about you as a person?' Confirmation again. 'So why couldn't you trust your own experience? What could it possibly matter to you if the rumour was true or not?'

What more could I say to this girl-woman? I could understand her misery. She had betrayed a friend: now that friend was dead. I tried to be more gentle than I felt. That's what Monica would have done.

Nicole was surprised when I showed up at the station again. For a week she had been chasing me all over town. Now suddenly I came to her twice in one day.

'It's about that motive,' I told her. 'I think I know why.'

'You know why Bannister killed Monica Harcourt?'

'Well, at the least I know why he *might* have murdered Monica when he didn't lay a hand on Jennifer Ward. But for this information I'll need a comfortable chair to sit on. My leg is killing me. And a decent cup of coffee.'

'Follow me. I'll even go so far as to get you brewed coffee

in a mug, from the percolator in Superintendent Neill's office. Greater love than this . . .' Nicole intoned as she trailed off down the corridor.

'This is how I see it,' I began, after approving of the coffee. 'Bannister has set his sights on Monica, his latest target. She's playing it cagey. Certainly not saying yes, but not yet telling him to stuff his secondment either. Hoping, I guess, that he'll relent and act honourably for once. He gets excited, thinks she's just playing hard to get. Meanwhile, some of the students in the Art Department get the idea that Monica is a lesbian. How they reach this conclusion, I don't know. Maybe it doesn't even matter. What *does* matter is that Samantha, one of Monica's tutees, freaks out. She can't handle it, rushes to put a great distance between herself and Monica. Monica was down as her project supervisor, but Sam requests a transfer to Ella. She tells Ella why. The Grimsby woman, who hates Monica for reasons of her own, finds some opportunity to tell the Provost, hoping to discredit Monica. That's why, when I went to see Bannister and told him I was a friend of Monica, he referred to me as a lesbian bitch. I thought it was just his little endearment.'

'So you reckon that Bannister had come across this rumour about Monica?'

'Oh yes, Bannister knew all right. And you can imagine how it affected him. Here he is, thinks of himself as the big Casanova, the Don Juan of Eastern. Hankering after Monica, thinking that at any moment she'll surrender to his charms. Well, when he hears the rumour, he'd be furious. I've met his type before. They take the information that a woman prefers other women, sexually I mean, as a slap in the face, an affront to their masculinity. He probably reckoned that Monica had put one over on him. That's why he went there on that Thursday evening, I'll bet – to confront her with it.'

Nicole looked thoughtful. 'I've seen the type. You reckon he could have confronted her, and been so outraged that he wanted to punish her then and there. To make her hurt for hurting him.'

'Do you recall the words in that telephone call to Helen Cochrane? The recording of Monica's last few minutes alive?

"I didn't mean to hurt you" was one of Monica's cries.'

Nicole had the final word.

'Christ,' was all she said.

CHAPTER 19

Over the next few days in London, Nicole kept me posted by telephone about the details of the police investigation. So enthusiastic were the accounts she gave that I reckon I couldn't have had much more detail if I had been present at the interrogations myself.

This vicarious involvement in police work did me a power of good. My leg seemed to mend in direct proportion to the strengthening of the case against Bannister.

The Provost had been asked, once again, to accompany the police to the station. Once again, he sauntered out of the front door of Eastern University confidently as if heading for a midday stroll. His mood changed at the station under the pressure of evidence, however. He was, after all, a bully, an abuser and a cheat, but he was not a professional criminal. And he was not used to systematic challenge, least of all from the police.

The statement from Bridget Cullers shook him. Nicole told me how he hedged and squirmed, how there was a delay while he organised a lawyer, how the lawyer provided only a feeble bulwark between him and the indisputable proof that he had hounded Bridget until she was forced to abandon her career.

'Is that what you did with the Harcourt girl?' they demanded. He denied it, of course. It was entirely different: he had scarcely known Monica, seen her only a couple of times in his office in connection with University business. Yes, she had invited him to visit on the night of her murder, but he had never contacted her at home or chased after her as he had 'in a moment of weakness' with Bridget Cullers.

Trina Thompson put paid to that story. Demure as ever,

she volunteered nothing spontaneously, but according to Nicole, her answers to police questions, delivered with an impeccable air of innocence, were devastating.

'Oh yes, the Provost often telephoned women lecturers at home . . . Why, I assumed it was on University business. Wasn't it? Yes, he asked me on five or six occasions to put calls through to Monica Harcourt at her home.'

Trina recalled one occasion when she had asked Monica to hold for the Provost, and Monica had begged her to tell Bannister that there was no answer at Monica's number. 'Please, Trina,' she had pleaded, 'I can't bear to speak to him again. Not now. *Please.*' Well, Trina had found this exchange so plaintive, so emphatic, that she was quite taken aback. But she decided there really wasn't any point in trying to connect them, so she simply told the Provost that Ms Harcourt's line was engaged.

'I'm sorry, sir,' she had apparently said at her interview, with a cool look at the scowling Bannister. 'It seemed the best thing to do at the time.' Hearing this, my admiration for this self-contained woman grew and grew. There was not a hint of insolence or impropriety in her tone, according to Nicole. Nor was there even a touch of deference or fear.

The Provost was being deserted, it seemed, by the women in his life. After Trina came Mrs Provost, her tears cushioned on a thick layer of anger. The news about Bridget, about Jennifer Ward (and about Mona Anderson, another victim who eventually came forward) didn't surprise her. It did make her furious. Nicole was convinced that Eugenie Bannister had long accustomed herself to private embarrassment, to the secret knowledge that her husband exploited his position for sexual gain. Whatever grief this had once caused, she had buried it for the sake of domestic and financial stability.

What she couldn't now stomach was the public humiliation. No stand-by-your-man and of-course-he-didn't-do-it from Eugenie. At least not yet. For now, she was telling all, including the fact that when Bannister had returned on the night of Monica's murder, he had done his best to avoid her, by-passing the sitting room where she was watching a rerun of *Cagney and Lacey*. He had gone straight to the shower-room and remained there for at least ten minutes. When he emerged he was in a particularly foul mood. Having had experience over the years of his foul moods (one such experience had landed her in the doctor's surgery with a dislocated shoulder), she kept out of his way.

By now there was no sign of Bannister's smarmy smile. And when confronted by Nicole with my thoughts on motive, his self-control cracked.

'She had kept you at arm's length, but not completely rejected you,' Nicole suggested. 'Eventually, with the date of the second committee looming, you signed the documents and sent off the letters of support, confident that Monica would reward you in kind. But you misjudged her. She was,' – and here Nicole quoted me quoting Trina – '"entirely straight" with you. You were too convinced of your own invincibility to see. The fact that she wanted to work in Oregon so badly, the fact that she hadn't run away, made you think she was willing to pay your price. Even after you signed the papers, even after she refused any longer to take your phone calls, you were sure you'd wear down her resistance. But then you heard – from Ella Grimsby of all people, who was jealous of your attentions to Monica – that Monica preferred relationships with women. Your confidence collapsed. *That* you couldn't forgive her. Heterosexuality, at least, was something you thought you were owed.'

The Provost at that point had to be physically restrained. His fury – the same fury that had driven him around to Monica's that night, uninvited, to confront her with her 'duplicity' – was unmistakable. His lawyer and the Police Sergeant managed to restrain him, but only just, from slamming Nicole against the wall. He hadn't yet admitted to Monica's murder, but if Nicole were to be believed, it was only a matter of time.

They say that sharing is an important part of a good relationship. Well, Sonny and I proved them right this week. First, we shared a rousing argument that focused on my failure to take care of myself and on his failure to take care of me. Then we shared the blow-by-blow description of Bannister's interrogation. Nicole would tell me, I would tell Sonny, and we'd take turns denouncing Bannister and revelling in his downfall. And along the way, we shared the fun of making up. I was so carried away by all this cosiness, that I even drove Sonny to Gatwick Airport for the early morning flight to Düsseldorf.

'Don't go thinking that this sets a precedent,' I warned, as I kissed him goodbye at the gate to the Departure Lounge.

'We'll see about that,' Sonny replied. He looked suspiciously like a tomcat that's been feasting on cream.

For most of Friday, I had the office all to myself. Dee was at home, hard at work on her lines. Stevie was still working the case for Customs & Excise out of Stansted, and wasn't expected back until Saturday. With everyone out, I had conditions for doing paperwork that were close to my ideal: no interruptions, answerphone on, old jazz tapes turned up as loud as my portable cassette player could manage. I worked quickly, improvising Leadbelly-ish lyrics in a throaty voice that competed with the drone of the heater. A one-woman karaoke night, that's me.

As I sang, I thought of Helen, at that very moment ambling along towards Wildfell. With Bannister 'behind bars', as Helen put it, she had finally felt confident enough to fetch Ginny back from Bristol. We were all looking forward to our first weekend together at the cottage since Monica's death. Helen had decided to drive to Norfolk while it was still light, and I had originally agreed to join her and Ginny there for supper.

But on my way out of Cambridge on Thursday, I had stopped by the library to let Helen know that my plans were somewhat altered. I couldn't locate her – the proverbial meeting, I suppose. Fortunately, I spotted the art students again, huddled around a display board, and the two young men patiently showed me the way to Helen's office. No one was there. I prised a coloured thumb-tack out of the doorframe, and used it to secure a note for Helen.

On my way to London. See you at Wildfell on Friday. Something's come up – don't expect me in until after 11. If you're tired, don't wait up. I'll bring the champagne. Love, L.

The something that had come up was the preview of the exhibition at the Sainsbury Centre, the one that contained Michael Loizou's award-winning picture. And though this appointment was genuine, I was pleased with the change of plan, glad that Helen would reach the cottage well before me, for another reason. Investigating a murder is one thing, but I didn't really want to set foot in Wildfell again until Helen and Ginny had exorcised Monica's presence.

I stopped singing for the moment, closed my eyes and enjoyed the thought of Helen driving out the spirit of the past. Drawing the curtains against the damp night air. Laying a fire, the sparks leaping into flame. Stretching out on the sofa with a novel, perhaps to read, but more likely to nap. Ginny on the hearthrug with her headphones on, playing with the neighbour's cat.

The champagne was not, of course, for celebration. It was for an ending, a punctuation mark. So we could move on. The thought of a return to a domestic sort of peace made me more optimistic than I had been for a very long time.

Late Friday afternoon, I met Angell and Emma for a quiet drink in the conservatory of the lovely house he had shared with Monica. Emma was unlike her sister in most physical respects: she was shorter, more rounded, more rooted to the ground. Where Monica gave you a sense of quicksilver, of someone about to take off and fly, you imagined Emma's sturdy brown legs going up and down mountains at an unhurried pace that would enable her to savour everything as she went along. But the sisters were also alike: the warmth, the laughter, the kindness were shared qualities. You knew for sure that in the years during which they had lived together, their household had been full of fun.

'I'll stay a while in England,' Emma confirmed. 'I have memories to cultivate here. You understand?'

Perfectly.

'Angell has said that I can have a room in this house for the time being. So I shan't need to rush away. Unless, that is,' and she smiled at him, a teasing look with no shading of awe, 'I get in the way of his writing. Then he'll have to turf me out.'

I understood that, too. And felt good about it.

Angell was grateful for the box of papers and the sketches I had culled from Monica's office. He had tentative thoughts of organising a retrospective exhibition for the year after next. With his contacts in the art world, he might just bring it off.

I mentioned to my two hosts that I was on my way to Norwich for the winter exhibition. They declined to accompany me, but Angell revealed something that was news to me: three of Monica's students, her ungainly young disciples, had won places in the show. It would please me to see what they'd done under her tutelage. It seemed a fitting goodbye to a woman who was aiming to be known by her work.

I had crossed London to Holland Park by Underground, and returned to my office in the same way. I was tempted simply to jump in the car, which was already packed, and set off for Norwich. But since no one had been receiving calls at the office for the past several hours, the answerphone was likely to be bursting with messages. I responded to the call of duty in the end, took a deep breath and ran up the stairs – my first such run since the injury to my leg.

At the top, I paused to take check my pulse-rate. Not bad. But standing there, with the fingers of one hand resting on the opposite wrist, I became aware of movement from the other side of the office door. Nothing dramatic, just a soft creaking such as you would expect from floorboards if someone standing near the door quietly changed their position. Braced themselves for attack.

I wasn't going to be caught off-guard a second time, not with my leg so nicely mending. My gun was in the car, three flights down. If I raced off to fetch it, whoever was waiting would know that I was on to them and they would be gone for sure when I got back. Perhaps if they *thought* I had gone, that would be my best bet.

I retreated noisily to the second-floor landing. Wrenching the fire extinguisher off its bracket with one smooth motion, I backed against the wall on the side of the stairwell away from my office. Sure enough, thirty seconds later, the office door opened quietly. There was a pause. Then footsteps, surprisingly light and even, raced down towards the second-floor landing. I hefted the fire extinguisher to shoulder height and held my breath. As the figure rounded the corner I managed to stop myself just in the nick of time from slamming the fifty-pound extinguisher hard into her stomach.

She was even taller than I had expected, with a narrow face, clear green eyes and a strong chin. She looked, as well she might, astonished. I set the extinguisher down, and extended my hand in greeting, deciding that an explanation would only embarrass us both.

'I'm Laura Principal. I'm sorry that I startled you. You were looking for me?'

She relaxed and smiled. 'Yes, I was. Your colleague, Dee, was upstairs when I arrived. She was kind enough to allow me to wait. My name is Elinor St James.'

'I know. I recognise you from your picture in the newspaper. Let's go upstairs and sit down.'

I didn't have much time, but luckily Elinor was not one to beat about the bush. 'Richard Dolby told me about your meeting with him. Is it really true that a friend of yours took photographs of us together on Holkham Beach?'

I explained about Monica and about the visit that Helen and I had made to The Eastings. For a moment she was silent.

'You were right, you know,' she said finally. 'I *wasn't* sure about the . . . operation. Maybe I should have kept the baby, my baby. And brought it up myself.' She shrugged her slender shoulders, the awkward movement of a girl younger than she looks. 'But Richard wouldn't hear of it. And he wouldn't even give me a chance to talk it over with my mother. Oh, she would have been furious, of course. And Father,' she added, almost as an afterthought. 'And I probably would have made the same decision anyway after talking to them. Though I feel upset about the abortion, I don't really feel ready for a baby. But what I resent,' she said, the chin lifting decisively, 'is that he didn't even allow me time to think it through. As if my feelings about it weren't important. As if it was just a matter of doing the rational thing.'

'Are you still involved with him?' I couldn't resist the question.

Elinor, wisely, took the long way around.

'He was all indignant after meeting you, you know. Regards you as a blackmailer, even though – or so I gather – you weren't interested in money at all.' She glanced at me for confirmation, and accepted my nod. 'But when I thought about it, I realised that he was the same way about that girl, Beverley Cattell, as he was about me. He knew what was best in connection with her pregnancy, too. Her feelings and her plans for her life had nothing to do with it either. Horrid, that kind of absolute certainty about other people, don't you think?'

'I do. So what would you like me to do about this?'

'I just wanted to say . . . thank you for noticing. It was your intervention that made me realise that Richard was wrong. Really wrong. I'm having dinner with my mother and father tonight, and I'm going to tell them about the abortion. I've broken off with Richard, so that will make it easier.'

The chin came up again. 'And I've told Richard,' she continued defiantly, 'that if he ever again tries to interfere with another woman's decision about her pregnancy, I'll go public myself. I'll tell the newspapers all about my termination and his involvement. And let him explain *that* to his supporters.'

And to his family, I thought.

Elinor hadn't quite finished. 'So, please,' she continued, 'leave this in my hands. Don't follow it up yourself. I've thought about it a lot over the past few days, and I think that I want to take responsibility for containing Richard.'

A good sign, that. Elinor didn't want an avenging angel, she wanted to reassert control over her own life. 'It's all yours,' I replied.

We talked a bit more – about her plans to follow up her studies, about Monica, about how Ellie had tried to distance herself from the Campaign for Family Revival. I promised to send her the photographs Monica had taken of her and Dolby at Holkham Bay. Perhaps they would help her work through her feelings about that painful time.

We wished each other luck. I meant it. I think she did too.

*

It had been a good end to the week so far: the mounting case against Bannister, the meeting with Angell and Emma, the positive news from Elinor St James. It was only after I had negotiated the Saab out of London traffic and onto the M11 that I allowed my anxieties to surface.

For the first time I confronted head-on the problem with the case against Bannister, a problem that I hadn't mentioned yet to anyone. Bannister's motive for the killing was rooted in what he said to me when I had accused him of visiting Monica on the night she was murdered: 'You lesbian bitch.' It was venomous, the way he hurled that at me, demonstrating not only that he had tagged Monica as loving women, but also that he was more than a little angry about it.

But as I had gone over this meeting in my mind, I had experienced a moment of total recall. The tone of voice Bannister had used, the nuance, indeed the precise words, came back with uncomfortable clarity:

'*You little bitch,*' he had hissed. '*You lesbian bitch. So you were there, with her. Laughing at me. You probably set it up together. You breathe a word of this – to anyone – and you'll regret it.*'

Nicole and Superintendent Neill had heard this part of my account, but hadn't seemed to notice its significance. I only fully registered its meaning this morning. Bannister was at Monica's door at the crucial time, yes. And he was undoubtedly in a state of fury. *But he never gained entry to Monica's flat.*

The person who had access to Monica's studio that evening, the person who had beaten her, who had tied her to a chair and sliced her up, who had spread her death out over a period of an hour, that person would know perfectly well that Monica didn't have a companion 'there, with her'.

I considered the possibility that this was Bannister's double bluff, that he had contrived to give the impression that he didn't know Monica was alone in order to divert suspicion away from himself. This idea wouldn't play for long. After all, Bannister's outburst provided a clear image of the urbane Director as a dangerous man; if he was the murderer he would have preferred to keep this under wraps. More importantly, that little outburst also offered the first indication of what motive Bannister might have for Monica's death. No double bluff, this, but an authentic cry of rage.

There was only one conclusion. When he arrived at Monica's house that night, Bannister might have had murder in his heart, but it wasn't he who slaughtered her . . .

And as if that wasn't enough of a headache, there were further unsettling developments with the Loizous. A pal of Stevie's who was Desk Sergeant at a Police Station near Soho, told her of a fracas outside a nightclub in the neighbourhood. Apparently, two heavies had set upon Dmitri Loizou as he was walking from the club to his car in the wee small hours of Wednesday morning. Sonia was with him. She screamed the parking lot down until finally a police car arrived and routed the bad guys. But Dmitri took quite a beating.

Stevie had a look at him in the hospital. 'He's not permanently injured,' she assured me, 'but he'll have to spend some of the money he stole from his brother on cosmetic surgery to reconstruct his nose. And his teeth.'

I felt a chill as I recalled again Michael Loizou's flawless smile.

This train of thought left me less apologetic than I might otherwise have been arriving late for my 'date' with the newly-liberated Michael Loizou. By the time I reached the outskirts of Norwich, the opening session of the exhibition was well under way. I parked in the car park adjoining the Sainsbury Centre, then dashed along the walkway that led to the main entrance, ignoring the fine spray of mud that splashed onto the hem of my skirt.

Michael Loizou was lounging to one side of a Barbara Hepworth figure. He wore a beautifully-cut Armani jacket and a dark green silk shirt. I wondered idly how many people in the foyer would take him for an ex-con. He looked graceful and relaxed. I wouldn't trust him for an instant.

He was about to pat my arm, a carefully-judged greeting: more friendly than a handshake, but less intimate than a kiss. I saw it coming and caught his wrist before it reached me. He looked startled and uneasy. It was a more aggressive gesture than I'd intended, but I wasn't in the mood for intimacies, however mild.

'I heard about Dmitri,' I announced. Quietly, so he had to listen. 'He looks as if he's been hit by a lorry. I thought you weren't angry?'

Michael relaxed again. What *had* he been expecting?

'I'm not angry,' he affirmed. 'Like I told you, I'm delighted that Dmitri and Sonia are leaving, but it wouldn't do for them to know that, would it? They might change their minds. They might decide to stay in England.'

In the end I let it pass. My relationship with Michael wasn't going very far, certainly not as far as Michael had in mind. But here I was at the exhibition, and I was curious still to see the Loizou *oeuvre*.

We obtained a catalogue and set off at a civilised pace. Many of the works on exhibit I simply blocked off. I like to guard against overload. A close encounter with a few interesting pieces is far more stimulating than a hectic glance at dozens. After we had taken in Michael's offering – a thoughtful line drawing, technically a bit clumsy but attractive nonetheless – I paused to locate the names of Monica's students in the catalogue. It wasn't difficult. This is largely a student exhibition, and the listings include the name of the college to which exhibitors are attached.

The pictures I sought were scattered over three different areas of the building, and we had less than a quarter of an hour before closing. I hurried Michael on.

The first painting was a menacing still life of objects that I took to be drug implements. It was highly stylised and not particularly interesting. The product, I thought in my uninformed way, of a young artist with little to say.

The second, an expressionist portrait in swirling oils, was more promising. Michael was quite taken by it, though nothing could have been further from the delicate style of his own work.

Turning steadfastly from the other rows upon rows of canvases, I led the way to the third location. One glance and my heart stopped. Something – adrenalin, I suppose – muddied my brain and I gazed raptly, like a madwoman.

The picture was compelling. Water colours – Monica's medium – subdued and skilful. An acre of dark forest. A rough wooden gate, a gracefully-arched apple tree. The corner of a cottage-barn, white Venetian blinds at a downstairs window. And leaning against the gate, a dull grey cone, a funeral vase, with a delicate spray of winter jasmine.

'Michael,' I exclaimed, clutching his arm. 'Listen to me. You've got to get this right. As soon as I leave, find a telephone and ring Cambridgeshire Police. Don't delay even for a second. Get through to Detective Sergeant Pelletier. Have you got that? *Pelletier*. Or if she's not in, Superintendent Neill. Tell them I've gone to Wildfell Cottage in Norfolk – they know where it is. Tell them Helen Cochrane's there, and she might be in danger. Her young daughter, too. Tell them to get a police car there immediately. And ring my office, leave a message to let Sonny and Stevie know where I've gone.'

I was speaking in a low voice, but the tone echoed in the vast silver spaces of the Centre and people were staring at us with disapproval. Michael looked confused. That's what you get when you invite a private investigator to a preview.

'Do it,' I commanded, and rushed off.

All around me there was indignation as I bolted through the hall, elbowing groups of visitors out of my way. To the car, fumbling for my keys, shouting at the car park attendant to lift the barrier. Shifting lanes, dodging lorries, negotiating the Norwich ring road as if it were a motorway.

At last I was out on the open road. The mobile phone wouldn't connect, the batteries were down. Leaping from the car at a roadside callbox, I dialled the cottage. Its phone was engaged. I dialled twice more, cursing British Telecom. Cursing my own stupidity.

Wildfell. I had known the meaning of the painting even before I could articulate it to myself. After Monica's first visit to the cottage, when she was keen but still undecided, one of her students had produced a painting that looked like Wildfell. An omen, she had said happily, and decided to cast her lot in with us. An omen, yes. But not the kind she meant.

Monica had been struck by the serendipity of the painting, its uncanny resemblance to Wildfell. Perhaps the detail hadn't been completed at that stage: the knocker on the door, the colour of the curtains, the ladder against the apple tree. Not coincidence, not resemblance, but identity. The student who made that painting had been to Wildfell. Had followed Monica there the first weekend she arrived. Had watched unobserved, perhaps from the meadow. And had left, for our next visit, a calling card – a tin vase of winter jasmine and alpine cyclamen, faithfully reproduced in the painting in the shadow of the wooden gate.

And I now realised, too late, what I should have known at the time. The tin vase was a funeral urn, its simple lines freighted with meaning. That was why Monica was so shaken when I told her how the flowers had arrived at the cottage. She was no stranger to death, and the significance of the vase had not been lost on her.

Suddenly I knew why I had been haunted by the feeling that I had known Monica before ever she arrived at Wildfell Cottage. A painting again: the portrait hanging on the wall in Mina Harrison's office. The wild and woolly hair, the cheek-bones, the angle of the head – sketchy, inexplicit, but no less certainly Monica for all that. And while I had stared at that painting, the audiotypist had talked to me incessantly – about her younger brother, who was a student in Cambridge. Of art, of course. Of *Monica*.

The name in the catalogue was Gregory Merrick. I could see him in my mind's eye, introducing Ruby and Amjud and Samantha to me outside the departmental office. He had a tentative manner, yes. But he was also tall, approaching six feet, and well-built. The same size as Mr Balaclava . . .

Greg. Often seen with Sam. Could it have been he who spread the rumour about Monica? Perhaps he imagined that a love for women was the explanation for Monica's indifference to him. Perhaps he was jealous of Sam's friendship with Monica, and had set out to create a distance between the women. Perhaps he even thought it was true.

Greg. Who had watched me pin on Helen's office door a note that revealed she would be alone at Wildfell this evening.

Greg. Longing, Monica mentioned, to be on intimate terms with the tutors. Always hanging around the office, within reach of the typewriter. It would have been an easy matter for him to type the invitation to Helen when the secretaries were out of the room. But why? What had he wanted with Helen that Thursday evening? What might he want with her now?

I thought of Monica's cold, bloodstained fingers and my foot pressed down on the accelerator.

CHAPTER 20

The gate was closed again. I didn't stop to loosen it, but swung myself over the top instead and plunged up the gravel driveway on foot. I could hear the branches of the apple tree creaking in the wind. They offered no contrast against the black sky and I was within touching distance before I could see the tree itself.

Ahead of me, ominously, Wildfell was bathed in darkness. The light above the front door was not switched on, the kitchen was dark. So much for my thoughts of a simmering casserole. I could detect an edge of light from the sitting-room window, but the heavy curtains obscured the room from view.

The keys were in my hand. I let myself in quietly, not wanting to acknowledge the reason for stealth. To my left, the sitting-room fire burned low, small sparks stirring as a draught followed the open door. The only light came from a table lamp that cast a soft golden glow.

Helen lay on her side on the sofa. Her knees were pulled up towards her chest, foetal fashion, and her head rested on one pale slim arm. A woollen blanket had worked its way towards the floor. Only a corner of it remained over her form. Her sleeping form.

I moved quietly towards her, a rush of relief forcing me to acknowledge the depth of my fear. To lose one friend is a misfortune. To lose two . . . I picked up the blanket from the floor and rearranged it gently over her legs. Helen stirred and stretched, opened her eyes and smiled at me, not yet awake enough to be surprised by my presence.

'Hi,' she said. 'How long have I been asleep?'

'Don't know. I just arrived. Where's Ginny, anyway?'

Helen sat up and twisted around, so she could consult the clock on the mantelpiece. 'She's upstairs having a shower, the last I heard. Gosh, I've been asleep for ages!'

No sound of running water. In fact, the upstairs was completely quiet. I moved towards the staircase, pausing at the turn where Helen couldn't see me to transfer the gun from the small of my back to my jacket pocket. I kept one hand in the pocket as I crept across the landing and peered into the bathroom: patches of water on the floor, sash window halfway open, cold air rushing through. Empty.

The door to Ginny's room was ajar. I stood back and pushed it open slowly with my left arm, scarcely feeling, my body on automatic pilot. The room was brightly lit by an overhead fixture. No one on the bed, the pink chenille spread unrumpled. No one on the rug. The door swung its full arc, and there was Ginny.

She sat at her child-sized desk, a coloured pencil in her hand, looking up towards me with big scared eyes. On the desk were three or four sheets of writing paper, covered with her neat handwriting. She was alone.

'Sorry, baby,' I said, putting the gun in my pocket. 'Did I startle you?'

'Why did you sneak up on me like that?' she demanded, rushing to give me a hug. 'You scared the life out of me. I thought it was that . . . well, you know.'

Yes, I did know.

'You were so quiet, I got frightened too. Sorry,' I apologised again. 'I guess I'm a little jumpy lately. Are you writing a letter?'

'To Karen. What do you think?' Ginny showed me an intricate pattern formed of lines in a dozen different colours, presumably the product of this evening's efforts.

'It's lovely – but didn't you just see Karen at school this afternoon?'

'What's that got to do with it? We always write when we're away, and make patterns for each other. Then we can talk about them next time we meet.'

'Sounds good to me. You going to be much longer?'

'I'm almost finished.' Ginny stood on tiptoe and stretched

her arm around my shoulders. 'Don't worry, Laura,' she advised, with a big-sister-type squeeze.

'Thanks, love. I feel better.'

Truer words were never spoken. I left her door ajar when I went out, closed the bathroom window, draped a towel over the wet patch on the floor, and made my way downstairs to Helen.

'Now or later?' Helen asked.

'Give me five minutes,' I replied, allowing time only to carry my bag in and doublecheck that all the downstairs doors were securely locked. The car could stay outside the gate until morning.

Then I fetched a pair of champagne glasses from the sideboard. The cork abandoned its grip on the bottle with a satisfying *thunk!* Settled cosily on the sofa, we raised our glasses first to ourselves, and then to Monica.

I was tempted just to leave it like that. Who wants to be Cassandra?

'Helen.' She looked up, relaxed and smiling for the first time in a while. 'Helen,' I tried again, 'it's not over yet.'

'What's not over?' She looked at me with mild curiosity. Then her brown eyes slid away from my face to a position behind me. Her expression changed. Without turning around, I set my champagne glass on the side-table and eased my right hand towards my jacket pocket.

At the same instant that Helen screamed, a slow-motion sort of scream, a high-pitched voice barked out behind me: 'I know you've got a gun. I want it. Right now, on the floor. Or—'

noises of fear issued from Helen's throat

'—or this little girl is dead.'

I turned at last. He was standing on the stairs, Ginny in front of him. A noose was tied around her neck. In his left hand, he gripped the rope, pulling it tightly towards him, so that Ginny's head and shoulders were crushed against his chest, her basketball boots scrabbling to maintain their purchase on the narrow stair. In his right hand he held a six-inch hunting knife, the angled blade slicing against the pale skin of Ginny's throat.

'You hear me?' he shouted. 'The gun!' Ginny began to gasp for breath.

'OK.' Soothing. 'OK, here it is.'

Slowly, I grasped the gun in my hand, slowly lifted it from my pocket, arm by my side, barrel pointed downwards. I bent my knees, set the gun on the floor.

The pressure eased slightly on Ginny's neck. She drew a shuddering breath.

Helen was silent at last. I hoped she wasn't in shock, but I didn't stop to look. I didn't for an instant take my eyes off Gregory Merrick's face.

He took a deep breath, feeling more in command of the situation. When he spoke, the reedy voice was an octave lower. 'Now, push the gun towards me. With your foot. Move slowly. Nothing unexpected.'

I did as he said. My kick was deliberately weak. The gun slid across the floorboards, came to rest halfway between him and me.

I was hoping he would send Ginny to pick it up. No such luck. He looked at the gun for a moment, then his eyes returned to me. Speculative, wary. Full of hate.

There was nothing to be gained by playing gentle with this guy. He wasn't here for fun.

'Gregory Merrick, isn't it? I've just come from the exhibition at the Sainsbury Centre, seen one of your water colours. Strange that you should use this cottage as a subject. The police thought it was very interesting. They're looking for you at the moment, want to talk to you about why you killed Monica. Me, I don't need to talk to you about that. I know why.'

'You know nothing,' he spat out. 'Nothing about Monica and me.' I'd touched a raw nerve.

'Oh, but I do. I know, for instance, that you liked Monica. Thought she was pretty, didn't you? Maybe even thought that she liked you? After all, she was kind to you, helped you with your water colours, praised them. I guess you thought that made you special, huh?'

He was breathing harder, the grip on the rope around

Ginny's neck was tightening again. Tears were coursing down her cheeks now, but she kept very still. Brave little girl.

Merrick's right arm, the arm holding the knife, was getting tired. It trembled ever so slightly. He took the bait. 'We had something going, Monica and I. I was her first successful entry in a national competition, did you know? She was proud of me. She told me I'd make her famous one day. But then she started spending time with that bitch Sam. She wasn't in her office when I called, I had to go looking for her, all kinds of times: had to ring her up at home, had to go to her flat at night. She started pretending she didn't recognise me. "Who's there?" she'd say when I telephoned, as if she didn't know it was me.' His cold grey eyes were only partly focused on the here-and-now.

He could stay in the past as far as I was concerned. 'So if you and she were such a hot number, why did you tell the others that Monica had relationships with women?'

'I did it to scare Sam off.' A look of cunning passed over his face. 'I thought if Sam was out of the way, Monica might be her old self again. God, talk about stupid. Next thing I know, Monica was trying to run away from me.'

'Run away?'

'To Oregon, arsehole!' His voice took on a macabre resemblance to Monica's. '"Look at my little house, Greg, by the sea. I'll live there with a poet," she said, "and paint." Taunting me with it.'

He was shaking now, not with exhaustion but with anger. He had loosened his hold, and Ginny slumped forward a fraction of an inch.

'And this place,' he growled, looking around with clenched teeth. 'I've seen it in my head so many times, even in my sleep. Couldn't make the images go away.' He turned to Helen. 'You and Monica. In bed together.'

Astonished, Helen blurted out, 'Monica wasn't my lover!'

'I saw you!' he screamed. 'Outside this cottage. I saw you both. Her hugging you, saying she was happy, she didn't want to leave. God, it made me sick. I should have killed you both there and then.' He struggled to control himself, his arm harsh again against Ginny's throat. 'Come here.' This at Helen. 'Here! It's you I want, not this child.'

Helen began to walk towards him, her eyes willing courage to Ginny. The gravel scrunched outside. The police? There were two sharp knocks on the door. 'Leave it,' Greg hissed at me. We all held our breaths. Seconds passed.

Knocks again. 'Helen? I know you're in there. Come on, you can't have forgotten our date. The others are on their way.' More knocks. Helen looked stunned. I immediately recognised Michael Loizou's South London accent.

Greg's teeth were clenched. 'Just the same as that fucking Provost, that Bannister,' he said. 'Thinks he has a right to come in here, to interrupt.' Pause. I edged a step closer to Ginny. 'Open the door, and get rid of him,' Merrick ordered.

Helen had to take two deep breaths before she could make herself walk to the door. She was trembling all over, her woollen tunic rippling about her as she moved, but her voice was firm. She planted herself in the doorway, and told Michael she didn't know who he was and she was busy and he would have to leave right away and she wasn't going to stand there arguing with him . . .

Greg was working up to a rage. Helen glanced fearfully at Ginny. Greg came down the stairs, shoving Ginny ahead of him, signalling ferociously with his right hand for Helen to shut the door.

I dived. I clenched my calf muscles and propelled myself across the six feet of floor space that divided me from Merrick, throwing my whole body between him and Ginny. Grabbing the rope with one hand so that he couldn't draw it back, I shouldered Ginny out of the way. The knife flashed towards me, ripping a channel of blood down my right arm, but missing my chest. I was forced to relinquish my grasp on the rope that circled Ginny's neck, and use both hands in desperation to grip Merrick's wrist, trying to prevent the blade from slashing down again. For five or six awful seconds, we stood there like statues, locked together. My shoulders shook from the effort of holding off that maniac arm, my mind recoiled from the sound of Ginny choking.

At last, there was a rush of movement from the doorway.

Stevie (Stevie?) grabbed the rope and pulled Ginny free. Someone else brought a poker smartly down on the side of Merrick's head, and with the release of the tension as his arm crumpled, I careered headfirst into the side of the chimney breast.

I wasn't out for long, maybe a minute or two. Already Stevie had applied a towel to the cut on my arm. The wound was deep, she said, but not particularly damaging. 'Press harder,' I instructed. No more transfusions if I could avoid it.

Ginny, bless her, was all right. Shaken up, of course, with a hideous-looking bruise on her throat. And inclined to cling rather close to Helen's side. But she was beginning to ask questions, and behind the shock in her eyes was a sheen of excitement. By tomorrow morning, I reckoned, she'd be weighing up the possibilities for show-and-tell at school.

Stevie and Michael tied Gregory Merrick to the captain's chair with a length of clothes-line from the shed. He was in some pain. While I was unconscious, Merrick had somehow acquired two black eyes, a cut lip, and what looked to my untutored eye like a broken nose. Michael seemed awfully pleased with himself.

'I owed you,' he said to me, and smiled his perfect smile.

I hoped that the police, when they finally did arrive, wouldn't make too much fuss about Merrick's injuries. In fact, when we pointed out to Nicole that the prisoner could do with medical attention, she peered at him and shrugged. 'These things happen,' was her official comment.

I returned from the emergency room in the hospital at Hunstanton shortly before midnight. It hardly seemed worth the trip, but my friends weren't taking any chances. And I have to admit that whatever the painkiller was that they injected me with, it would fetch a pretty price on the rave scene. I was flying.

The first thing I did after greeting everyone was to take a look at Ginny. Given the hour, I wasn't at all surprised to find that she was stretched out on her back in her pink-covered bed, fast asleep. A fat letter to Karen was propped up against the mirror. Helen followed me up, and dropped a kiss on Ginny's forehead – not for the first time tonight, I reckoned.

The second thing I did was to turf the neighbour's cat out of my armchair and snuggle down, legs stretched out in front of me. Stevie held up a hand to signal that we couldn't begin the serious conversation yet. She strode into the kitchen, and returned with a platter containing, among other things, prawn dumplings of such delicacy that I tuned out of the conversation until the last one was demolished.

'I didn't know you could cook like that.'

'Lots of things you don't know,' Stevie enjoined. Not original, but certainly true.

'So go on. Tell me how you came to be here.' I was suddenly struck by an absence. 'Where's Michael, by the way?'

'He had a matter to attend to at Heathrow Airport. Something about watching an early-morning flight boarding for Caracas.'

I tried to get Stevie to account for her arrival at Wildfell at the crucial moment, but Helen interrupted.

'Do me a favour, Laura. Everything seems to have happened so quickly, I'm completely at sea. You're the only one who knows the whole story. How about treating us all to a systematic account, in decent chronological order.' She wanted, like Alice, to begin at the beginning . . .

'But where *is* the beginning?' I asked. This kind of question doesn't suit me. Blame it on the painkillers.

Helen tactfully overlooked my attempt to signal a deeper philosophical agenda. 'How about starting with the theory of the evil eye?' she suggested. 'Can I take it you've junked that completely? Monica wasn't fearful because she felt threatened by her own success. She was nervous about what Bannister was up to. And she was scared of Gregory Merrick. Right?'

'Largely,' I replied. 'Only difference is, she didn't know it was Merrick who frightened her. To her, Greg was just a kid who was kind of needy and hung around her a lot. She probably realised he fancied her, but thought it was just a crush. The man she was afraid of was the one who stalked her, who stood outside her house in the middle of the night, who made threatening telephone calls. The man she referred to in her diary. And it didn't occur to her that that man and Gregory Merrick were one and the same.'

'And Merrick even followed her here?'

'Sure did, the little slimebag. When she told her students the good news about Oregon, Merrick was outraged that she should think of leaving Cambridge. He regarded it as a betrayal. It's after that that he became *really* obsessive. He followed her in his car to Burnham St Stephens, parked on the High Street and crept down through the meadow. He kept watch on the house for most of the period she was here. He even snuck into her room when we were out picking mushrooms. Remember that Monica had this idea that someone had moved her bookmark? Well, it was Merrick, going through her things. Of course when he saw the book, he was even more furious. She was reading—'

'Oh, I remember now,' Helen interrupted. 'One of my favourites: *Murder at the Nightwood Bar*. A Kate Delafield thriller, set in a lesbian bar in LA. No wonder he got worked up.'

'That's it. Psychotic as Merrick is, he took this as confirmation that the story he had made up for Sam, about Monica being a lesbian, was true. And the next day, when he saw that Helen and Monica were fond of one another, he put two and two together and made five. It can't have helped his mood that Monica joked to us as she said goodbye about being bored with whingeing students. Anyway, it's after those goodbyes that he became set on killing Helen too.'

'Then that's why he sent me that invitation,' broke in Helen, 'pretending it came from Monica. He intended—' she cast her eyes towards the stairs leading to Ginny's bedroom and automatically lowered her voice to a whisper '—to kill us both.'

The neighbour's cat had taken up residence on Stevie's lap, and Stevie looked as if she liked the arrangement. She suspended her stroking duties for a moment to point to something which she found implausible in the story so far. 'Look,' she objected, 'one thing about all this bothers me. If Monica was so jumpy, whyever would she let Merrick into her flat the night she was killed? The police said, as I recall, that there were no signs of a break-in.'

I took up the thread again. 'Well, as I said before, Monica

didn't suspect Merrick in the least. But more importantly, Angell had cancelled his arrangement to visit, and Monica needed someone to help her shift some furniture. So when Merrick "happened" along, she must have thought it was a stroke of good luck. It's he who lifted the bookcase into the hired van.'

Helen glanced at the clock which was chiming its way towards the wee small hours. 'Laura, you must be exhausted. Can you manage one more question before we all call it a night?'

'Dozens more, actually. Fire away.' The combination of adrenaline and painkillers had left my brain racing. Might as well have some ideas to chase.

'OK, let's go back to the attack in your office. I take it that Mr Balaclava was Gregory Merrick? That we have to drop the idea of Dmitri Loizou as the bad guy here?'

I nodded agreement.

'But I still haven't got a clue what he was doing in your office. Do you think he came specifically to try to kill you, or what?'

'Or what,' I replied. 'My guess is that he had come to search the office, expecting not unreasonably that it would be empty in the evening. You see, that was the same day that I found Monica's diary in the back of her filing cabinet. I told Mary McKinnon that I was taking the diary to London, and that I'd read it there. There were a group of students hanging around filling in forms while we were talking. Greg must have overheard – his ears would prick up at the mention of Monica's name. In his own twisted way, thinking that he was someone important in Monica's life, he probably suspected that she might have written about him in her diary. So he got the office address from my business card on Mary's desk, and raced down to London, intending to locate the diary and get rid of it before I came across his name and handed him over to the police. He had no idea that I would turn up in the office. When I did, true to form, he attacked.'

Helen made an elaborate point of consulting her watch. 'Do you folks realise that it's after 1 a.m.? We librarians can't do without our sleep, even on days like this. To be blunt, it's time I hit the sack.' She stood up, straightened her cardigan over her shoulders. Then she paused and sat down again.

'No. I can't go to bed without a bit of background on our rescue. The thing I can't figure out, Stevie, is how you and Michael managed to show up at the crucial moment.'

'No mystery about it. Michael rang the Cambridge Police and got through to Superintendent Neill. Nicole was out. Neill was sceptical about the urgency of the call. He was still investigating the Provost, and as far as he was concerned, the case was virtually closed. So all he did was ask the North Norfolk Constabulary to look in on their way past.'

'I'm surprised the cops came at all in that case,' I exclaimed. 'Friday's a busy night.'

'Ah well, you can thank your pal Nicole for that. When she saw the message in the records book, she set off all the alarms. 'Course, by the time she got here herself, it was all over.'

'I thought you were going to explain how *you* got here,' Helen insisted.

'All part of the same story,' Stevie reassured her. 'When Michael realised that Neill was soft-pedalling, he rang our office. Left a message on the answerphone. I collected the messages on my carphone in Stansted, and ate up the road between the airport and Norfolk in record time.' She smiled contentedly. 'The Mercedes needed a workout.'

Stevie looked smug. Well she might.

'You could have knocked me over with a feather when I heard Michael's voice,' I admitted. 'How did you dream up this crazy scheme for knocking on the door, and so on?'

'Now, this part is astonishing,' Stevie warned. 'I hare-tailed it here from Stansted, and Michael drove from Norwich. Nevertheless, I entered the driveway about thirty seconds behind him. I immediately had Michael pegged for the killer, skulking around outside your cottage in the dark. I was within a hair's-breadth of tackling him, when he announced who he was.'

What a farce that would have been! Michael and Stevie scuffling in the driveway, while Merrick held a knife on Ginny inside.

'The rest took place in a flash,' Stevie said. 'The sight of your car outside the gate gave us a pretty good idea of what was up. We reckoned there was no point in trying to take the place by storm. If the guy had a weapon, someone would get hurt. So we decided to create a distraction, give you an opportunity to catch him off-guard. Which of course,' she announced with a flourish, 'you did.'

'What can I say, Stevie? That's the second time in a fortnight you've come to my rescue. You're going to have to start thinking what I can do to even up the score.'

'Well,' said Stevie, pouring herself another glass of wine. 'I've been doing some thinking about that. I've got some money put by, and weekends in London are hell. Are you two,' she asked with a nod at Helen and me, 'still looking for a third person to share Wildfell? When you both feel ready, I'd like to talk about it.'

Helen nodded, and tossed me a hopeful look the meaning of which was easy to decipher. I thought of those prawn dumplings. 'Let's talk,' I said.

A half-hour later, round about the time we had settled dates for Stevie's move, Sonny arrived. He had received a message from me as he disembarked from the Düsseldorf flight, and a British Airways hostess, who'd clearly enjoyed his company on the way over, squeezed him onto a late flight which was just leaving for Norwich. A hired car, a dash through the night, and here he was, too late for the fun but in time for the last part of the retrospective.

Sonny offered me a kiss and a half-case of red wine from an exquisite vintage, all the way from his favourite stockist in Düsseldorf. I accepted both offers with pleasure.

Then he took up my former seat in the big armchair. Instead of shifting somewhere else, I snuggled down on his lap, and gave him as serious a kiss and hug as my bandaged arm would allow.

'Hey,' he exclaimed, pleased but a little embarrassed. 'I've been gone less than twenty-four hours!'

'Yes,' I said, embracing him again. 'And don't think I haven't missed you.'